SEND FOR PAUL TEMPLE AGAIN!

Francis Henry Durbridge was born in Hull, Yorkshire, in 1912 and was educated at Bradford Grammar School. He was encouraged at an early age to write by his English teacher and went on to read English at Birmingham University. At the age of twenty one he sold a play to the BBC and continued to write following his graduation whilst working as a stockbroker's clerk.

In 1938, he created the character Paul Temple, a crime novelist and detective. Many others followed and they were hugely successful until the last of the series was completed in 1968. In 1969, the Paul Temple series was adapted for television and four of the adventures prior to this, had been adapted for cinema, albeit with less success than radio and TV. Francis Durbridge also wrote for the stage and continued doing so up until 1991, when *Sweet Revenge* was completed. Additionally, he wrote over twenty other well received novels, most of which were on the general subject of crime. The last, *Fatal Encounter*, was published after his death in 1998.

Also in this series

FRANCIS DURBRIDGE

Send for Paul Temple Again!

COLLINS
CRIME
CLUB

COLLINS CRIME CLUB

An imprint of HarperCollins*Publishers*
1 London Bridge Street
London SE1 9GF

www.harpercollins.co.uk

This paperback edition 2015

First published in Great Britain by
LONG 1948

A catalogue record for this book is
available from the British Library

ISBN 978-0-00-812564-6

Set in Sabon by Born Group using Atomik ePublisher from Easypress

Printed and bound in Great Britain by
Clays Ltd, St Ives plc

CONTENTS

CHAPTER I

Death at the Brains Trust

ARTHUR MONTAGUE WEBB had occupied the position of ticket inspector for over fifteen years. It was a position of which he was more than a little conscious, as those unfortunate passengers who tried travelling 'first' on a third-class ticket had reason to aware. Even during the war years, when he fought his way endlessly down jammed corridors, his attitude seldom relaxed. Very occasionally, he might install a harmless old lady in a first-class compartment, with an apologetic and slightly anxious glance at the other occupants.

Mr. Webb's raucous, 'Tickets, please!' echoed down the corridors of the Manchester–Euston express one rough night in the late autumn. He paused to pull up a window in the corridor which was admitting a half-gale, then opened the door of a compartment which had a single occupant who was stretched full length along the seat. The occupant of the carriage was rather a dark young man of about twenty-seven, with unruly black hair and glistening white teeth, which he exposed in a pleasant smile. He seemed in no way upset at the inspector's intrusion.

1

'Sorry to wake you, sir,' said Mr. Webb mechanically. It was his inevitable formula on night trains.

'That's all right,' yawned the young man, fumbling in his pocket for his ticket. 'Lordy, I was hard on!'

Mr. Webb's ears, attuned to dialects from every corner of the country, immediately registered the young man as being of Welsh origin.

'What time is it now?' asked the passenger, inserting a finger and thumb in his upper waistcoat pocket.

'It's half past ten, sir,' announced Webb, producing a large silver watch, and glancing at it for corroboration.

The Welshman yawned again.

'About another hour before we get into Euston?' he queried.

Webb nodded, and waited while the young man found his ticket.

'Not many people travelling tonight,' said the young man, his Welsh accent as pronounced as ever.

'Haven't had it as quiet as this for months,' the inspector informed him, clipping the ticket and handing it back. 'Thank you, sir. Good night.'

The young man nodded and composed himself to sleep again as the door of the compartment slid softly to, and Mr. Webb went on his way.

Webb muttered a soft imprecation to himself as he came out into the corridor again, for the window he had closed had slid down, and once more he got the full force of the biting wind. He snatched at the strap, pulled up the window and passed on to the next compartment. There was no light in this compartment and the blinds were drawn, but in the faint glow reflected from the corridor Webb could discern the figure of a woman slumped in the far corner with her back to the engine.

'Ticket, please, miss!' called the inspector. At that moment the express began to rattle noisily over a viaduct, and she gave no sign of having heard him. Webb repeated his request and advanced a step into the compartment.

'Cor blimey!' muttered Webb, who never ceased to marvel at the way people slept on trains. The girl remained indifferent to his presence, so he moved across and shook her shoulder vigorously.

'Come along, miss, wake up!' he urged in an authoritative tone. 'Wake up now! I want to see your ticket.' He shook her again. Suddenly and quite without warning her head jerked forward.

Webb released her shoulder and, turning, switched on the lights in the compartment. The girl was in the early thirties, with red-gold hair and large eyes. Beneath an elaborate makeup the face was ashen.

'Strewth!' murmured Webb expressively under his breath. Then, without any further ado, he turned and went back to the compartment he had just visited.

The young man looked up in some surprise as the inspector's head appeared.

'What is it? What is it, man?' he demanded. 'Have you seen a ghost or something?'

'Would you mind coming into the next compartment, sir?' asked Webb in a very agitated tone. 'It's – it's a young lady, sir. I think she's been taken ill.'

The young man sat up with a start and at once rose to his feet.

'Why, yes, of course,' he murmured, following the ticket inspector into the next compartment. They found the young woman had now slid to the floor, where she was lying in an ungainly heap.

'Take her shoulders,' ordered the young man, catching hold of the woman's feet. Rather awkwardly, they lifted her on to the seat and laid her full length. The Welshman placed a finger and thumb beneath her eyes, then felt her pulse.

'What is it? What's the matter with her?' demanded Webb in an anxious tone.

'What's the matter with her! Why, lordy, man, she's dead!'

The inspector's jaw dropped. He bent forward and eyed the body intently, as if he could not believe what he heard. For some seconds there was no sound but the mournful scream of the engine's whistle and the unceasing clatter of the wheels.

'Shouldn't we pull the communication-cord?' suggested the Welshman, an excited flush mounting in his cheeks.

'Don't see that can help much,' replied the other gruffly.

'But, man, we should get a doctor . . .'

'I'll see if there's one on the train first. No sense in losing time if we can help it. We're running seven minutes late as it is.'

A sudden draught swept through the compartment. The window in the corridor was open again. The breeze stirred the curtains, which were closely drawn. Something caught the Welshman's eye, and he drew back one of the curtains. He leaned forward and gazed intently at the corner of the window near where the dead woman had been sitting.

'What are you staring at?' demanded Webb.

For a moment the other did not reply. Then he suddenly gave to an exclamation.

'Look what's chalked on the window,' he said, moving out of the light, so that the inspector could see for himself.

Rather laboriously, he spelt out the three letters that were scrawled in vivid red capitals. 'R-E-X.'

'Rex?' repeated the little Welshman, with a puzzled frown. 'Now what does that mean, I wonder?'

Arthur Montague Webb slowly shook his head. He was very puzzled.

It did not take the police long to discover that the dead woman was Norma Rice, the well-known actress, and within a few hours a dozen newspaper reporters were busily ferreting for facts to add to the rather scanty information about the lady in question which they found in their libraries.

Norma Rice's career had always been something of a mystery, true, she made no secret of her origins. She was the daughter of a wardrobe mistress from the Theatre Royal, Drury Lane, and had spent her childhood in Peabody's Buildings, within a stone's throw of that famous theatre. Her *gamin* qualities and their potentialities had soon come to the notice of a certain Madame Terrani, who ran the famous Starlit Juveniles, and it was not long before Norma Rice was the 'stooge' of the outfit – the girl who always does the wrong thing and is a couple of beats behind the rest of the talented troupe.

Norma stuck it until she was fifteen, then she mysteriously vanished, to reappear four years later as the star overnight of a new Broadway musical, *Glamour Incorporated*, in which she sang and danced with such gay abandon that even the dour H. L. Mencken professed himself enchanted.

Norma remained in the show for six months, then staged another of her strange disappearances, re-emerging two years later as the lead in a sophisticated Hollywood film, *Never Marry Strangers*. Once again, the critics acclaimed her as a new star, but when the film company endeavoured to foreclose their option upon her services, she vanished again without leaving the slightest clue.

Back in England, she invested most of the money she had earned in founding a repertory company which appeared at a tiny theatre in a small town in Dorset. Later she scored a considerable success as Lady Teazle in a revival of *The School for Scandal* at the Viceroy Theatre in London, and was afterwards seen in several other costume parts. She had, in fact, only deviated from costume comedy on one occasion, to play the lead in *The Lady Has a Past*, by an unknown young dramatist named Carl Lathom, whose first play it was. It had proved a sensation in theatrical circles, yet once again Norma Rice had disappointed her public by withdrawing from the cast after six months, after which the play slowly fizzled out, despite the fact that the most expensive young actress in the West End had taken Norma Rice's place.

It was not surprising that the more sensational newspapers found Norma Rice's career more than a trifle intriguing, and engaged certain practised freelance journalists to 'play it up'. You can't libel a dead woman, so let's have a double-page spread with plenty of pictures!

But none of the articles provided the solution as to how Norma Rice could have taken a large dose of Amashyer, a little-known drug with a delayed action, which had caused her death. Nor could they offer any clue to the identity of the melodramatic individual who had scrawled 'Rex' on the carriage window.

True, the police had discovered that a clever young actor named Rex Wilmslow had played opposite Norma on her last appearance in the West End, but as he had performed in a matinee and evening show in London on the day that she had died, it was difficult to prove that he could possibly have had anything to do with the tragedy.

A murder of a well-known person like Norma Rice presented many difficulties – always presuming she had been murdered – for a woman in her position was likely to have made enemies in almost any sphere of life, and such enemies might just as easily be in America as over here. It was a by-word, for instance, that she had alienated at least half a dozen big executives in the stage and film world by her impetuous actions, which had cost them thousands of pounds, and by her vitriolic tongue, which she never made the least attempt to restrain. As long as stage people could remember her, there had been rumours about Norma Rice. She was said to have slapped three dramatic critics' faces, one after the other, during a first-night party; she was said to have extorted thousands of pounds from the Earl of Dorrington, whose son had been infatuated with her during his Varsity days; she was reputed to have obtained the famous Calcutta Pendant by a trick; she was said to spend months under the influence of opium, hence her mysterious disappearances . . .

Few people had liked Norma Rice, but her bitterest enemies had to admit that she possessed that certain something which held an audience from the first moment she set foot on the stage.

Naturally, all these sidelights on Norma Rice's character ended to confuse the issue, and the Special Branch Commissioner of New Scotland Yard was more than a little worried when he attended the third conference in the office of Lord Flexdale, Secretary for Home Security. It was by no means the last conference. The Norma Rice murder was followed by two more within a comparatively short space of time.

Newspapers made Rex the subject of leading articles which cast no uncertain aspersions at the efficiency of the police force.

The name Rex could be overheard in conversation upon almost any public vehicle as passengers opened their morning and evening papers, and the Sunday Press indulged in a shoal of speculative articles, signed by so-called experts. When the total of Rex murders was up to four, Lord Flexdale decided it was high time drastic action was taken, and bluntly intimated as much to Sir Graham Forbes.

Sir Graham protested at some length. He was one of the old school who disliked the private affairs of New Scotland Yard being dragged into the limelight. He maintained that the Yard would get its man in the long run, and he chafed at the impatience of government officials who panicked at a few articles in what he called the 'Scare Press'.

But on this occasion Lord Flexdale was adamant.

'It's no use, Forbes,' he declared flatly. 'We can't hope to tell where this fellow Rex is going to break out next. There appears to be no connection between any of his victims, and his motives are all quite obscure so far. We've got to call for wider co-operation from members of the public. It's been done before, and it worked. I see no reason why it shouldn't work again.'

'That's all very well,' grunted Forbes, 'but remember you're giving a devil of a lot away to Rex if you admit—'

Lord Flexdale broke in impatiently.

'I shall admit as little as possible.'

'Then what do you propose?'

'I have already arranged,' Lord Flexdale informed him, 'to speak after the nine o'clock news.'

Forbes grunted again. Privately, he thought Lord Flexdale welcomed any opportunity to address himself to the nation.

The discreetly shaded reading-lamp near the fire revealed a room furnished in a manner sufficiently unusual to arouse a visitor's curiosity as to the character of its owner. There was a strange jumble of small ornaments of Oriental origin, an assortment of Persian daggers on the walls, a life-size bust of a Chinese idol standing on a pedestal, two enigmatical pictures by Picasso or one of his disciples – it was difficult to judge in the subdued light – and a wide assortment of cushions ranging through a spectrum of colours.

The recumbent figure in a large armchair stirred as a clock in the hall outside softly struck nine, and a slim, perfectly manicured hand stretched out and switched on the radio. It seemed that the clock in the hall was slow, for the announcer was just concluding the news. There was an impatient exclamation from the armchair.

After a suitable pause, the announcer continued: 'As listeners to our earlier bulletins will already have heard, we have with us in the studio this evening Lord Flexdale, Secretary for Home Security, who is broadcasting a special message to listeners, both in this country and the United States of America. Lord Flexdale.'

There was a slight cough, a shuffling of papers, then the measured tones of the Cabinet Minister.

'It is exactly two months since we read in the newspapers about the murder of that distinguished young actress, Miss Norma Rice. As you will no doubt recall, the body of Miss Rice was discovered in a railway compartment in the night express from Manchester to London. The official who discovered the body has already recounted at some length how he noticed the word "Rex" marked on the window of the compartment. Since that particular night, there have been three more murders, all as yet unsolved, and in each case the perpetrator has left this solitary clue to his or her identity.'

The minister paused, as if to allow this statement to impress itself upon the listening public. Then he continued with slightly more emphasis: 'I am authorised by His Majesty's Government to state that a free pardon will be given to any person, other than one actually guilty of wilful murder, providing the said person will furnish the evidence necessary to secure the arrest and conviction of the criminal responsible for these tragic misdeeds, which are a menace to the existence of social security.'

Lord Flexdale was obviously making the most of this opportunity to enlarge upon one of his pet themes. With the merest suggestion of a chuckle from the armchair, the slim fingers reached out once more and switched off the radio.

'We shall see, Lord Flexdale, we shall see,' murmured Rex, sinking back into the large armchair.

The news-room of the *Daily Clarion* was in its customary state of turmoil. At tables ranged found the room, reporters hammered out their stories. Copy-boys moved quickly in and out of the sub-editors' room, carrying messages and bundles of copy. Under a large window, one of the staff artists put some finishing touches to a drawing. A dozen people seemed to be joking at once, and doors marked 'News Editor', 'Assistant News Editor', 'Chief Sub-Editor' were forever opening and closing.

George Dillany, the crime reporter of the paper, sat at his little table, moodily jabbing at the space bar of his typewriter.

George had been overworked of late, and it was beginning to show in his face and manner. He was a little worried, too, that his work might be suffering. After a couple of drinks, however, he would reassure himself with the consolation that if Scotland Yard couldn't deliver the goods, how could he be expected to turn in a reasonable story? The *Daily Clarion* paid him to report crimes, not to solve them. All the same, a really good story, particularly an exclusive, made a hell of a difference to one's outlook on life. You could walk down Fleet Street and look people in the face, reserving a particularly generous greeting for rivals who had been unlucky enough to miss the scoop. Unfortunately, George would be in the position of one of those rivals today, for he had missed a scoop himself. It had appeared in a morning edition of the *Evening Courier* under the large black headline:

SCOTLAND YARD SENDS FOR PAUL TEMPLE

'All ruddy headline and no story,' grumbled George *to* himself, reading the ten lines that followed the heading:

> *'It is understood that Sir Graham Forbes, Special Branch Commissioner of New Scotland Yard, is consulting with Mr. Paul Temple, the popular novelist and private investigator, on the question of the "Rex" murders. Mr. Temple has been staying in the country working on his latest novel, but is coming to London to appear in this evening's Brains Trust broadcast. It is not yet known whether Mr. Temple will agree to co-operate with the Yard in solving these crimes which are agitating the whole country.'*

George Dillany ruffled his hair thoughtfully.

What did it all amount to? he asked himself. It was one hundred per cent conjecture. He himself had called twice at the Temples' flat during the last twenty-four hours, and had found it empty. He had rung up Bramley Lodge and spoken to Steve, Temple's wife, who had somewhat coldly informed him that to the best of her knowledge her husband was not contemplating embarking upon another case.

A copy-boy came running up to tell him that Hawkes, the news-editor, wanted to speak to him, and George levered himself up rather moodily and went over to the room in question.

Hawkes was just slamming down the telephone receiver as Dillany entered. His beady black eyes snapped as he asked: 'What about the Paul Temple story?'

Dillany shrugged.

'I've tried to get hold of Forbes – in fact, I've been through to half a dozen people at the Yard. They're not talking.'

'You and your pals at the Yard!' sneered Hawkes. 'It's a damn' lucky thing for you and all of us I had the sense to send a man down there. And, what's more, he's landed a story, and it confirms this!'

He indicated the report in the evening paper.

'You don't mean Temple has been to the Yard?' queried Dillany sceptically.

'No, I mean the Yard has gone to Temple. Wilkinson was hanging around about an hour ago when he saw Forbes leave. He followed him to Temple's flat. They're there now.' Dillany whistled softly to himself. 'Then it looks as if they're calling Temple in after all,' he mused.

'Of course they're calling him in,' rasped Hawkes impatiently. 'What the hell do you think they're doing? Drinking each other's health?'

Which, in point of fact, was exactly what they were doing at that particular moment. Temple was reflecting that Forbes looked just a little greyer and the lines of his face were a shade more pronounced. Forbes was thinking that Temple, with his slight sunburn, appeared amazingly young, and he envied him his comparatively carefree existence. How very pleasant to disappear into the heart of the countryside to write a novel when one was in the mood. Like many people who have never written a book, Forbes imagined it was merely a matter of filling in an occasional hour in the evenings, with a pipe and a drink at one's elbow to assist one's pleasant ruminations.

The third member of the party, Inspector Emmanuel Crane, had never even given the matter a thought, though he did read a novel occasionally. A well-built, seemingly unimaginative individual, he sat four-square in one of the upright chairs, clutching his tankard. As he looked round Temple's well-appointed lounge, he reflected for the first time that there must be money in this writing game. This fellow Temple had a place in the country too – yes, there must be a lot of money in it. More writing about crime than in tracking down criminals. He began to wonder how much . . .

Inspector Crane had a nasty habit of lifting a corner of his upper lip from time to time, thus giving his face a sneering expression which was more than a little unfortunate, and which created a none too favourable impression upon strangers. Temple, who had only met him casually once or twice previously at the Yard, was lazily trying to assess Crane's possibilities, for he was apparently a very active personality at the Yard of recent months, according to reports he had received.

Meanwhile, Temple made pleasant conversation with Forbes, enjoying renewing his acquaintance with the rather brusque but none the less likeable personality.

'What the devil have you been doing with yourself lately?' Forbes was asking. 'I tried to telephone you about a fortnight back.'

'Steve and I have been at Bramley Lodge, and the village telephone exchange out there is, well, a bit happy-go-lucky,' smiled Temple. 'I'm writing a new novel – at least, I'm trying to write one.'

Crane suddenly came to life.

'I read your last novel, sir,' he announced with a note of pride in his voice.

'Oh, did you, Inspector?' Temple was just a shade taken aback.

'So did I,' grunted Forbes. 'The detective was a bigger fool than ever!'

Temple laughed.

'He had to be, Sir Graham,' he replied with a twinkle. 'Wasn't he practically the Chief Commissioner?'

Crane's hearty guffaw seemed to shake the glasses on the sideboard, and Forbes could not restrain a grim chuckle.

Temple got up to fill Forbes' glass again, and as he returned the Assistant Commissioner said: 'I suppose I don't have to tell you why we're here, Temple.'

Temple looked from one to the other, then said very quietly: 'Rex?'

Forbes nodded, hesitated, then took a sip at his sherry.

'Well?' he queried, with a lift of his bushy grey eyebrows.

Temple slowly shook his head.

'I'm sorry, Sir Graham,' he murmured. 'I'd like to help you if I could, but I must finish this novel by the end of the month and make a start on a series of articles I've been commissioned to write for an American magazine.'

Forbes put down his glass and gazed earnestly at the novelist. 'Temple, I don't think you realise just how serious this business is. It's damned serious! I saw Lord Flexdale this morning—'

14

'I heard him on the radio last night,' interposed Temple with a trace of a smile. 'A remarkable display of oratory, if I may say so.'

'Oratory never caught a murderer yet in my experience,' rejoined Forbes grimly. 'And nobody knows that better than Flexdale. When I saw him this morning, he sent you a message.'

'This is an unexpected honour.'

'He said to me: "We must call in Paul Temple, and there isn't a minute to lose. Get hold of Temple immediately!"'

Temple flicked the ash from his cigarette.

'You tell Lord Flexdale with my compliments that if he will finish writing my novel I will catch Rex for him,' he retorted lightly.

Crane did not appreciate this.

'You'll catch Rex, eh, Mr. Temple?' he ruminated ponderously. 'Just like that?' He snapped his fingers expressively.

Temple still refused to take the matter very seriously. 'Well, after all, Inspector,' he murmured, 'I was lucky enough to catch the Knave, the Front Page Man, Z 4, and, if I remember rightly, even the Marquis.'

'Yes, that's all very well, Mr. Temple,' insisted Crane heavily, 'but, if you'll forgive my saying so, this is a different proposition.'

Temple gave him a friendly smile.

'I quite appreciate that, Inspector,' he said reassuringly. Then he turned to Forbes and asked: 'When did you first hear about Rex? Forgive my asking such elementary questions, but I've been buried in the country.'

'It was about six months ago,' supplied Crane.

'Yes,' nodded Forbes.' A man called Richard East was murdered – he was found in his car on the Great North Road. Chalked on the windscreen of the car was the word—'

'Let me guess,' smiled Temple. 'And that was Rex's first appearance?'

'The very first time.'

'How was East murdered exactly?'

'He was shot through the head.'

'Motive?'

Forbes stirred uneasily in his chair, and looked across at Crane, whose dour features were inscrutable.

'There didn't appear to be a motive,' said Forbes at last. 'There never does! That's the extraordinary part about it, Temple, damn it, we just don't know what we're up against!' He rubbed his chin with an impatient gesture.

'Well, it certainly wasn't money,' ventured Crane. 'East had about a hundred and fifty quid in his pocket when we found him.'

Temple was obviously getting interested.

'And after the East murder?' he asked.

'After that came the Norma Rice affair. You remember that surely, sir?' put in Crane.

Temple nodded slowly.

'Oh yes, I read about Norma Rice. I knew her slightly. I even dallied with the idea of writing a play for her at one time. She was a very remarkable actress.'

'That's right, sir,' nodded Crane. 'She was found in the express from Manchester. The word "Rex" was scrawled across the window.'

'So it was,' nodded Temple. 'This Rex would appear to be something of an exhibitionist.'

'Yes, and there again, you see, Temple, there didn't seem to be a motive,' interposed Forbes eagerly.

Temple lighted another cigarette and asked: 'Could it have been suicide?'

Crane's upper lip twitched sardonically.

'Suicide?' he repeated in an amused tone. 'Not a chance!'

'Surely with a temperament like Norma Rice's—' began Temple diffidently, but Crane interrupted.

'She'd just opened in a new play at Manchester that had been a big success, and was coming to London in a fortnight's time. What's more, she'd got herself engaged to be married, so you might say everything in the garden was rosy. Couldn't possibly have been suicide, whichever way you look at it.'

Temple frowned and looked across at Sir Graham, who appeared to be lost in thought.

'Was Miss Rice shot through the head?'

Forbes came back to earth with a start.

'Good God, no!' he exclaimed. 'As a matter of fact, when the ticket-inspector found her he thought she was asleep.'

'She'd been poisoned,' added Crane. 'Obviously somebody had given her an overdose of Amashyer.' He turned to Temple. 'It's a delayed-action narcotic that takes about six hours as a rule to prove fatal, Mr. Temple.'

'Yes, I've heard of Amashyer, Inspector,' smiled Temple, who had been among the first to discover the presence of this drug in London some years previously. He refilled Crane's tankard, then turned to Sir Graham.

'How many of these murders did you say there had been, Sir Graham?'

'Five.'

'And in every case you came across the word "Rex"?'

Forbes nodded slowly. 'On the window of a railway carriage, on the windscreen of a car, on a small lace handkerchief written in lipstick, on the face of a watch—'

17

'And don't forget the tattoo mark on the dead man's wrist,' put in Crane, who seemed to take a morbid delight in the more gruesome aspects of the case.

Forbes sipped his sherry, wishing Temple would make up his mind whether he was going to work on the case. He was anxious to get back to his office, acquaint himself with any recent developments and get his team of picked men launched on their respective lines of investigation. He had not been particularly enthusiastic about Lord Flexdale's decision to call in Temple, for he had the impression that during the past year or so Paul Temple had become rather more interested in writing about crime than in active participation. No doubt Steve had something to do with this, and you couldn't blame her. Temple made a packet of money out of his books, so why should he go rushing into danger just for the fun of the thing? Yet Temple seemed more than a little interested in this case – that was a part of the man's charm, decided Forbes. He had a capacity for taking a lively interest in whatever you chose to talk about.

'Is this word "Rex" the only link between each particular murder?' Temple was asking, his dark brown eyes alight with eagerness. 'Is that your only reason for suspecting that each murder was committed by the same person?'

'Yes, of course,' nodded Forbes. 'Except that in one case . . .' Forbes seemed to hesitate.

'In one case . . .' prompted Temple.

'We found a card on Richard East, a visiting-card,' admitted Forbes. 'Of course, it may mean nothing at all – just the merest coincidence. After all, most men have a habit of tucking an odd visiting-card in one of their waistcoat pockets.'

'You mean it was one of his own cards?'

'Yes – but there was a name scribbled on the back,' broke in Crane.

'Oh,' said Temple. 'Anyone we know?'

'It conveyed nothing to us at the time. But we found the same name scribbled in the back of a diary which was in Norma Rice's handbag.'

'This is most interesting,' said Temple, leaning forward in the chair. 'And what was the name?'

'It was just "Mrs. Trevelyan".'

'Trevelyan,' mused Temple, obviously more than a little intrigued. 'No address?'

'No address.'

Forbes shifted uncomfortably in his chair.

'And now you know as much as we do, Temple,' he murmured dryly. 'If I didn't think this business was damned serious, believe me, I wouldn't be bothering you. In fact, when Lord Flexdale mentioned it, I told him you were up to your eyes in work, but he insisted.'

Temple sighed.

'I'd like to help you, Sir Graham, I really would,' he admitted. 'But you see after that business with the Marquis, I made Steve a promise. I promised her faithfully that under no circumstance would I take on another case.'

He was about to explain further when the door handle turned and Steve herself came in, wearing an attractive costume and what was obviously a new hat. Temple raised his eyebrows the merest fraction. There was a flicker of amusement round his mobile mouth as he welcomed her.

'Hello, darling. Look who's here!'

Steve was patently delighted to see Sir Graham, and went across to shake hands.

'It's good to see you again after all this time, Sir Graham.'

'And you look younger every time we meet,' he responded gallantly.

19

'She certainly looks a very different woman,' supplements her husband. 'I say, what the devil have you been doing to yourself, darling?'

Steve could not repress a smile.

'It's the new hat, darling. Don't you like it?'

Temple put his head on one side and scrutinised the article in question with a serious air.

'Is it back to front?' he asked at last.

'Of course it's not back to front!' retorted Steve indignantly and they all laughed.

Forbes introduced Crane to Steve and they chatted for some minutes about minor matters. Then, suddenly remembering the hours of work awaiting him at the Yard, Forbes said: 'Well, I suppose we'd better be getting along. Thanks for the sherry, Temple. Good-bye, Steve. I hope we'll be meeting again fairly soon. Don't bury yourself in the country quite so long next time.'

He picked up his hat and gloves from a chair.

'Why don't you come to dinner one night while we're up here, Sir Graham?' asked Steve. 'We'd love to have you.'

Forbes nodded. 'Let's make it one night next week. May I give you a ring to let you know?'

'Do,' urged Temple, accompanying the visitors to the door.

When he returned, Steve had taken off her hat, and was sitting on the settee placidly knitting. This was an accomplishment she had acquired recently from the housekeeper at Bramley Lodge, and one which she found both soothing and satisfying. Intent upon turning the heel of a sock – the second of the first pair which she intended shortly to present with pride to her husband – she only looked up for a second as he came in.

'You seem very pleased with yourself,' smiled Temple, going to pour himself another glass of sherry, then changing his mind. 'Is it the new hat?'

'Yes. It's a model, you know. Don't you really like it?'

'It's got unconditional surrender written all over it!' laughed Temple.

'No, seriously, what do you think of it?'

'It's stupendous! It's terrific! It's colossal!' he enthused, rescuing her ball of wool which had rolled under a chair. He went on, 'How much did it cost?'

'You'll never know!' laughed Steve. 'I paid cash.' She went on knitting for a while and her husband idly rolled the ball of wool along the edge of the settee.

'What did Sir Graham want?' asked Steve presently, doing her utmost to make the inquiry sound casual.

Temple dropped the wool and felt for his cigarette-case.

'Oh, he just happened to be passing,' he answered lightly.

She did not speak again for a minute or two. Temple wandered rather restlessly round the room, lighting a cigarette and stubbing out after a few puffs. Presently Steve gave vent to a sigh of relief. 'Thank goodness, that's the heel finished!' she announced. Then, apparently as an afterthought, 'Paul, have you seen the evening paper?'

He turned quickly.

'No, darling. Why?'

Steve reached for her handbag, opened it and took out a small, neatly folded square of paper, which she opened out and passed over to him. The first thing to catch his eye was the streamed headline:

SCOTLAND YARD SENDS FOR PAUL TEMPLE

He glanced quickly at the report, then tossed the paper on the floor.

'Darling, you know what they're like in Fleet Street,' she murmured apologetically.

'I know,' Steve nodded, the memories of her newspaper days always fresh in her mind.

'I can't think where they could possibly get this information from,' went on Temple hurriedly. 'Considering we only got here last night—'

'Did Sir Graham mention this Rex affair?' asked Steve in the same casual tone, though her heart was beating much faster than she would have cared to admit.

'Oh, he mentioned it, of course, in a general sort of way,' replied Temple vaguely, glancing at his wrist-watch, and suddenly leaping to his feet. 'I say, I must be off. I'm supposed to be at Broadcasting House at seven sharp.'

'I'll drive you down,' she offered.

'Good!' he agreed. 'Then if you pick me up later we can have a spot of dinner together and I'll tell you all the blunders I made.'

'Yes, let's do that,' she nodded. But she seemed to have suddenly become restrained and on the defensive. He could see that she was troubled.

'Steve, don't worry,' he begged. 'I'm not going to get mixed up in anything more dangerous than the Brains Trust. I promised you last time, remember?'

Her face seemed to clear.

'All right, darling.'

'So come along, put on that ridiculous hat of yours and let's go and earn an honest living.'

'Okay. And don't make a fool of yourself any more than you can help.'

She thrust her knitting under a cushion and went out into the hall with him.

'Good heavens, why should I? Just because I'm in the Brains Trust!'

'Well,' murmured Steve, standing in front of the mirror and adjusting her hat to the correct angle, 'what shall you do if they ask you some pretty awkward questions?'

'That will rather depend,' smiled Temple. 'But I imagine I shall give them some pretty awkward answers!'

It took them rather less than five minutes to reach the dignified entrance to Broadcasting House, but the clock showed three minutes to seven as Temple passed into the hall, and he chafed impatiently as he waited to announce himself to the receptionist, who dispatched a pageboy to accompany him to the studio immediately.

He found the announcer talking to Donald McCullough and both eyeing the clock anxiously, while the members of the Brains Trust were sitting round a table in the centre of which was a microphone. They were all looking extremely cheerful and engaging in desultory bursts of conversation.

'I'm afraid you've missed the "warming-up" question, Mr. Temple,' said the announcer, 'but you'll be all right.' He briefly acquainted Temple with the procedure, and a minute later they were ready to go.

'Remember, although this is a recording, it's the real thing! So get right on your toes,' smiled the announcer.

'Really, I've never felt so nervous in my life,' admitted Lady Weyman, a tall woman with piercing eyes, who rather surprisingly proved to be an expert on international affairs.

Next to her sat A. P. Mulroy, editor of the *London Tribune*, and a very young man for the job – a man who never hesitated to print what he thought.

Sitting next to him was Sir Ernest Cranbury, Professor of Economics, who had a large following in America by reason of his readable book on the subject of the gold standard. He was a man in the early fifties, with pale, watery eyes, iron-grey hair and a protruding forehead.

As he slipped into his seat next to C.E.M. Joad, who favoured him with a murmured greeting, Temple was overcome for a moment by the collection of such distinguished individuals, and wondered what he could possibly add to the remarks of such a company. However, he nodded and smiled at the producer, who was sitting behind Donald McCullough. Suddenly McCullough began to introduce them.

He paused for a moment, then continued: 'Our first question this evening comes from Mrs. Palfrey, Chorley Forest, Abingale. She would like the Brains Trust to explain what is meant when one speaks of the Science of any particular subject. Is it correct, for instance, to speak of the Science of History?'

McCullough looked round his team, who were reading duplicates of the question on slips of paper passed round by the producer. Presently, Joad raised a languid hand, and McCullough nodded to him.

'Well, of course, it all depends what you mean by the word "science",' Joad was beginning in his inimitable fashion, when there was a strangled gasp from Sir Ernest, who suddenly fell forward across the table, knocking a carafe of water and two glasses on to the floor. Lady Weyman could not suppress a scream and Joad stopped speaking.

Meanwhile, the announcer had gone to the microphone and given the curt order, 'Stop recording!'

'It's my heart!' gasped Cranbury, clutching aimlessly at his coat. 'I can feel it . . . racing . . .'

'Are you all right, Sir Ernest?' cried Lady Weyman rather unnecessarily.

'I'll be all right presently,' Cranbury told them. 'I'm most terribly sorry.'

'Get some more water,' said McCullough, and one of the studio assistants ran to obey.

Sir Ernest tried to struggle into an upright position.

'Don't try and get up, Sir Ernest,' advised Temple, who was feeling Cranbury's pulse. The sick man gave a little cry of pain and relapsed into his former position.

'Don't excite yourself, and lie perfectly still,' insisted Temple still holding Cranbury's wrist. He turned to tell McCullough that it would be advisable to get a doctor, and the latter replied that the staff doctor was on his way.

Cranbury took a sip at the glass Temple held to his lips, then said in a weak voice: 'Temple, listen! There's something I want you to know, just in case anything happens.'

'Nothing's going to happen,' Temple tried to reassure him though he felt far from confident on the subject.

'It's just a sort of giddy turn,' said Mulroy comfortingly. 'We all get 'em at times.'

'No!' gasped Cranbury. 'I know it isn't! Listen, Temple – I want to tell you about—about Rex!'

The word was spoken very softly, but they all heard it, and there was a tiny gasp of astonishment.

'Rex!' repeated Mulroy, alert as ever for news.

'That's right,' breathed Cranbury heavily. 'Now listen . . . when I first received the letter . . .' His voice faded away. Temple and Mulroy had both leaned forward to catch every word, but suddenly Cranbury's head dropped helplessly.

'Here's the doctor,' said Mulroy. 'Perhaps an injection . . .' Temple shook his head.

'No, it's too late,' he said, dropping the lifeless wrist. 'He's dead!'

CHAPTER II

Paul Temple Takes Over

WHEN the body of Sir Ernest Cranbury had been taken away conversation seemed to flow more easily, and there were three or four animated groups in the studio, busily discussing what could be done, what had caused Sir Ernest's death, whether or not he could be replaced on the Brains Trust at such short notice – and what precisely had Rex to do with his sudden and mysterious death?

They apparently expected Temple to enlighten them upon this last point, but discovered that he seemed to know as little as they did. For one thing, he had never met Sir Ernest before and had not the least idea why he should be singled out by Rex in this manner. It was this aspect of the case which intrigued Temple. Rex's victims appeared to come from all classes of people – as far as Temple could judge the only thing they had in common was a certain degree of financial stability, though this was by no means absolutely certain. On the face of it, Norma Rice was a successful actress, but that did not necessarily mean she had a great deal of money.

Temple mused upon these and other things, taking little part in the conversations that seethed around him. Meanwhile, the producer of the programme was busily telephoning the Programme Controller.

It was eventually decided that it would be advisable to cancel the present session of the Brains Trust and substitute a recording of a much earlier session in the programme.

Temple breathed a small sigh of relief and asked if he could telephone his wife. In the tiny control-cubicle which the engineers had now deserted, he managed to get through to Steve and ask her to pick him up right away. In reply to her startled query about the broadcast, he told her that there had been an accident and the programme was cancelled. Having twice reassured her that he himself was in no way involved, she agreed to come right away.

Accompanied by Mulroy, who was still trying to pump him, Temple took the lift down to the private bar in the basement. He drank a large glass of whisky, refused a second, and made his uncertain way along endless corridors and upstairs until he came into the entrance hall once again.

A little knot of reporters had already gathered there, and among them was Rex Bryant, of the *Evening Post*, who had been considerably involved in one of Temple's earlier cases. He caught sight of the novelist and came over to him eagerly. After various mutual inquiries, Rex Bryant said, 'Well, now, what about a story on this Rex affair?' Temple shook his head.

'I'm sorry to say you're probably just as wise about it as I am,' he confessed.

'Then tell me if that story's true about your being called in on the case. Are you really going to work on it?'

'That rather depends,' murmured Temple.

'On what?'

'Well, you've heard of actors appearing by kind permission of some management or other?'

'Yes, of course, but what—'

'I', explained Temple, 'also take on a case by kind permission of a lady who's waiting for me outside in a car.' He turned to go. 'Give me a ring a bit later on, Bryant, and I'll help you if I can.'

He found Steve sitting in the car outside with a tiny worried frown corrugating her forehead.

'Are you sure there's nothing seriously wrong, darling?' she asked as he opened the door of the car and got in beside her.

'Nothing wrong with me,' he replied. 'But Sir Ernest Cranbury has had a nasty heart attack, and I'm afraid . . .'

She guessed the rest.

'Have they told his wife?' was her next question.

'Sir Ernest, so they tell me, is a bachelor who lived in a nice flat just off Park Lane,' explained Temple.

Steve nodded thoughtfully, started the car, and they set off along upper Regent Street.

As they waited for the traffic lights to change, Steve said, 'It must have been a dreadful shock to everybody in the studio.'

'Frightful,' nodded Temple. 'We didn't know what the devil to do. It was all so sudden. No doubt if we'd had to answer a question on how to deal with just such an emergency, we should have given long and plausible replies, but when the event was beneath our noses it was quite a different kettle of fish!'

'What did the doctor say?'

Temple shrugged.

'There was nothing much for him to add to what we'd guessed. There'll be an inquest, of course.'

Steve nodded thoughtfully and released the clutch as the lights changed.

'Do you think it was heart failure, just over-excitement?' she asked presently, trying to make her voice sound as casual as possible.

Temple did not speak for a few seconds. Then he said thoughtfully, 'No, I don't.'

'Why not?'

'Because just before he passed out he said to me, "I want to tell you about Rex",' replied Temple unemotionally, thinking he might as well enlighten Steve now, for she would be certain to hear or read his evidence at the inquest. She took it with comparative calm.

'Rex . . .' she murmured thoughtfully, pulling up again at another set of lights. 'What do you think he could have meant?' she asked.

'I don't know. I've been thinking about that. There was something else too that rather intrigued me.'

He began to fumble in his coat pocket, then leaned forward and switched on the overhead light in the car.

'We had to search Sir Ernest's pockets to try and find his address. Inside his wallet there was this piece of paper – it dropped on the floor. No one else noticed it, so I – er – naturally . . .'

'Naturally,' smiled Steve. The lights were still against her, so she took the paper and looked at it quickly.

'There's nothing on it,' she said.

'Look in the corner – it's written rather faintly in pencil.'

She held the paper closer and read, 'Mrs. Trevelyan.'

He took the paper and nodded. Steve suddenly sat bolt upright.

'Paul, that was the name you told me about, the one on the visiting-card and in the diary belonging to Norma Rice.'

'Exactly. Hi—look out, the lights have changed!'

The car shot forward again, and they travelled for about two hundred yards without speaking. Then Temple happened to look through the side window and noticed a large black saloon edging dangerously near them and moving at a fair speed.

'By Timothy, he seems to be in a hurry!' commented Temple as the car came almost level. With a sudden impulse he switched off the roof light.

Quite suddenly, the overtaking car seemed to lurch towards them. Temple grabbed the hand-brake as Steve swerved to avoid the passing car. There was a scraping of metal and a slight bump as Temple's car hit a lamp standard a glancing blow. The black saloon roared away down Regent Street, swung into a side turning, and was lost.

Steve sat for a moment trying to regain her composure. 'He nearly forced us into that shop window,' she said breathlessly. Temple nodded.

'It was done deliberately, no doubt about that.' He was debating in his mind whether to give chase to the black saloon, but the arrival of a constable forestalled that. Temple briefly gave him particulars, but on an impulse refrained from giving the number of the saloon, of which he had caught a fleeting glimpse. For one he was not quite certain, for another he thought he might like to follow up this clue himself. Unfortunately, neither he nor Steve had been able to recognise the man who was driving – he had worn a hat pulled well down, and his overcoat collar was turned up round his ears. After making one or two notes, the constable allowed them to proceed.

'Why did you hesitate when he asked you the number?' said Steve, as she changed gear.

'Because,' he answered softly, 'I think I saw it. I wouldn't be quite certain, but it looked like DVC629.'

'Can't you have it traced?' asked Steve eagerly.

'I didn't want an official job made of it, in case I happened to be wrong. What's more, number plates can be changed pretty quickly. And then again . . .'

'Yes?'

'Well, supposing this business has got something to do with Rex?'

'With Rex!' echoed Steve, completely staggered. 'But it can't have.'

'But supposing it has!' insisted her husband.

'Well?'

'Well – would you still want me to trace that car number?'

Steve suddenly swung round, a determined light in her eye.

'Yes!' she replied in a definite tone. 'Yes, I would. Forget that promise if you really want to.'

Temple slapped his right fist into his left palm. 'Okay, Mrs. Temple! If that's how you feel, pull up for a minute and we'll change places.'

She did so. Then a thought seemed to strike him as he caught sight of a telephone-box, and he asked Steve to wait while he made a call. When he returned he looked very pleased with himself.

'All right, darling, we're all set. Hold on to that precarious hat of yours, and off we go.'

'But, Paul, where—?'

He smiled.

'To a little pub in Limehouse known as the "Twisted Keys".' He noted her expression. 'It's all right, darling, it's not such a dive as all that. They've even got a saloon bar!'

However, the Twisted Keys certainly did not look very inviting from the outside when they arrived there, though Steve could find little fault with the saloon bar, which had obviously been modernised.

'I take it we're supposed to be meeting somebody here,' said Steve, as she settled in a corner with a pink gin.

Temple looked round cautiously.

'Yes, an old friend of mine named Spider Williams. He specialises in car jobs – knows who's out on the road and what they're up to. If ever a car gets stolen, trust Spider to hear about it in next to no time. I told him to 'phone his pals and let me know if he heard anything about a Milford saloon – gave him the number, of course, though that may not mean much.'

He did not seem inclined to talk any more, but thoughtfully drank half a pint of ale and then ordered another. Half an hour slipped by; people drifted in and out, some eyed them suspiciously, others seemed intent only upon quenching their thirst, and minding their own business. Temple fetched Steve another pink gin and grinned at her cheerfully.

'You don't seem very impressed by this establishment,' he said.

'Is one supposed to be?' asked Steve.

'Of course! It's one of the most famous pubs in London. At least it was, before the brewery decided to modernise it. Since then, the place has lost its tone. I don't suppose there's been a free fight here for months. Of course, they still get a few of the old-timers, but you have to know when to catch them – and they never use this bar.' He grinned reminiscently. 'That's why Spider sounded surprised when I told him I'd be in here.'

'What sort of man is this Spider Williams?' inquired Steve, rather more intrigued.

Temple shrugged.

'Oh, he's just a little chap who knows most of the answers.'

'Why do they call him Spider?'

'Possibly because his web explores most of the corners of the underworld as far as his own particular line is concerned.'

Steve smiled somewhat wistfully. 'I can't understand you, darling. I really can't. Surely Sir Graham could have found out about the car?'

Temple took a gulp at his beer.

'If I'm going to investigate this business, I'll do it in my own sweet way,' he announced calmly. Then the door swung open and he said, 'Ah, here's our friend. Now don't laugh – he takes himself very seriously.'

Under the large peak of his cloth cap, the beady eyes of Spider Williams swiftly surveyed the room. Then he caught sight of Temple and came over at once. He was the type of man familiar to *habitués* of racecourses, where his prototypes abound in hundreds – hangers-on who somehow contrive to make a living at the game.

'Ah Mr. Temple!' he began breezily. 'Sorry I'm late. 'Ad a bit of a job gettin' 'ere.'

'Sit down Spider,' smiled Temple, turning to introduce his wife.

'You don't 'ave to tell me who this is!' grinned Spider. 'Could spot her a mile off. Glad to know you, Mrs. Temple. Sorry I'm late, Mrs. Temple. 'Ope you ain't tired of 'angin' about. I 'ad a bit of a job gettin' 'ere.'

Temple obtained a drink for the newcomer.

'Any luck, Spider?' he asked, when they had gathered round the table.

Spider shook his head. 'Not a blamed thing, guv'nor,' he replied, taking a swig at his beer and wiping his mouth with the back of his hand. 'I bin through to five or six what's in the know, but they ain't 'eard nothin'. What sort of car did yer say it was?'

'I told you,' said Temple rather impatiently. 'So far as I could see, it looked like a Milford.'

'And what time was this?'

'I couldn't say to the minute. I left Broadcasting House soon after seven-thirty, and we were on our way down to Piccadilly.'

'It couldn't have been much after eight when you 'phoned me,' said Spider. 'You'll 'ave to gimme a bit more time, guv'nor. Maybe something'll turn up. These cars ain't so easy to trace, yer know—'

He was interrupted by the barmaid, with whom he seemed on be on rather more than familiar terms. She told him that he was wanted on the telephone, and with a knowing wink at Temple he went out to take the call.

Temple took the opportunity to order another drink, and was about to make some remark to Steve when he noticed her looking at someone behind him. The next instant he felt a resounding smack between the shoulders, and a voice said in a pronounced Welsh accent: 'Hello, Simon! Who would have thought of seeing you here!'

Temple looked round inquiringly, and saw a dark young man who now appeared highly embarrassed.

'Lordy!' he exclaimed in a half whisper. 'You're not Simon!'

'I'm rather afraid I'm not,' smiled Temple, not a little amused at the other's dismayed expression. It was, in fact, the little Welshman who had been present at the discovery of Norma Rice's body, though Temple was not yet aware of this.

'Well now, just fancy my patting you on the back like that. Good gracious me, what a stupid thing to do! I can't think what came over me.'

'This is the first time I've heard that I've got a double,' smiled Temple.

35

'But you have indeed! When your back was turned towards me I was sure it was Simon Phipps.'

'I should like to meet Mr. Phipps sometime. By the way, my name is Temple.'

'Temple!' cried the little Welshman, with a dramatic gesture. 'Not Paul Temple?'

'I'm afraid so.'

'Why, yes, of course – I recognise you now. I have seen pictures of you on your novels.'

'No wonder you didn't know me!' grinned Temple.

'It's very sporty of you to take it like this, I must say. But I do feel such a fool! And to think I've only just finished reading one of your novels.'

'Oh?' murmured Temple, in a somewhat indifferent tone.

'Yes indeed,' continued the Welshman with gathering enthusiasm. 'The one called *Murder on the Mayflower*.'

'I hope you liked it.'

The other nodded vigorously.

'It was most ingenious. There was only one thing I didn't quite like – when that man jumped off the boat so suddenly. Of course, you know I go in for that sort of thing quite a lot.'

'Jumping off boats?' asked Temple.

'Oh no, no! I mean detective novels.'

'You write them too?'

'Mercy, no! I read them. I have always got one with me.' He fumbled in his coat pocket and produced a shabby paperbacked specimen. 'I read them all day long. Why, in the last two years I have read four hundred and sixty-three detective novels. That's pretty good going, isn't it?'

For a moment Temple seemed quite stunned. 'Yes,' he agreed at length in a subdued voice, 'whichever way you look at it, that seems to be pretty good going. You must be fully qualified to embark upon a career of crime.'

'You will have your little joke, Mr. Temple. But I am an absolute glutton for anything to do with murder, crime or criminology. It is very strange for a docile man like myself. I could not hurt so much as a fly.'

'Anyhow,' said Temple, 'I hope you haven't remembered quite everything you've read, or your brain must be in a considerate state of turmoil.'

At that moment Spider Williams loomed up once more, and the Welshman again made his apologies and withdrew. As he was moving away, he turned and said to Temple in a serious voice, 'If it's any consolation to you, Mr. Temple, my friend Phipps is a very good-looking man. Good night, Mr. Temple. Goodnight, Mrs. Temple.'

When he was out of earshot, Steve said, 'Now what made him think I was Mrs. Temple? You never introduced me.'

'You look like Mrs. Temple,' her husband assured her. 'But, what's more to the point, what made him think I was Simon Phipps?' He hesitated a moment, then added thoughtfully, 'If he really did think I was Simon Phipps.'

But he had no further opportunity to speculate upon this, for Spider was breathing hoarsely in his ear.

'Bit o' luck we've 'ad, guv'nor,' he wheezed. 'One of my blokes, Bert 'Arris struck oil, as yer might say.'

'Go on,' nodded Temple.

'That car was a six-cylinder Milford. Black saloon. DVC629 like you said – 'ad a G.B. plate on the back.'

'Yes, I seem to remember that,' said Temple, wrinkling his forehead.

'I saw it too,' agreed Steve. 'Whose car is it?'

Spider Williams chuckled.

'Quite the little detective, ain't she, guv?' Then he became confidential once more. 'That car belongs to a bloke named Doctor Kohima, 497 Great Wigmore Street.'

'You seem to have it all off pat,' said Temple. 'Has this doctor ever been mixed up in anything?'

'Not that I know of, Mr. Temple. All you asked me was to find whose car bumped you – and I've got you the lowdown.'

'Are you sure of this, Spider?' asked Temple rather dubiously.

The little man nodded emphatically.

'We don't make mistakes in our racket, Mr. Temple. You know that.'

'Doctor Kohima,' repeated Temple thoughtfully. 'I seem to recall the name. I believe he's an Egyptian nerve specialist – some sort of psychiatrist.'

'That's right,' nodded Steve. 'He's very fashionable just now. I've overheard women talking about him at the hairdresser's or somewhere.'

Temple opened his wallet and passed a couple of banknotes over to Spider, who stowed them away in an inside pocket.

'If it was Doctor Kohima driving that car,' said Temple, 'there doesn't seem to be much wrong with *his* nerves.'

They bade Spider good night and went out.

Temple was very silent as he drove back, turning over in his mind the startling events of the evening. Could there be any connection between Sir Ernest's death and the attempt to smash up their car? And who was that little Welsh fellow? And Doctor Kohima . . . he found himself more intrigued by that name than any of the others. Why should a fashionable psychiatrist spend his evening charging around the streets in his car? And why should he have homicidal intentions towards Paul Temple?

He was still more than a trifle puzzled the following day when Steve drove him slowly down Great Wigmore Street.

They drew up outside a Georgian mansion and noted the neat brown plate with 'Charles Kohima' in white lettering.

'Did you make an appointment?' asked Steve.

'Yes, I 'phoned through this morning. What are you going to do – wait for me in the car?'

She considered this for a moment, then decided that she would pay a visit to a servants' registry office which was just round the corner.

'Still looking for a maid?' smiled Temple. 'By Timothy! You are an optimist!' He slowly climbed out of the car and said, 'I don't suppose I shall be very long. If you're not outside, I'll probably go straight back to the flat.'

She nodded and drove off.

A young maid answered Temple's ring and conducted him into the waiting-room, which looked much more like a private sitting-room. Lounging on the settee was a fair-haired, sensitive-faced man of about forty-five, carelessly glancing through an expensive American fashion journal. He wished Temple good afternoon in a rather agreeable sort of voice, and started the usual aimless sort of conversation about the weather. As he was obviously waiting to see the doctor, Temple began to wonder if his own appointment would take place at the agreed time.

'Our friend seems as busy as ever,' said the man on the settee, when the conversation was showing some signs of lagging.

'Our friend?' repeated Temple, slightly puzzled.

'Doctor Kohima.'

'Oh!'

The man on the settee eyed Temple keenly. 'Oh, I'm afraid I was rather jumping to conclusions,' he said. 'This is your first visit, perhaps?'

'Well, yes,' smiled Temple, 'I suppose in a manner of speaking it is.'

The other leaned forward and said in an earnest voice, 'You won't regret it.'

'I hope not,' said Temple, secretly wondering if the other man was quite normal.

'Kohima's a brilliant man. Really brilliant. Absolutely first class. Take my word for it.'

Temple did not speak for a moment, but quietly eyed the fair-haired man very carefully. Then he said, 'Forgive my asking, but haven't we met before somewhere?'

The other shook his head, and with just a shade too much emphasis replied, 'I don't think so. My name is Lathom – Carl Lathom.'

'I thought so,' nodded Temple, whose memory for faces was as reliable as a card index. 'It was about six years ago, at Lady Forester's.'

Carl Lathom frowned.

'I'm afraid I don't actually remember the occasion,' he admitted.

'Then you'd hardly remember me. My name happens to be Temple.'

Lathom's face cleared.

'Oh yes, of course. You write detective novels and things.'

'Chiefly detective novels.'

'Oh, please forgive me,' said Lathom apologetically. 'I didn't mean to be rude.'

'That's all right,' laughed Temple.

'But I really must apologise. I know how sensitive one feels about one's work. You see,' he added, with a rueful sort of smile, 'I once wrote a play myself.'

'I remember it very well,' Temple assured him.

'Yes,' nodded Carl, in a more indifferent tone, 'it had quite a good run. Made me a lot of money.'

'Congratulations.'

Carl Lathom shrugged.

'Oh, that was a long time ago,' he murmured, as if the memory was not entirely pleasant.

But Temple had suddenly recollected something else.

'Tell me,' he went on, in a casual tone, 'wasn't Norma Rice in your play?'

'Yes, she had the lead. It was her first big chance in the West End. She was awfully good, too. Awfully good. The play was quite hopeless without her.' After a brief pause, he added, 'I say, did you see that in the newspapers? About Norma? It was a hell of a shock to me.'

'A most distressing business,' agreed Temple.

'Oh, most distressing. A charming girl, too. Temperamental, of course, but that's understandable. I got to know her quite a bit during rehearsals of the play, and it seemed to me that she had a morbid streak in her nature which might run away with her one day. When I first read about her death I should have been willing to lay ten to one that it was suicide.'

Temple smiled.

'But surely she would hardly have taken an overdose of Amashyer and then gone to the trouble to scrawl "Rex" on the carriage window . . .'

Lathom shook his head.

'That's just the sort of crazy thing Norma would do – specially if she had happened to read about the Rex murders.' He sighed. 'There's no accounting for some women. All the same, she was a great actress.'

'Have you written anything else since that play?' asked Temple.

41

'Not a single word. I got caught up in the advertising game and then I had a sort of breakdown. I've been very ill during the past three or four years.'

'Oh, I'm sorry,' sympathised Temple.

Lathom smiled. 'Oh, I'm much better now, thank you.'

'Thanks to Doctor Kohima?'

'Entirely. He's really first class. It's difficult to explain without sounding rather schoolgirlish, but he is really, quite frankly, such a distinctive personality. Something keeps telling you that he is doing his utmost to work with you and straighten out all the kinks.' He laughed a trifle self-consciously and added, 'You can imagine that's rather important with a psychiatrist.' Opening a slim gold cigarette-case, he passed it over to Temple.

After they lit their cigarettes, Lathom went on in a conversational tone, 'Yes, I've been very groggy. Had one or two very nasty turns – the brain can play some devilish queer tricks, you know, Mr. Temple. As a matter of fact, strictly between ourselves, I've been suffering from – well – hallucinations.'

Temple managed to conceal his surprise by taking a draw at his cigarette and slowly expelling a stream of smoke.

'Of course, I'm cured now,' continued Lathom rather more assertively. 'But it was distinctly unpleasant while it lasted.'

'I should imagine so,' nodded Temple.' Did the – er – hallucinations take any consistent form?'

'Why, yes, I had the impression that everywhere I went I was being followed—'

'Not by the police?' queried Temple, who had often heard of this particular type of illusion.

'No, nothing as lurid as that,' laughed Lathom. 'This was a girl who was following me around. A very attractive girl, too. I can see her now just as clearly as I see you sitting there.

She had brown shoes – brown costume – brown handbag – perky little hat – silk stockings! I suppose, really, it was quite the nicest type of hallucination.'

'Did you ever try to, well, to sort of corner the girl in brown?' asked Temple, in an interested tone.

'Time and again. But of course she was never there. She'd vanish quite completely – almost into thin air. It was quite uncanny. I don't mind telling you it had me badly rattled.'

'And you mean to say Doctor Kohima convinced you that she did not exist?'

'That's just what he did,' Lathom assured Temple earnestly. 'It's taken him literally months of exhaustive research, but he's done it! I can't quite tell you how, but suddenly the lady in is no more. She's vanished for the last time. No doubt about the doctor is brilliant – really quite brilliant.'

He appeared to be about to enlarge further upon this question when the door opened, and a well-dressed woman of about thirty-five stood there.

'The doctor's sorry to keep you waiting, Mr. Temple,' she announced. 'He'll be able to see you in about five minutes.'

'Thank you,' said Temple. The woman looked round and suddenly saw Lathom, who was sitting behind the door.

'Your appointment wasn't till four, Mr. Lathom,' she said. 'Didn't you know that?'

Lathom rose politely and smiled at her.

'Oh yes,' he replied suavely. 'But I'm afraid I found myself in the neighbourhood with half an hour to spare, so I thought I'd come in and relax, as the doctor always advises.'

'It's quite all right,' smiled the secretary, 'as long as you don't mind waiting.'

'Not at all.'

'I'll tell the doctor you're here,' she said as she went out, silently closing the door after her.

Temple looked round for an ash-tray and stubbed out his cigarette.

'Was that Doctor Kohima's secretary?' he asked.

'That's right. An awfully nice person.'

'Yes, she seemed very helpful when I spoke to her on the 'phone,' nodded Temple. 'You don't happen to know her name?'

'Well, I always call her "nurse" for some silly reason. But the doctor did introduce us when I first came here. Her name is Mrs. Trevelyan.'

CHAPTER III

Steve Finds a Treasure

TEMPLE glanced somewhat suspiciously at Lathom, but the letter's expression was completely matter-of-fact.

'Are you quite sure that's the name?' asked Temple.

'Of course I'm sure. Why?'

'Oh—nothing.'

Temple imagined he caught a glint of amusement in Lathom's somewhat steely blue eyes, but decided he had been mistaken. Lathom picked up a glossy magazine, glanced aimlessly through it then turned to Temple again.

'Come to think of it, Mr. Temple, I've been seeing your name the papers once or twice lately in connection with this Rex case. Was the report true in the *Evening Courier* a couple of nights back?'

'Which report was that exactly?'

'The one that said Sir Graham Forbes had finally decided to send for Paul Temple.'

Temple shrugged, took out his cigarette-case, and offered one to Lathom.

'Are you interested in this Rex affair?' he asked.

There was silence for a moment, then Lathom said, 'Yes, as a matter of fact I am. I don't actually take an interest in murders and sordid crimes, but this business rather intrigues me. Maybe it's partly because I knew Norma Rice.' He gave an apologetic laugh, then added somewhat self-consciously, 'I'm afraid I've even got quite a little theory of my own.'

'What is it?' asked Temple quietly.

'Oh, really! You must get dozens of people trying to foist their wild ideas on you. Doesn't it get rather boring?'

'I'm not easily bored, Mr. Lathom,' Temple assured him, he lit his cigarette. 'In a case of this nature, one has to consider every possible angle, and there's an old story about the onlooker seeing most of the game.'

'Then, if you really want my opinion, Mr. Temple,' said Lathom earnestly, 'I think this fellow Rex is nothing more than a homicidal maniac.'

'What makes you think that?'

'Well, look at the Norma Rice affair. If Rex really was responsible for murdering Norma Rice, what possible motive could he have had?'

'I suppose Norma Rice had enemies, the same as anyone else. I believe she had rather a gift for alienating people.'

'But poor old Norma never meant any harm. Everyone knew it was just her temperamental moods. And then take this murder of Cranbury in the Brains Trust. It sounds fantastic to me.'

'Then you've heard of Sir Ernest's death?'

'Good lord, yes. Haven't you seen the papers today? They gave you a pretty good show. But why did Rex pick on poor old Cranbury?'

'Who says Rex killed him?'

'Why, the papers. Anyhow, you were there – you know what happened.' He paused, evidently expecting Temple to supply some further information.

'There was nothing very dramatic about it,' said the novelist. 'Sir Ernest simply collapsed – it just appeared to be heart failure.'

'Then why are the newspapers saying that he was murdered by Rex?'

'Because,' Temple quietly informed him, 'Sir Ernest mentioned Rex just before he died.'

'Did he?' Lathom's eyes widened. 'Did he, by Jove! I didn't know that. Can you tell me what he said, or is it a secret?'

Temple smiled.

'It wasn't as startling as all that. He simply said, "Temple, I want to tell you about Rex."'

Again there was silence. Then Lathom asked:

'That was all?'

'All there was time for.'

Lathom nodded his head thoughtfully, as if he were busy fitting facts into his theory. Suddenly he exclaimed, 'Well, there you are! Obviously this fellow Rex is a lunatic. Must be as crazy as a hatter. Good heavens, why should anyone want to murder poor old Ernest?'

'You knew Sir Ernest?' put in Temple quickly.

'Good lord, yes! He was quite a man about town, you know. He wasn't exactly a friend of mine, but we were always bumping into each other in clubs and places. Seemed quite a harmless old stick – completely wrapped up in his work – the last sort of person you'd expect to find at cross-purposes with a murderer.'

As Lathom finished speaking the door opened, and Mrs. Trevelyan said, 'The doctor will see you now, Mr. Temple.'

Temple rose and thanked her. As he went to the door, Lathom murmured, 'We shall meet again, I hope, Mr. Temple. I hope my theories haven't bored you too much.'

'Not at all,' replied Temple politely, and there was some degree of truth in his answer, for he had not made up his mind about Mr. Carl Lathom. And one is invariably intrigued by a stranger who retains some element of mystery.

Outside, Mrs. Trevelyan closed the door behind them. 'Before you see Doctor Kohima, could I have a word with you?' she said.

Her voice was low and urgent, and Temple detected an expression of alarm in her eyes.

'Yes, of course,' he answered.

She led him a little way along the corridor, then turned once more.

'Listen! I've got to talk to you!' she whispered, and there was a note of urgency in her voice. 'I've got to talk to you about Rex.'

She looked round cautiously as if she were scared of being overheard. Then she went on, 'Please believe me, it's desperately important.'

Temple said, 'I'm sure it must be.'

'We can't talk here,' she said nervously, looking at the row of doors, as if she expected any one of them to open suddenly.

'Then what do you suggest?'

She placed a forefinger and thumb inside a belt she wore, and produced a slip of paper.

'Could you possibly come to this address – tonight?'

Temple took the paper and glanced at it casually.

'Tonight, at what time?'

She moistened her lips, hesitated, then said:

'Half past ten. You will come, won't you?'

'Yes, all right.'

'You promise?' she insisted anxiously.

Temple eyed her keenly, noting the attractive high cheek-bones and keen grey eyes set widely apart.

'Yes, I promise,' he slowly assured her.

Obviously relieved, she went to a door opposite where they stood and opened it. 'This way, sir, please,' she called, raising her voice.

The room into which she showed him was quite plainly furnished. There was, however, a very comfortable couch in an alcove farthest from the window, and there was also a large armchair beside it.

Doctor Kohima was sitting at a large desk in the middle of the room, and he rose to shake hands with Temple as he came in. The doctor was quite obviously an Egyptian. His skin was honey-coloured and he had a handsome profile that would most certainly find favour with a large feminine clientele. When he spoke he had a soft voice rather like the purr of a contented cat, a voice calculated to extract the most intimate confidences, however unwilling the patient.

Temple had already looked up his record and had discovered that he was fully qualified in medicine, but had devoted five years to psychological analysis under the celebrated Pulitzer in Vienna. He was, in fact, reputed to have been a favourite pupil of the great man.

At a first meeting, Kohima always gave the impression of holding a tremendous reserve of very vital mental power which it was difficult to describe. There was a warmth in his handclasp, and he nodded to Temple to take a chair.

'I am so sorry to have kept you waiting, Mr. Temple,' he apologised in a sincere voice with the merest trace of accent.

'Do sit down, please. According to your 'phone message, you wish to consult me upon a purely personal matter.'

He swung round in his swivel chair and smiled frankly.

Temple could not restrain the feeling that here was a man with whom one could put the cards on the table. But this feeling was tinged with caution, for he was aware that the doctor must be an adept at breaking down defences, and knew every gambit to suit all types of individuals.

'To be quite frank, Doctor Kohima,' he began carefully, 'I should simply like to ask you a few questions.'

A tiny frown puckered the loose skin round the doctor's dark eyes.

'This is not a newspaper interview?' he asked, still in the same pleasing tone, though Temple noticed that his expression had changed.

'No,' he said. 'Nothing like that.'

'Then I shall be delighted,' said the doctor. 'It will make such a pleasant change. It is always I who am asking the questions, hour after hour – day after day – probing into people's private thoughts. However, you will not be interested in that. Please go on.'

Temple hesitated a bare second, then suddenly shot the question.

'Have you a car, Doctor?'

'A car?' repeated Kohima, obviously a little surprised. 'Why, yes – is that unusual for a doctor?'

'What make is your car?'

'It's a Milford. A six-cylinder Milford.'

'Black?'

The doctor nodded.

'Registration number?'

'DVC629,' replied the doctor, his voice betraying the fact that he was considerably puzzled. 'Why do you ask?'

'Thank you,' said Temple. 'Now I'll tell you exactly why I am here.'

He went on to detail the story of the accident of the previous evening, telling it in a level, unemotional tone, and noting that his listener paid close attention to all the facts. Doctor Kohima was a perfect audience. When Temple concluded by repeating the description of the car that had forced them into the kerb, the doctor was patently startled.

'You must have been mistaken!' he urged.

'No,' replied Temple calmly. 'I have every reason to believe that my description is accurate to the last detail.'

'But it couldn't have been my car, Mr. Temple,' replied the other, a little worried now. 'Why, my car was never out of the garage at all last night.'

'Where do you keep it?'

'Well, actually at my house near Regent's Park. But all this week it's been at Sloan's Garage in Leicester Square for one or two minor repairs. As a matter of fact, I'm supposed to collect it tonight.' He hesitated, obviously more than a little puzzled, then suggested, 'Why don't you 'phone the garage, Mr. Temple? Please, I wish you would.'

'You've no objection?'

'But of course not!' He picked up a little black notebook and turned the pages. 'The number is Temple Bar 7178.'

'Thank you,' said Temple, and drew the telephone towards him. The doctor poured himself a glass of water from the carafe on his desk and began to sip it slowly.

'Sloan's Garage?' said Temple into the mouthpiece. 'I am speaking for Doctor Kohima. Would it be convenient for him to pick up his car this evening? . . . yes, the Milford . . . oh . . . it was ready yesterday? I see. Could you tell me, by any chance, if the car was taken out last night?' There was a pause while Temple listened to a lengthy explanation.

'Have you any idea what time that was?' he said presently. 'Half past seven? Who brought it back? Oh, the chauffeur – at about a quarter to ten. Right—thank you very much.'

He slowly replaced the receiver and turned to the doctor.

'Do I understand that the car was ready yesterday?' asked Doctor Kohima.

'That's so. It was also taken out of the garage last night by your chauffeur. He had it between half past seven and a quarter to ten. And of course it was during that period that our little accident happened. So you see it was obviously—'

'But I don't understand—' interrupted Doctor Kohima in a bewildered tone. 'In fact, I'm afraid you're going to get rather a surprise. . .'

But Temple did not seem in the least surprised. With the merest suggestion of a smile playing around his lips, he said: 'I don't think so, Doctor Kohima. You are simply going to tell me that you haven't got a chauffeur!'

As Steve was not waiting with the car outside, Temple decided to walk back to the flat. As he strode along the wide pavements of Wigmore Street he turned over the mystery of Doctor Kohima's car in his mind. The doctor's surprise had seemed genuine enough, which was no more than one could expect, for one could hardly suspect an established psychiatrist of repute to be connected with an incident of this character. It was probably a sheer coincidence that his car had been chosen from the hundreds or more in the garage.

And yet there was Mrs. Trevelyan.

No doubt about it, this woman was in some way connected with Rex. There had been those clues on the dead bodies, and she herself had almost admitted as much. She was supposed to be going to tell him more tonight. In fact, she seemed terribly anxious to tell what she knew. Could it be a case of a guilty conscience? Mrs. Trevelyan might even be Rex herself, and tonight's appointment some sort of trap. All the same, Temple meant to keep the appointment. He had found more than once that if one walked into a trap knowingly and kept one's wits, the trapper was often himself caught. His mind went back to the elaborate and ingenious plans laid by the Marquis at the October Hotel . . . but they had culminated in an episode which had revealed the identity of *The Marquis*. There was such a thing as baiting the trap too generously.

Temple pondered upon these and other similar ideas as he came into Oxford Street and crossed it to turn down into Mayfair. Finding that he had left his latchkey in his other suit, Temple had to ring the bell to be admitted to the flat. He was beginning to wonder if Steve had returned when the door swung quickly open, and a bland yellow face smiled up into his.

'Good afternoon. You are Mr. Temple, yes?' said a cheerful voice which was of obvious Oriental origin.

'Er – yes –' murmured Temple, somewhat taken aback.

'Welcome home, Mr. Temple,' continued the little man, with a slight inclination of his head as he stepped aside for Temple to enter.

'Thanks very much,' was all Temple could manage by way of reply.

As the door closed, the man said, 'I will take your hat and coat, thank you.'

'Thank *you*,' murmured Temple politely, secretly wondering what all this was about.

'Not at all,' smiled the other, quite unabashed. 'It is a pleasure to serve you, sir.'

At that moment, to Temple's great relief, Steve came out of the lounge.

'Hello, Paul,' she greeted him. Then turned to the little man. 'Oh, Ricky – this is Mr. Temple.'

Ricky smiled even more widely than before.

'I recognise him,' he announced proudly. 'We get on pretty well together – I hope.'

Even Steve seemed slightly at a loss.

'Yes, well, that will be all now, thank you, Ricky,' she said, and the little man bowed and went into the kitchen. In the lounge, Temple said, 'Steve, where on earth did you pick him up?'

'At the registry office. He was waiting for a job there – and I was looking for someone – and they hadn't another soul on their books, so I thought, well, there's no harm in giving him a trial.'

'By Timothy, what next?' exclaimed her husband. 'Ever since Pryce left, there's been one long succession—'

'Paul, you don't seem to have any idea just how difficult it is to get servants,' said Steve, faintly exasperated.

'Difficult!' echoed Temple. 'We've had three Czechs, a Viennese, a Hungarian, a Greek . . . and now, for Pete's sake, a Chinese!'

'Siamese, darling!' she corrected him. 'And, anyway, he's got awfully good references. I was lucky to catch him before he registered, or he'd most certainly have been snapped up by some film star. As it was, I only got him through mentioning your name.'

'My name?'

'Yes, he's quite an admirer of your books. He says he reads them to improve his English!'

Temple caught Steve's eye and could not repress a smile.

'Okay, we'll give him a trial,' he grinned. 'But chop-suey for breakfast just once and he'll need all those references!'

'Oh, I forgot to tell you,' said Steve quickly. 'Sir Graham's in the study.'

'What does he want?' asked Temple.

'I've no idea, darling. He's been talking most interestingly about the weather. Inspector Crane's with him – you know – the sandy one with the unfortunate manner.'

'Must be something in the wind,' mused Temple, as they went along to the study.

Forbes and Crane were talking rapidly, but they stopped as soon as the door opened. Forbes looked as if he had not slept very well of late – the lines on the rugged face were more deeply marked than ever. But he smiled as Temple and Steve entered the room.

'Sorry to have kept you waiting, Sir Graham. Good afternoon, Inspector,' said Temple, noting that Crane looked even more surly than usual.

Steve brought them a drink, and after a short interchange of noncommittal pleasantries, Temple lay back in his chair and asked:

'Well, what goes on now? Any more developments, Sir Graham?'

Sir Graham took a deep breath.

'Oh yes,' he said, 'there's always something moving on this case. That's one thing to be thankful for, anyway.'

'Then what is it this time?'

'Well, it looks as if we might be on to something at last.' Forbes paused for a moment, then said, 'Temple, do you happen to have heard of a man called Hans Muller?'

'Hans Muller,' repeated Temple thoughtfully. 'Yes, I know the gentleman. Big, fair man. Dutch extraction. Has he turned up again?'

'What do you make of him?' demanded Crane bluntly.

'Oh, well,' shrugged Temple, 'the man's a crook, of course but a fairly intelligent one. Why do you ask?'

'We've received a letter from him – or, rather, the inspector has. Show it Mr. Temple, Inspector.'

Crane fumbled in an inside pocket and produced a thin blue envelope.

'Here it is, sir,' he replied.

'Then are you a pen-friend of Muller's?' queried Temple in some surprise.

Crane shook his head.

'I can't think why he picked on me, sir. I've never actually been in contact with Muller, and I must say this rather surprised me.'

'Do you mean the contents surprised you, or the fact that you received it?'

'Well, in a manner of speaking, both, sir.'

Temple extracted a single sheet of notepaper and read:

Inspector Crane,
I am given to understand that you are personally in charge of the Rex case. I would respectfully suggest, therefore, that you meet me tonight, shortly before midnight, at Granger's Wharf, Rotherhithe. I can enlighten you on the identity of Rex.
Sincerely yours,
Hans Muller.

Temple read it through again, then returned the note to its envelope, which he passed back to the inspector.

'It seems genuine enough – though I get the impression that Muller seems to know you rather well,' he commented.

Crane shook his head.

'I've never set eyes on the fellow,' he insisted. 'To be perfectly honest, I'd never even heard of him till this morning.'

'Then why should he write you a friendly sort of letter like that? It isn't as if there were any reward offered for information about Rex,' put in Steve.

'I've never seen the man in my life,' Crane reasserted stubbornly.

'We don't even know much about Muller at the Yard,' said Forbes. 'That's why I wanted to have a word with you, Temple. We know that Muller is a Dutchman and that he came over here in 1934, but that's about all.'

'Very well,' smiled Temple, 'now let's see what I can do.' He went over to his desk, unlocked the bottom right-hand drawer and produced a thick, indexed ledger, with an attractive leather cover.

'What's that, Temple?' asked Forbes, with interest.

'Oh, just a sort of personal "Who's Who" I've been keeping for years. I meet a lot of interesting people, and it seemed a good idea to keep a record of them. Useful when I'm stuck for a new character in one of my books.'

His long fingers flicked over the pages.

'Ah, here we are . . . Muller, Hans. Born in Amsterdam, probably about 1898 . . . suspected of receiving stolen diamonds . . . nothing proved . . . first-class linguist . . . Dutch, Flemish, Danish, French and English . . .'

He stopped, then said quietly, 'I say, this is interesting. Apparently, Muller is very well off. In 1939 he inherited quite legitimately nearly a quarter of a million . . .'

Forbes whistled expressively.

'Have you ever met the man?' asked Crane.

'Why, yes.' Temple referred to the book again. 'Paris in February 1938 and the Hague, January 1939 – that was before he came into the money. At that time, we suspected he might have had a hand in disposing of the Falkirk Diamond when it was smuggled out of this country.'

'Oh yes, I remember,' said Forbes, who had indeed been closely concerned with the case.

'Well, if you know this man, Mr. Temple,' interposed Crane, 'it seems to me it might be a very good idea if you came along with us tonight.'

'Yes, by all means,' agreed Forbes. 'We'll pick you up at eleven, if that's all right with you.'

'No,' replied Temple quickly. 'I'm afraid I have an appointment at ten-thirty.'

'An appointment, darling?' queried Steve.

'Yes,' said Temple casually, 'I'll tell you about that later.' He turned to the Assistant Commissioner. 'Where are you starting from?'

'We're taking a police-launch from Westminster.'

'That'll suit me,' nodded Temple. 'I'll see you there – at the Pier – about eleven-fifteen?'

'No later.'

Temple nodded.

'Right,' agreed Forbes, slowly rising and putting down his empty glass. 'See you at eleven-fifteen. Better wear a couple of overcoats – it'll probably be damned cold on the river. Come on, Crane.'

They had not reached the door before it had already opened, and there was Ricky with their hats and coats.

'Sir Graham and Inspector Crane are leaving, Ricky,' Steve announced rather superfluously.

'Okay, missie,' smiled the little Siamese. 'This way, please, Sir Graham. . .'

When they had gone and Ricky had carefully closed the door, Temple turned to Steve.

'I say,' he murmured, 'he'll have to stop this "okay, missie" business.'

Steve laughed.

'Poor Ricky! You must admit, darling, he makes the place seem more colourful, somehow.'

'If his cooking's up to the same standard,' grinned Temple, 'we're on velvet.'

'What's this appointment of yours tonight at ten-thirty?' asked Steve, becoming serious at once.

'I suppose you wouldn't believe me if I told you it was with an extremely attractive, sophisticated woman in the early thirties,' smiled Temple.

'I might.'

'Oh, well, I'd better start at the beginning. I had a chat with Doctor Kohima about the car that bumped us. It was his all right.'

'But – but – hadn't he any explanation?'

'He had. A very plausible one, too. You know, Steve, there's something damned queer about that affair.'

'In what way exactly?'

'Well, in the first place, his car is supposed to be at a garage in Bicester Square, where it's being repaired. The doctor said it would be ready today, and asked me to check that with the garage. They said it was actually ready yesterday, and, what's more, that Doctor Kohima's chauffeur took the car out of the garage last night at seven-thirty and brought it back at nine forty-five.'

'Then, there you are!' exclaimed Steve. 'That was when the accident happened. The chauffeur must be mixed up somehow—'

'That's just the point,' interrupted Temple. 'You see, Doctor Kohima doesn't happen to have a chauffeur.'

Steve was momentarily nonplussed, then rallied with: 'But it's quite simple. Someone pretended to be the doctor's chauffeur.'

Temple nodded thoughtfully.

'In which case, how did he get the car? They're pretty smart at that garage – they told me the system they have, and it's fairly foolproof. There's only one way he could have got it, by producing a ticket, and that ticket must be the same as the one originally given to Doctor Kohima.'

'So that means the doctor was lying?'

'Seems like it. But it doesn't mean that he drove the car himself. In fact, I'm sure he didn't. What's more, his being a psychiatrist doesn't simplify matters. You always have a feeling that he's one jump ahead of you, and it's rather an uncomfortable feeling.'

Steve wrinkled her forehead thoughtfully.

'Surely he realises that this is a very serious business?' she said. 'Doesn't he propose to do anything? I mean, after all it was his car, and if you notify the police—'

'No, I don't propose to do that just yet,' replied Temple. 'He was quite helpful up to a point. Seemed to be telling me all he knew.'

'But where does this beautiful woman come into the picture?' demanded Steve suddenly. 'Or doesn't she?'

'She comes into it all right. The woman in question is Doctor Kohima's secretary – and her name is Mrs. Trevelyan.'

Steve dropped the bundle of knitting she had just picked up.

'Darling, you're joking!' she cried.

Temple slowly shook his head.

'So your appointment tonight is with Mrs. Trevelyan?' continued Steve.

'I'm afraid so. D'you mind?'

'It doesn't look as if I shall have much say in the matter.'

'Oh, but you have, darling. I wouldn't dream of going without you. I told you that Mrs. Trevelyan is a very attractive woman. And my experience is that if a very attractive woman means mischief, she is far less dangerous if another very attractive woman happens to be present.'

'So even a detective's wife has her uses,' smiled Steve. 'Well, where do we meet the lady?'

He passed over the slip of paper, and she read the address.

'That's not far from here,' she commented. 'Does Doctor Kohima know about this appointment?'

'No, and she seemed pretty anxious that he shouldn't get to hear of it. The woman is frightened, Steve. I don't know what she's scared of, but she's as frightened as hell!'

'Many actresses are very beautiful,' said Steve softly.

'The converse doesn't necessarily apply.'

'Still, acting is often instinctive to a good-looking woman. She knows how men fall for beauty in distress. Are you sure you want me to come with you?'

Temple looked at her earnestly.

'Of course. But I ought to warn you that there may be a certain amount of danger.'

'In that case,' declared Steve decisively, 'I'm most certainly coming.'

'Good,' smiled Temple. 'Better bring your knitting. The needles might come in useful – I read somewhere that they can be dangerous weapons. Ah well, I think I'll change.' He yawned prodigiously and announced, 'I feel like a bath.'

The door opened softly and Ricky stood there impassively with folded hands and imperturbable smile.

'What is it, Ricky?' asked Steve.

'So sorry to interrupt,' murmured the little Siamese, experiencing just the merest difficulty with his r's. 'Your bath is ready, Sir.'

Temple looked at Steve, then back at Ricky.

'Oh – er – thanks very much,' he said, slowly getting to his feet. 'Just a minute, Ricky,' he called, as the little man turned to go. 'How did you know I was thinking of taking a bath?'

The smile on the yellow face grew even wider for a moment, then vanished, as Ricky seriously announced 'It is the duty of the good servant to anticipate the wishes of the good master. So sorry I interrupt – so sorry.' The door closed behind him.

'That, I take it,' said Temple, 'is an old Siamese proverb.'

'Darling,' cried Steve, 'he's going to be wonderful!'

'I don't believe it!' said Temple, who was obviously amused nevertheless. 'It isn't true. It's done by mirrors! It's a mirage! It's Oriental necromancy!'

Steve laughed, then folded her hands and in a recognisable imitation of Ricky's voice, said, 'It is the duty of the good servant to anticipate the wishes of the good master.'

'In other words . . .' grinned Temple. 'You look as if you need a bath!'

CHAPTER IV

Rex Strikes Again

As HE LAY in his bath, Temple found his thoughts drifting to Hans Muller. He remembered the big Dutchman quite well, particularly his capacity for evasiveness in the face of all sorts of questioning retaining at the same time the politest and most unruffled air and an expressionless face that would have brought him a fortune at poker. Muller had puzzled the police of five countries in his day; they had never been able to 'pin' anything definite on him, although they had the strongest suspicions that he had been involved in many a deal in stolen gems.

How had Muller come up against Rex? There were a number of possibilities upon which Temple idly began to speculate. Rex could have discovered some conclusive piece of evidence against Muller and started to blackmail him. Muller was the last person who would stand for blackmail. He would set about fighting the blackmailer in his own way.

On the other hand, Muller might be acting for someone who was suffering from the attentions of Rex. He was that sort of man. Now he had no need to engage in a life of crime himself, he might be amusing himself pitting his wits against master criminals.

A third possibility was that Hans Muller was an agent, willing or unwilling, of Rex himself, and that the message was in the nature of some sort of decoy that would lead to trouble. Temple turned on the shower and the rush of water swept these speculations temporarily from his mind.

Temple noted that Steve was wearing a completely new and very becoming dress as they set out for the address Mrs. Trevelyan had given them. It was in the Lancaster Gate district, and they had little difficulty in finding it.

Forty-nine, Marshall House Terrace was a three-storey mansion standing back a short distance from the road and approached by a short flight of steps. They left the car outside and went up to the front door, noting that it sadly needed a coat of paint. Somewhere in the distance a church clock chimed the half-hour. Temple scanned the front of the house and noted that none of the windows were lighted.

He jerked the old-fashioned knob in its circle at the side of the door, and a bell echoed far away in the lower regions of the house. There was no sign of life. A policeman walked slowly past on his beat, and looked up at them for a moment. Then Temple pulled the bell again. Once more it tinkled its mournful refrain.

'There's no one here, Paul,' said Steve at last.

'Yes, the place does seem deserted,' agreed Temple, in a puzzled tone.

'Are you sure this is the right address?'

'Well, it's 49 Marshall House Terrace . . . the same as on the paper.'

'Yes,' said Steve, turning and leaning lightly against the door. She gave a sudden exclamation.

'Paul!'

'What is it?'

'The door, it's not fastened—'

'Good Lord!' exclaimed Temple under his breath. He pushed the door gently open a few inches.

'She's probably expecting us to walk in,' he said. 'Follow me, Steve . . .'

'But, Paul, we can't just walk in as if we lived here,' she began to protest, but Temple was already well inside the entrance hall, and Steve had no alternative but to follow him. He pushed the door to after them.

'We can always walk out again if we're not wanted,' he said lightly. A dim red light burned at the far end of the hall and there were two doors on their right with a flight of stairs on the left.

'The house seems deserted,' said Steve in a low tone.

Temple pushed open the nearest door and managed to find the electric-light switch.

'Yes, but it's not empty,' he whispered. 'This room is quite well furnished.' They went inside. The long green curtains were drawn, and chintz covers to match had a fresh appearance. There were two large divans, a couple of deep armchairs and a large bowl filled with dark red roses occupied a prominent position in the centre of the room.

An expensive ormolu clock was the only ornament on the mantelpiece.

'Do you suppose that she lives here?' asked Steve.

'If she does, she's pretty well off. This room would cost a pretty penny to furnish and—'

He paused and stood listening intently.

'What is it?' asked Steve. There was complete silence except for the steady ticking of a clock and the rattle of a lorry at the end of the avenue.

'Didn't you hear something?' he asked.

'No.'

'That's funny. I thought I heard somebody moving over-head. I must have been mistaken.'

He walked across to the window and pulled the curtains a little apart.

'What are we going to do if she doesn't turn up?' asked Steve.

'Oh, she'll turn up all right. She's bound to. Unless . . .' He hesitated.

'Unless what?'

He paced the room thoughtfully, then stood looking down at a suitcase that stood between the end of a divan and the wall in a corner by the fireplace.

'Hallo, it looks as if someone has just arrived, judging by this case,' he murmured, almost to himself. 'Now I wonder if—'

Once again he stopped speaking suddenly.

'Steve! Listen! Can't you hear something?'

'It's only the clock, Paul.'

'No, no, I don't mean that.'

'Darling, you're imagining things.'

'Steve!' he whispered tensely.

They held their breath. Faintly from the room above came the wail of a violin.

'Now do you hear it?' he asked.

'Yes – yes, it's a violin,' she nodded breathlessly.

It was rather louder now and Temple recognised the music. They listened for quite two minutes. Then Temple said, 'I heard it before. I knew damn' well I heard it.'

'Where's it coming from?' asked Steve.

'One of the bedrooms, I should imagine.' His brain was working rapidly, and a minute later he said, 'You stay here,

Steve, and I'll go upstairs and see if this violinist can tell us anything.'

He moved quickly to the door, then stopped and looked over towards the fireplace.

'What are you staring at?' asked Steve.

'The clock!' he whispered.

She followed his gaze. The hands of the clock indicated twenty past four. She went over to the clock and put her head near it.

'Why – it's stopped!' she exclaimed in surprise. Then she straightened herself and listened again.

'That ticking . . .' she breathed. 'It isn't this clock . . .'

'There's no other clock in the room.'

Temple stood in the middle of the room now, all his senses fully on the alert. Suddenly he sprang towards the suitcase. As he picked it up a growing certainty filled his mind.

'Stand clear of the window, Steve!' he gasped, and hurled the case at the dividing line in the curtains. There was a loud crash of glass, silence for a split second, then an explosion which shook the rafters. Fortunately, the curtains protected them from flying glass. Steve had instinctively dropped to the floor behind one of the divans and Temple crouched at the back of an armchair. The explosion had blown out the lights, and it was a matter of seconds before Temple produced a pocket torch, and noted with relief that Steve was quite safe.

'Thank goodness it landed in the flower beds!' he said hoarsely. 'It won't exactly improve the garden, but that can't be helped.' The curtains at the paneless windows flapped in the evening breeze.

'Darling, this is beyond me,' admitted Steve, looking round helplessly.

'Come along, let's get back to the car,' he suggested, taking her arm and helping her to her feet.

'But what about that person upstairs – he's still playing the violin,' said Steve, standing up and listening intently. The strains of the music floated down to them.

'Whoever can it be?' whispered Steve.

'I'm pretty sure it's Fritz Kreisler,' smiled Temple.

'Fritz Kreisler – but how on earth—'

'An automatic gramophone,' he replied, in rather a rueful tone. 'I ought to have guessed that. It's a simple idea, but quite effective.'

Steve was more bewildered than ever. 'But, darling, why on earth should Mrs. Trevelyan take all the trouble to set a gramophone working?'

Temple glanced at his wrist-watch.

'I'll explain later,' he replied. 'Come along, Steve. I've got to meet Sir Graham down at Westminster in about twenty minutes. Let's hope we don't meet much traffic.'

Steve, however, felt she had had enough for one evening.

'You can drop me at our corner and I'll walk back to the flat,' she announced. Temple noticed that she was rather white.

'All right,' he agreed. 'And you'd better tell that Chinese puzzle of ours to mix you a good, stiff drink.'

'He probably has it mixed already,' she said, with an attempt at a laugh.

On their way out they were confronted by a policeman, to whom Temple gave a brief account of the accident. It was fully five minutes before they were able to make their way through the small group of onlookers and restart the car.

The nearest church clock had already struck eleven before they emerged from Lancaster Gate and headed for Mayfair. Having dropped Steve on the corner of Half Moon Street, Temple forgot about such things as speed limits as he drove expertly down the emptying streets in the direction of Westminster.

He found Forbes and an Irish sergeant named Bannion, whom he had met before several times, pacing impatiently up and down the landing stage and looking up at the huge dial of Big Ben which pointed to eleven-twenty. In the background, Crane leaned against a wooden building and moodily smoked a cigarette.

'It's gone a quarter past,' he growled.

'All right, we'll give him another five minutes,' said Sir Graham. 'How long will it take us to get there, Sergeant?'

'About a quarter of an hour, sir,' replied the sergeant.

At that moment Temple came running down the iron steps, buttoning his overcoat against the cold wind blowing from the river.

'Just in time, Temple,' Sir Graham greeted him. 'We nearly gave you up as a bad job!'

'Sorry, Sir Graham,' Temple apologised, then nodded to Bannion.

'Hello, Sergeant. Still with the old barge?'

'That's right, Mr. Temple,' grinned the sergeant.

Crane came out of the shadows and nodded curtly to Temple. 'Evening, sir.' He turned to Bannion. 'All right, Sergeant. Let's get started.'

They clambered into the boat which was rocking unsteadily against a swift tide. At the second attempt, the motor roared into life, and Crane cast off. The sergeant slowly opened the throttle, and they lurched their way into midstream on the slightly choppy waters. A tug towing three large barges chugged its way past them. The sergeant snapped on his searchlight for a second, just to make sure it was working. From time to time they ran into a patch of mist that curled over the water. A ship's siren echoed mournfully across the river from the neighbourhood of the docks. Temple shivered and wondered why he had not agreed to meet Sir Graham at Granger's Wharf and travelled there in his car. It would certainly have been a much warmer journey. What was more, it would probably have been quicker.

The cold night air pushed past them, and they crouched in the well of the launch to find what little protection there was from wind and spray.

'The mist seems to have cleared,' commented Forbes presently.

'Lucky for us,' nodded Crane.

'Getting near it now, sir,' murmured the sergeant, peering into the night.

'Where is it exactly?' asked Temple.

'Away yonder on the left there,' was the reply. 'We'll be there in two or three minutes.' He changed the direction of the boat slightly, and they began to head towards the left bank. Straining his eyes, Temple could just discern the dim outlines of a large warehouse towards which the sergeant was steering.

'There we are, sir. That's Granger's Wharf.'

'Know anything about it, Sergeant?' asked Forbes.

'Not much doing there lately,' replied the sergeant. 'I think some of their cargoes have been diverted to places abroad. They take mostly foodstuffs . . .'

He manoeuvred the launch gently towards the small landing stage.

'This is the warehouse, sir – and that's a checking office.'

'And what's that?' asked Crane, indicating a large, wooden shed to their right.

'I think they park lorries in there. If you're meeting anybody, I expect you'll find them in the checking office. Most of 'em have a stove or a gas fire.'

The launch bumped lightly against the piles, and Temple leapt on to the landing stage.

'Throw me a rope, Sergeant.'

'Here y'are, sir.'

Temple secured the rope to a ring in the floor of the landing stage, and while he was completing a nautical knot the others had also disembarked.

'You wait here, Sergeant,' ordered Crane, as they stood for a moment looking round to get their bearings. There were no lights of any description, apart from a street lamp shining dimly some eighty yards away. Temple shivered as a bleak gust of wind whistled round the warehouse. But Crane showed no sign of making a move.

'What are you looking for, Inspector? The reception committee?' asked Temple.

Crane's face remained completely wooden.

'I'm looking for Muller, sir,' he replied.

'He doesn't appear to be here,' grunted Forbes, who was also becoming a trifle impatient.

And indeed the wharf seemed completely deserted.

Temple suddenly shone his torch on the ground. Then he bent down to examine the muddy surface.

'What is it, sir?' asked Crane.

'They look to me like fairly recent footprints.'

Forbes came over and peered at the patch of ground lit by Temple's torch. 'Yes, quite recent,' he agreed. 'They seem to point towards the checking office.'

Temple at once led the way in that direction.

The checking office proved to be a fairly old brick structure surmounted by a corrugated iron roof. Forbes knocked sharply at the door, but there was no reply. Crane peered into the grimy iron-framed window, but declared that he could see nothing.

'Doesn't seem to be anyone here,' he commented. 'Maybe we'd better make the round of the other places.'

'It's possible our friend Muller got cold feet and backed out at the last minute,' said Forbes.

Crane made another attempt to look through the window. 'Can't see a thing – maybe they've still got some sort of blackout up. Have you tried the door?'

'Yes, it's locked all right.'

Crane was just debating whether to shine his torch through he window, and risk attracting a possible bullet, when there was a soft exclamation from Temple, who had suddenly shone his small pencil-torch on the top right-hand corner of the door.

'Good God!' breathed Forbes. 'What is it, sir?' asked Crane, coming up quickly. And then he noticed it.

The word 'Rex' splashed in vivid red letters diagonally across the top corner. Temple snapped out the torch.

'What are you going to do?' asked Forbes.

'Stand back, Sir Graham,' said Temple in a low voice. 'I'm going to break the door down!'

He measured the distance and leapt at the centre of the door. It splintered almost immediately. Crane pushed a burly shoulder against the one side and the door burst open. Temple shone his torch and the beam picked out the ponderous figure of a man slumped over the back of a chair. Blood dripped steadily from his head into a large pool on the floor beneath the chair.

'My God!' exclaimed Crane, advancing into the office.

'It's his throat . . .' mumbled Forbes, and Temple switched the beam away from the red gash.

'Mr. Temple,' said Crane in a low voice. 'Is this our man?'

Temple did not answer immediately. They stood in the heavy darkness and in complete silence save for the mournful sound of a ship's siren somewhere in the distance. Then Temple abruptly switched the light full on the dead man's face.

'Yes,' he said quietly. 'It's Hans Muller.'

At first, Crane was jubilant over the footprints they had discovered, but on investigation they proved to be those of the dead man. Around the checking office there were dozens of footprints, and those of Rex – if it were Rex who had committed the crime – had probably been trodden over by the Scotland Yard party. Crane eventually gave it up as a bad job, announcing that he would return the next morning and see if he could do any better with the help of daylight.

On the way back, Temple related his experiences of the day – how he had met Doctor Kohima and Mrs. Trevelyan, but did not mention the strange sequel of that meeting. They welcomed any diversion to distract from the thoughts of the ghastly sight they had just encountered. When they reached the landing stage at Westminster, Temple invited Forbes and Crane back to the flat for a drink, and as it was considerably nearer than either of their homes they accepted the invitation with alacrity.

The clock in the hall struck one as Temple fitted his latchkey in the lock, and he was amazed to find Steve sitting up and waiting for them.

'You're back earlier than I thought,' she said as they came in. She pushed her knitting beneath a cushion and looked at him critically as he went to pour out drinks.

'You look tired, darling,' she commented.

'It's not surprising,' said Forbes, lying back in a comfortable armchair and stretching out his legs. 'We've had quite a night!'

'What happened?' asked Steve. 'Did you see Muller?'

Forbes exchanged a glance with Temple and shrugged.

'We saw him, Mrs. Temple,' said Crane at length, 'but not quite under the circumstances we expected.'

'He was dead,' explained Temple. 'Murdered, I'm afraid.'

Steve made an effort to fight back the feeling of horror which swept over her whenever she heard of the latest addition of Rex's victims.

'Thank goodness you weren't there, Steve,' said Forbes quietly, accepting a large whisky from Temple and draining it at a gulp. Crane did likewise, and Temple refilled their glasses.

'You're looking pretty pale, Steve,' he commented shrewdly. 'Sure you won't have a drink?'

'Quite sure thanks, darling. I expect I'm over-tired.'

'Did you get back all right after you left me?' he asked.

'Yes . . .' she hesitated.

'Is anything wrong?' asked Temple, eyeing her intently. 'It's all right, darling, you can talk. I've told Sir Graham about Mrs. Trevelyan and Doctor Kohima. Nothing else has happened, has there?'

'Well, I suppose it's nothing really,' murmured Steve reluctantly. 'All the same, it was rather queer—'

'Go on,' prompted Temple.

'I expect you'll think it's all nonsense, but—'

'Indeed we shan't, Steve,' Forbes assured her seriously. 'We're only too glad to hear the slightest thing that might possibly have some bearing on this business.'

'Well, after I left you, Paul, I came back here and drank a small glass of brandy. Then Ricky made me some coffee and I sent him to bed. After that, I felt that if I went to bed I'd never sleep—'

'You shouldn't have had the coffee,' he murmured.

'Perhaps not. Anyhow, I felt that if I had a breath of fresh air, would help to soothe my nerves. So I slipped on my coat, and went out. I walked into Piccadilly and turned into Park Lane. It was fairly late and there weren't very many people about. Along Park Lane a strange sort of feeling seemed to creep over me – don't ask me why – but I felt quite certain that somebody was following me.'

'Who on earth would want to follow you?' asked Forbes, then suddenly looked very embarrassed. 'Well, you know what I mean, Steve – after all, if it had been one of the gay lads he would most certainly have tried to catch up with you.'

'That's just it,' said Steve. 'I couldn't see anyone. I couldn't even hear footsteps, and yet I felt sure that someone was there.'

'Perhaps it was some sort of hallucination, Mrs. Temple,' suggested Crane slowly.

'Oh no!' cried Steve. 'Because, as I turned into Curzon Street I saw someone.'

'Good old feminine intuition vindicated again,' said Temple lightly, in an attempt to dispel the worried look in Steve's eyes. 'So you saw the person who was following you?'

'Yes, I saw her pass quickly under the lamp at the end of Curzon Street. I got a good look at her – then she seemed to vanish. I think she realised I had spotted her.'

'Are you telling us this mysterious person was a woman?' asked Temple in some surprise.

'I'm quite certain, Paul. For about two seconds, I saw her almost as clearly as I can see you now.'

'Then you can describe her?' queried Forbes eagerly.

'I can,' replied Steve with quiet confidence.

'Well?' said Temple, taking a drink of his double brandy.

Steve drew a deep breath.

'Well,' she began, 'the girl was smartly dressed. She was young – a brunette – and dressed in brown. Brown handbag, sun-tan silk stockings, brown costume, perky little hat—'

The three men looked at one another without speaking. Then Temple took a sip at his brandy.

'Quite the nicest type of hallucination,' he said slowly.

CHAPTER V

Concerning Doctor Kohima

STEVE came near to losing her temper. She was over-tired, had been through a trying experience that night, and her nerves were somewhat on edge.

'I'm not joking, Paul,' she said with a note of asperity in her voice. I tell you it was no hallucination.'

He leaned forward and patted her hand.

'Of course it wasn't, Steve. I've already heard all about it once before today – or rather yesterday!'

It was Forbes' turn to sit up and take notice. 'D'you mean you know this girl Steve's talking about?' he queried sharply.

'No,' said Temple absent-mindedly, feeling for another cigarette and carefully lighting it.

'Then why d'you say you've heard all about it?'

Temple settled back in his chair once more and began to review the facts, as much for his own benefit as the Assistant Commissioner's.

'It's like this, Sir Graham. When I visited Doctor Kohima's I met a man called Carl Lathom. He told me that he had been suffering from hallucinations for quite some time.'

'What sort of hallucinations?' interrupted Crane in a harsh, impatient voice.

'Quite the usual type in some ways – he was under the impression that everywhere he went he was being followed.'

'But what the devil's this got to do with anything?' snapped Forbes irritably.

Temple held up his hand.

'Just a minute, Sir Graham. Let me tell you about this girl who was following Lathom. He described her to me. Lathom said: "I could see her as clearly as I can see you now. Brown shoes – brown costume – brown handbag – perky little hat—"'

There was a gasp of astonishment from Steve and a slight exclamation of surprise from Forbes. Crane looked completely dubious.

'Are you sure about all this, Temple?' asked Sir Graham incredulously.

'Good heavens! It's fantastic!' exclaimed Crane.

Temple slowly shook his head.

'No,' he said, 'when one really thinks about it, Inspector, it simply means that Doctor Kohima was mistaken.'

'Mistaken?' repeated Crane in some mystification. 'Mistaken about what?'

'Well,' replied Temple, faintly amused, 'about the hallucinations.'

Forbes rose and began to pace heavily across the room. The case was beginning to take on an eerie aspect which frankly bewildered him.

'Look here,' he growled in a dogmatical tone, 'you can say what you like about this business, but I've got a hunch this Mrs. Trevelyan's at the back of it all.'

'In point of fact,' interposed Temple gently, 'you think Mrs. Trevelyan is Rex?'

'Yes,' replied Forbes stoutly, 'I do. Look at the evidence against her. The way her name has cropped up in most of the murders. You can't tell me she knows nothing about this business.'

'I wouldn't dream of telling you that, Sir Graham. But a lot of people know something about this business without being responsible for the murders. What do you think, Crane?'

'I don't know,' replied Crane stolidly, though he was obviously cherishing his own theories.

'Of course,' continued Forbes, 'if that fellow Lathom was – er – unhinged, it's just possible that this doctor fellow could have – well – planted the description of that girl in his mind.' Forbes looked rather pleased with himself as he advanced the theory.

'Then you think Doctor Kohima is somehow connected with Rex?' asked Temple.

'Never set eyes on the fellow yet,' retorted Forbes bluntly. 'I'll tell you more when I see him. But it's more than likely he's in with this Mrs. Trevelyan—'

'But what would be the point in planting such a description in Carl Lathom's mind?' asked Steve, who found the discussion becoming more and more involved. This obviously puzzled Sir Graham.

'There must be some reason, of course,' he grunted. 'I should say that doctor's up to some trickery – wants to plant that girl somehow to distract us—'

'But there really is a girl in brown,' said Steve. 'And how could the doctor know she would always be wearing it?'

'He could order her to do it.'

'For all you know, Steve,' continued Sir Graham, 'this girl you saw might have been Mrs. Trevelyan. You've never met her, have you?'

'Well, no . . . but Paul described her to me, and I don't think—'

'Don't be too sure, Steve – you know how women can change their appearance,' said Forbes.

'Well if it was Mrs. Trevelyan, she's certainly had a busy evening,' commented Steve, 'what with that little surprise she prepared for us earlier on.'

Forbes looked up quickly.

'What's all this?'

Temple frowned. He had purposely refrained from telling Forbes and Crane about their adventure that evening because he knew that such information would most likely result in Forbes interviewing or even arresting Mrs. Trevelyan, and he wanted to let events develop naturally for another day or so. However, he reflected that the policeman's report about the bomb explosion would be sure to reach Sir Graham fairly soon, and any further concealment would be impossible. Temple smiled reassuringly at Steve, who was looking rather guilty, then said, 'I had an appointment tonight with Mrs. Trevelyan at a house in Lancaster Gate.'

'The devil you did!' whistled Forbes. 'What time was that?'

'Half past ten.'

'And what happened, Mr. Temple?' demanded Crane curiously.

A whimsical smile curved round Temple's lips. 'I took Steve along to make the lady's acquaintance. But instead we were introduced to a time-bomb! You'll get a notification about it in the morning, I should imagine, Inspector.'

'Good heavens!' said Forbes.

'And not only a time-bomb, Sir Graham,' pursued Temple, 'but a rather ingenious little trick to keep us sitting on top of it. Someone had fixed an automatic gramophone in one of the bedrooms, so that we should hear music and presume the house was occupied. Then, while we were waiting—'

'You'd stand in the hall and get the full force—' put in Crane.

'Yes,' nodded Temple, 'but how did you know that the time-bomb was in the hall, Inspector?'

'I – I – just guessed,' replied Crane, somewhat taken aback.

'And what happened?' put in Forbes. 'You say the damn thing went off?'

'I managed to fling it into the front garden – just in time, I should imagine. It must have blown out every window in that side of the house.'

'It was horrible!' said Steve almost in a whisper. Forbes went over and placed a reassuring hand on her shoulder.

'This settles one thing at any rate!' he announced firmly. 'I'll get out a warrant for Mrs. Trevelyan's arrest first thing in the morning.'

Temple sighed.

'No, Sir Graham, I beg of you not to do that,' he said quietly.

'But you can't overlook a damnable thing like that, Temple!'

'All the same, Sir Graham, I'm pretty certain if you gave it another day or two, well – she might even lead us to Rex.'

'Then you don't think she *is* Rex, in spite of all this?' demanded Forbes incredulously.

'I'd prefer to say she is a first-class contact with Rex,' replied Temple thoughtfully. 'And we have to step very carefully or Rex will quite deliberately destroy that contact – that's my theory at any rate. I'll admit that Mrs. Trevelyan is in a highly suspicious position at the moment, but I still think we've got to go carefully.'

'I agree with Mr. Temple, sir,' said Crane rather surprisingly. 'It wouldn't be a wise move to arrest her – not simply on a charge of attempted murder.'

The Assistant Commissioner mused upon this for a little while. At last he turned to Temple.

'Where did you say this house was?'

'Forty-nine, Marshall House Terrace, Lancaster Gate.'

'I expect there'll be a report when we get back, sir,' said Crane.

'I'd like to see it, if you don't mind,' put in Temple.

'Yes – of course,' nodded Forbes. 'I'll 'phone you in the morning. Are you ready, Crane?'

Temple went out with his guests and Steve rather absently gathered the glasses and placed them on a tray, ready to he washed. Then she replaced the bottle and decanter in the sideboard. When Temple returned, she said:

'I don't think I care for that man Crane very much.'

'More feminine intuition?' he smiled.

'How long has he been at the Yard?'

'About six years. Has quite a reputation as a go-getter. Shouldn't wonder if he's in the running for the A.C.'s job when Forbes retires. Why don't you like him?'

Steve shook her head. 'I don't quite know. Maybe it's just that he's got an unfortunate manner.'

'H'm, that's one way of putting it,' mused Temple, who had pondered several times that evening if Crane had anything up his sleeve, and if so whether he was holding it back in order to obtain some special kudos for the discovery of Rex. It was nearly two o'clock now, but Temple did not feel the least bit sleepy.

'What do you make of this Rex affair, Steve?' he asked suddenly.

She looked at him in some surprise. 'I don't know what to make of it,' she replied in a slightly bewildered tone. 'Sometimes, I think that Rex must be a – well – homicidal maniac. Why should he want to murder Sir Ernest Cranbury and Norma Rice?'

'It's just a question of finding the motive,' said Temple softly, almost to himself.

'Motive?' repeated Steve. 'Have you hit upon the least trace of a motive?'

'Perhaps not. But that isn't to say there isn't one,' he replied enigmatically. He picked up a large volume, a French book on criminology, and began to turn the pages absent-mindedly.

'Well, I think I'll go to bed,' said Steve.

He looked up. 'No, don't go for a minute or two,' he said casually. 'She should be here any second now.'

Steve turned in the doorway. 'You're expecting somebody at this time?' she demanded incredulously.

'Yes,' he replied quietly. 'I'm expecting Mrs. Trevelyan.'

Steve came back and leaned on an armchair. 'You really mean that Mrs. Trevelyan is coming here – at two in the morning?'

'Well, I shall be very surprised if she doesn't.'

'But, Paul – how do you know?'

'Because I caught a glimpse of her – in a large car at the end of the mews. It was there when I got back with Sir Graham.'

'A blue car with disc wheels?' put in Steve quickly.

'That's it.'

'Why, it was there when I got back here. She must have been expecting you – and she was probably afraid to come in when she saw Sir Graham and the inspector. And, Paul—'

'Yes, darling?'

'She wasn't the woman in brown, was she?'

The sound of the front-door buzzer vibrated in the hall outside.

'You'll have a chance to see for yourself,' murmured Temple softly as he went out to open the door. Before he reached it, the buzzer sounded again.

When Temple opened the door, Mrs. Trevelyan stood there, nervously clutching her handbag, and obviously very much on edge. Her mouth was working in tiny spasmodic jerks and her eyes were unnaturally bright. Temple gave no sign that he was in any way surprised to see her.

'Mr. Temple – I've got to have a talk with you!' she began in an unnatural, somewhat hysterical voice.

'Come in, Mrs. Trevelyan. I've been expecting you.' He stood politely aside and closed the door after her. In the hall, she looked round for a moment, then moved to the lighted doorway of the lounge. She started perceptibly as she saw Steve, who was standing over by the fireplace.

'Good evening,' said Steve quietly.

'Good evening, Mrs. Temple,' mumbled the visitor somewhat uncertainly.

'Please sit down, Mrs. Trevelyan,' said Temple in a pleasant voice, as he indicated a vacant armchair. 'Would you like a drink?' She shook her head.

'No, I haven't a great deal of time, and—'

For a moment she hesitated then, 'Mr. Temple . . . would you mind drawing those curtains, please?'

'No one can see you from the street,' he reassured her.

'But the flats opposite – I'm so frightened –' she clasped her hands nervously.

'All right, darling, I'll do it,' put in Steve, going over to the windows and carefully drawing the curtains.

'Oh – thank you – thank you so much, Mrs. Temple.'

Mrs. Trevelyan seemed perilously near to tears. She swallowed hard and said, 'I'm most terribly sorry about what happened tonight at Marshall House Terrace.'

'So are we,' said Temple drily.

'I can't tell you how upset I am—'

'It very nearly upset us too. However, it might have been worse.'

Steve swung round and levelled her keen brown eyes upon those of the visitor. 'Did you know there was a time-bomb in the house?' she demanded,

Mrs. Trevelyan clenched her hands.

'No!' she replied desperately. 'No, I swear I didn't. I watched you both go into the house – I was at the other end of the road. When the bomb exploded I . . . I didn't know what to do!'

She sank into a chair and burst into tears. Temple looked across at Steve. After a minute or two, Mrs. Trevelyan seemed to recover.

Temple and Steve were both unable to convince themselves as to whether their visitor's grief was genuine or not, and consequently experienced several uncomfortable moments.

Mrs. Trevelyan calmed down a little and dabbed her eyes with a small lace handkerchief. Then Temple began to speak very slowly and seriously.

'I want you to listen very carefully, Mrs. Trevelyan, because the position is pretty serious, as I think you realise. About six months ago, a man called Richard East was murdered by Rex. A visiting-card was found on him, and on the back of the card was the name "Mrs. Trevelyan".'

She sat upright with a jerk.

'I don't believe it!' she cried.

'Soon afterwards,' continued Temple evenly, 'there came the Norma Rice affair. You remember that?'

85

She nodded. 'She was found dead in a railway compartment, wasn't she?'

'Exactly. And scribbled in the back of a diary belonging to Norma Rice was the name "Mrs. Trevelyan".'

She caught her breath, then rounded on him.

''You're lying! This is some sort of plot against me—'

'I haven't finished yet, Mrs. Trevelyan,' went on Temple quietly, taking his wallet from his pocket and extracting a slip of paper. 'You see this?'

Her eyes were almost starting out of her head as she snatched the paper.

'My name . . . again . . .' she whispered hoarsely. 'Where did you get it?'

'The paper was found on Sir Ernest Cranbury.'

'Oh, my God!' There was a note of helplessness in her voice. She let fall the paper and it fluttered gently to the carpet. Temple picked it up and carefully restored it to his wallet. Mrs. Trevelyan had fallen back into a corner of her chair, and her face was very white.

'Paul – she's going to faint!' cried Steve in alarm.

Mrs. Trevelyan gripped the arms of the chair and seemed to make an effort to recover.

'I'll be all right,' she gulped.

'Let me get you a drink,' said Temple, crossing to the sideboard.

Mrs. Trevelyan looked up at Steve and essayed a feeble smile.

'I really am sorry about tonight, Mrs. Temple. It was ghastly. Were you hurt at all?'

'No,' replied Steve, 'thanks to my husband.'

'I'm so glad,' said Mrs. Trevelyan, looking quite relieved. 'If anything had happened to you, I – I—'

Temple came across with her drink, and she sipped it gratefully.

'Is that better?' he asked presently.

She nodded, and handed him back the glass.

He hesitated a moment, then said, 'I suppose you know Sir Graham Forbes was here a little while ago with Inspector Crane?'

'Yes, I saw them leave.'

'Then you know Sir Graham?' he queried at once.

'Only by sight. I've never actually met him.'

He toyed with her empty glass.

'You know, Mrs. Trevelyan, Sir Graham isn't a fool by any means.'

'Well?' she said, a note of challenge creeping back into her voice.

'Well, I think you might be interested to know that Sir Graham has a pretty strong theory about you.'

'You mean he thinks I'm Rex,' she put in quickly.

Temple paused, then said, 'Yes.'

Her face was set in more severe lines, but she relaxed once again and finally said in a comparatively quiet voice: 'Do *you* think I'm Rex, Mr. Temple?'

Temple thrust his hands deep into his trouser pockets, leaned against the mantelpiece and looked down at her. 'When I investigate a case, Mrs. Trevelyan,' he said, 'I always make a point of trying to find out right at the very beginning what exactly it's all about. Sometimes, this isn't quite so simple as it seems. Take this particular case, for instance. Why did Rex murder Richard East? Why did Rex murder Norma Rice and Sir Ernest Cranbury? There doesn't appear to have been a motive – on the face of it the murders are haphazard and unconnected. But I'm quite sure that there is a motive, Mrs. Trevelyan, and I'm equally sure that you know what that motive is!'

He spoke the last words with quiet emphasis. Once more, she folded into a corner of the armchair and was silent for some seconds, her fingers pulling at the dainty handkerchief in her nervous apprehension. At last, she looked into Temple's eyes and said quietly: 'Yes, I know.' There was still a note of desperation in her voice as she continued. 'About six or seven months ago I got the first letter from Rex. I thought it was some sort of joke, but the next letter soon dispelled the idea. There were things in that letter that I imagined were known to no one.'

'And Rex asked for money?' prompted Temple quietly.

'Three thousand pounds. He said if I didn't pay the money, then that would be the end of my secret.'

'So you paid the three thousand.'

Mrs. Trevelyan sighed.

'Yes, I paid. But not immediately. It was only after the murder of Richard East that I lost my nerve.'

Temple seemed slightly puzzled.

'But how could you associate Richard East with your own affairs. Was there any connection?'

She shook her head. 'Not directly. You see, Rex sent me a list of eight names. Richard East was the first name on the list. Then I knew that East was murdered because he refused to be blackmailed.'

There was a surge of agonised terror in Mrs. Trevelyan's low tones. Steve could not repress a subdued murmur of sympathy. Temple was turning over in his mind this latest bit of information; it seemed to tally quite consistently with most of his theories. What was more, this list of names gave him a definite line of investigation.

'And after you had paid the money? I take it that was not the end of the matter?' he said.

'I didn't hear any more until about three months ago. Then I received a note – it was on my desk one morning. It simply asked for certain information about one of Doctor Kohima's patients.'

'Did the letter end with the usual threats?'

'No. But it was written in a sort of dictatorial style, as if it took for granted that I should do as I was asked.'

'And did you?'

'Yes,' she said quietly. 'And I've been terrified ever since that it would cost me my job. As you know, Mr. Temple, it's a very serious matter to divulge the secrets of one's patients, but I was so terrified – it was soon after Norma Rice's death. It was like the hand of Nemesis drawing nearer and nearer . . . I lay awake night after night . . .'

'And I take it that Rex told you to arrange our meeting tonight? Was that so?' She nodded helplessly.

'Yes. The note was on my desk this morning when I got to the office. I'm almost afraid to look at my desk these last few weeks – in fact, it takes a tremendous effort for me to go at all. If Doctor Kohima weren't so kind, I'd have resigned months ago.'

'These notes come through the post?'

'Oh yes, they have a West End postmark.'

'H'm, that doesn't convey much.'

She took a small envelope from her bag and also a sheet of cream-laid notepaper.

'I brought this morning's note with me – and here is the list of names—'

Temple read the note and passed it to Steve. Then he took the other paper, on which were typed eight names:

Richard East
Norma Rice
Conrad Stephens
Felicity Mayne
Ernest Cranbury
James Barton
Norman Steele
Barbara Trevelyan

Steve looked over his shoulder and whispered, 'The first five names, Paul . . . they're all . . . dead.'

'They've all been murdered,' said Mrs. Trevelyan. 'And now there are only three names left. Goodness knows how long before there are only two and then—'

'Don't upset yourself, Mrs. Trevelyan,' urged Temple. 'We're catching up on Rex pretty fast, you know. It may be that Messrs. Barton and Steele are playing for time, too. Maybe they've followed in your footsteps and agreed to play ball—'

'I had no choice, Mr. Temple,' said Mrs. Trevelyan earnestly. 'It almost ruined me to find that three thousand pounds – all I have now is my salary – I even had to sell my home. But if that secret of mine had been made public, well, there'd have been nothing much to live for, I do assure you.'

Temple thoughtfully studied the papers she had given him while Steve and Mrs. Trevelyan carried on a whispered conversation. He wondered just how far Mrs. Trevelyan could be trusted. She seemed sincere enough, and there was no mistaking the fact that her visit had called for a considerable effort on her part. But there was always the possibility that Rex was offering Mrs. Trevelyan as bait to effect a large-scale coup. During a pause in the conversation between Steve and their visitor, Temple said, 'This information you obtained about one of Doctor Kohima's patients, Mrs. Trevelyan – you sent it direct to Rex?'

'Yes,' she replied quickly. 'I posted it. To the Royal Falcon Hotel at Canterbury.'

'Just simply to the hotel?'

She hesitated for a fraction of a second, then said: 'No, I addressed it to Miss Judy Smith.'

'Miss Judy Smith? Do you know her?'

She shook her head.

'And what about the three thousand pounds? Did you send that to the same place?'

'I was told to make the money up into a small parcel and take it down to the hotel.'

'Addressed to Miss Smith?'

'Yes.

'Did you see anyone when you called?'

'Only the receptionist. I simply left the parcel at the desk.'

'Then you don't even know if Miss Judy Smith was staying at the hotel?' asked Steve.

Mrs. Trevelyan shrugged. 'I don't even know if there is such a person.'

It was a common enough name, certainly, reflected Temple, and sounded as if it had been chosen on the spur of the moment as a matter of convenience.

So far, Mrs. Trevelyan had answered his questions with apparent frankness and with practically no hesitation. He decided to try a different line.

'Tell me, Mrs. Trevelyan,' he began slowly, 'how long have you been working for Doctor Kohima?'

He noticed the muscles of her face contract slightly.

'About six years,' she replied in a low voice.

'That's quite a time,' he mused. 'You must have got to know each other pretty well.'

She leaned forward and exclaimed impulsively, 'Please don't think that Doctor Kohima has anything to do with this awful business. If I suspected he knew I had anything to do with it, I couldn't face him . . . I couldn't—' Her voice choked with emotion. She recovered a little and said, 'You see, he's such a decent person . . . above all this sordidness—'

'But surely a psychiatrist comes into contact with a certain amount of unpleasantness in his patients' egos,' said Temple with a smile. 'I was always under the impression that it was part of his work to eliminate such negative qualities—'

'Yes, that's true,' she agreed, 'but don't you see it's just his job – it isn't the man himself – any more than you could be judged by the characters of the villains in your novels.'

'Heaven forbid!' laughed Steve.

'I'll give you that point,' conceded Temple. 'However, I suppose you use a typewriter at the office, Mrs. Trevelyan.'

She nodded.

'Do you know anything about typewriters?'

'Well, I've used a few in my time,' she said, a little surprised. Then she noticed that he was again examining the notes he was holding. 'I can tell you this, Mr. Temple. All the notes I've had from Rex have been typed on the same machine.'

'How do you know that?'

'Well, if you look very carefully you can see that—'

'That the "a" isn't very clearly formed, and there is a definite blur across the letter "d". I had already noticed that. And the earlier letters were the same?'

'Exactly.'

'I suppose,' he murmured diffidently, 'these notes couldn't have been typed on the machine you use at the office?'

'Good gracious, no!' she exclaimed. 'These notes have been typed on a portable.'

'I think,' said Temple slowly, 'that I recall seeing a small portable standing at the side of Doctor Kohima's desk. Am I right?'

She bit her lip. For a moment she frowned as if in deep thought. Finally, she said, 'Yes, that is a portable . . . but I don't ever remember seeing him use it.'

'One rarely pays twenty pounds for a portable if one has no intention of using it,' he commented drily. 'And I want you to use it, Mrs. Trevelyan.'

'But the doctor keeps it locked, I think—'

'Then I suggest that your own machine should develop some little fault which would mean that you would have to borrow the portable. I want a specimen of all the lettering by ten-thirty in the morning. I'll call for it myself.'

'But if the doctor sees you he'll wonder what—'

'If the doctor sees me,' interposed Temple, 'you can tell him that I'm still making inquiries about his car.'

Mrs. Trevelyan appeared more worried than ever. She looked much older now than when he had first set eyes on her, for her tears had certainly not improved her make-up. But she was still a striking looking woman, who would have been outstanding in any company.

'Surely you don't suspect Doctor Kohima, Mr. Temple,' she said at length. 'Why I've known him for ten years – he's the soul of integrity – you couldn't possibly—'

'In a case of this kind, Mrs. Trevelyan,' he interrupted, 'I make a point of suspecting everyone. It's as much a question of procedure as anything. One has to work to a routine like a scientist making tests and eliminating one formula after another until he hits upon the right one. Experience has taught me that a person isn't necessarily innocent just because you happen to have known them for ten years, or just because they happen to be living or working under the same roof. Literally thousands of people have a private life which is a complete secret even to their nearest relatives and friends.'

He was about to enlarge upon this but there was a gentle knock at the door and Ricky appeared. Mrs. Trevelyan could not conceal a start of surprise, but she regained her composure at once as Steve said, 'What is it, Ricky?'

'So sorry I startled you!'

'I thought you were in bed,' said Steve.

'Oh no – I was reading master's excellent book – *The Lady in Danger*. I heard voices, so I thought perhaps you would like some coffee. It is all ready.'

'That's a very good idea, Ricky,' applauded Temple. 'I dare say you got it from an old Chinese proverb, but it's still a good idea.'

'Thank you, sir,' smiled Ricky, looking even more pleased with himself than usual. Just as he was closing the door, Temple called after him, 'Oh, while I think of it, Ricky. Mrs. Temple and I are probably going away for a day or so. You might sort out one or two things for me.'

Ricky appeared to be about to ask a question, then seemed to think better of it.

'Yes, sir,' he said softly. 'And you would like coffee for three?'

'For three, please.'

When Ricky had gone, Mrs. Trevelyan seemed to relax, and Temple did his utmost to set her at ease.

'You'll appreciate, Mrs. Trevelyan, that I'm in no way responsible for the actions of New Scotland Yard,' he began, lighting a cigarette for her. 'Sir Graham Forbes is a man who believes in swift action. Like most of us, he makes mistakes. He might even make a mistake in your case.'

She blew out a cloud of smoke.

'You mean he might arrest me,' she said. 'Well, in some ways that would be a relief. At least, I would be fairly safe in a prison cell . . . I wouldn't jump every time a door opens, every time I pass a dark alley, every time a car backfires. It's sheer torture!'

Steve nodded sympathetically.

'I don't altogether agree with Sir Graham's point of view,' continued Temple. 'My own idea is that you would be much better going your own way – under observation perhaps – but free to move around. However, if Sir Graham does decide to – act, I hope you won't get alarmed.'

She smiled as Ricky came in with the coffee.

'It's all right, Mr. Temple,' she said. 'Being arrested is a very minor ordeal compared with some I've been through lately.'

'Have you been arrested before?'

She shook her head.

'No . . . I can't say I have. But I can imagine it – with the help of newspapers and crime novels!'

She drank her coffee and rose to go.

'If there is anything more I can tell you, Mr. Temple, I'll be only too pleased,' she said, holding out her hand. 'But you'll remember what I said about the doctor? He really is a wonderful man, and I hate to see his work disturbed, or to have him upset in any way.'

'I'll bear it in mind, Mrs. Trevelyan,' Temple gravely assured her. Ricky appeared as from nowhere to usher out the visitor, but Temple insisted on accompanying her back to her car. They hardly spoke during the short walk, partly because both were a little on edge, for the deserted street with its patches of shadow had a slightly sinister aspect in the small hours of the morning.

But the excursion passed without incident, the car purred into life at a touch of the starter, and vanished round the corner of Half Moon Street towards Piccadilly.

When Temple returned he found that Steve had gone to bed and was already half asleep.

'Well, what d'you think of Mrs. Trevelyan?' he asked as he unfastened his tie.

'I'm so glad, darling,' she murmured drowsily. 'So glad about what?'

'That she isn't the girl in brown,' said Steve, and immediately fell asleep.

CHAPTER VI

Canterbury Tale

PROMPTLY at ten-thirty the next morning, Temple rang Doctor Kohima's doorbell, and was admitted by a maid. He told her that Mrs. Trevelyan was expecting him, and was shown into the waiting-room. At first, he thought the room was empty, until a cultured voice from behind the door wished him a cheerful good morning.

'This is a pleasant surprise, Mr. Temple,' declared Carl Lathom, who, as usual, looked particularly well-groomed.

Temple was just a little startled to see this young man so soon, but he did not show it, and merely returned the greeting with a pleasant smile.

'I didn't expect to see you here, sir,' said Lathom. 'At least, not at this time of the morning.'

Temple laughed.

'The surprise is mutual,' he remarked. 'I suppose it is a little early in the day to have one's ego probed.'

Lathom shook his head seriously.

'On the contrary, my dear Mr. Temple, the doctor assures me that in my case this is quite the most suitable time for treatment. One's vitality is at its peak, and I am particularly amenable to certain psycho-therapeutical experiments. Of course, as I told you, mine is rather an unusual case.'

'I quite appreciate that, Mr. Lathom,' replied Temple seriously. 'Though naturally every case is individual in its way.'

'I quite agree. And I trust that you were suitably impressed yourself when you consulted the doctor yesterday.'

Temple had a feeling that Lathom was more than a trifle inquisitive to find out why he was there. Of course, it was probably natural for patients of this type to be curious about each others' illness and symptoms. So he merely replied noncommittally: 'Oh yes – very much impressed I assure you.'

'Ah, I knew you would be,' nodded Lathom. 'A really remarkable man, Doctor Kohima. Absolutely first class.'

'I should imagine so.'

'I don't know whether I told you or not, but he cured me of a most extraordinary hallucination. Everywhere I went I was under the impression that—'

'That you were being followed,' put in Temple. 'Yes, you told me.'

'Looking back now,' continued Lathom almost nonchalantly, 'it seems quite fantastic, but at the time it really got me down. One has to be fairly desperate before one ventures into a place of this sort, don't you think?'

'Yes,' replied Temple. 'I suppose one does.' The feeling that Lathom was quietly probing into the reason for his presence there returned with growing force, but Temple showed no sign, and continued to chat politely with him on the subject of hallucinations.

'Of course, I was lucky in one way. Mine was quite the nicest type,' Lathom was saying for the second time, when Temple quietly intervened.

'If by any chance your hallucination returns, Mr. Lathom – though I don't suppose for a moment it will—'

'Yes?' said Lathom curiously. 'Are you offering me any special advice?'

'I should advise you,' said Temple with a slow smile, 'to consult me instead of Doctor Kohima.'

For a moment there was a startled expression in Lathom's eyes, and he appeared to be about to ask a question, but the door opened to admit Doctor Kohima.

'Right you are, Mr. Lathom,' he said briskly. 'I'm ready for you now.' Then he caught sight of Temple.

'Why, good morning, Mr. Temple. I – er – I don't recall making an appointment.'

'No,' replied Temple casually. 'I called to see Mrs. Trevelyan.'

The doctor pursed his mouth thoughtfully, then gave Temple a shrewd glance.

'Now I come to think of it, there is a little matter I'd like to talk to you about. Will you excuse us a moment, Mr. Lathom?'

'Of course,' said Lathom politely. Kohima held the door for Temple, and they went into his consulting room. Temple noted that the portable typewriter was no longer standing on the floor beside the desk.

They were no sooner in the room with the door closed than Kohima turned swiftly, and demanded: 'What exactly did you want to see Mrs. Trevelyan about?'

Temple showed no sign of being perturbed by the question, but replied quite pleasantly: 'Oh, it was just about your car, Doctor.'

Kohima frowned.

'But I've told you all there is to tell about my car. You 'phoned the garage yourself, I was perfectly frank with you—'

'Yes, of course,' replied Temple suavely. 'But with your permission I should like to have a chat with Mrs. Trevelyan.'

'Very well,' said Kohima at last, unable to conceal a faint note of annoyance in his voice. He pressed a button at the side of his desk. Almost at once, a second door opened, and Mrs. Trevelyan came in.

'Ah, Mrs. Trevelyan,' said the doctor, 'this is Mr. Temple.'

'We met yesterday,' Mrs. Trevelyan reminded him.

'Yes – of course. Well, Mr. Temple would apparently like a word with you.'

'Very good, Doctor,' replied Mrs. Trevelyan in an expressionless voice.

'I imagine Mr. Temple wants to ask you one or two routine questions, Mrs. Trevelyan. Satisfy his curiosity if you can.' The doctor's voice sounded faintly bored now. 'Take him into your office, and tell Mr. Lathom I'll see him. No, don't bother, I'll tell him.'

As Temple and Mrs. Trevelyan were leaving, the doctor called: 'Oh, and before I forget, Mrs. Trevelyan. I appear to have mislaid my silver pencil – the one with my initials on it. You haven't seen it by any chance?'

'It was on your desk last night, Doctor,' she told him.

'Yes, I'm aware of that,' he replied, faintly irritated. 'I saw it myself last night. But it's gone this morning.'

'I'll try and find it for you, sir,' she smiled, and Temple followed her out of the room and carefully closed the door.

Her little office was small and very plainly furnished with a flat top desk and a large filing cabinet, with a couple of chairs. On the desk stood a portable typewriter, from which she snatched a sheet of paper.

'Here you are, Mr. Temple,' she said.

He examined it closely. After a moment, he said: 'The typing isn't the same.'

'Of course not,' she replied, repressing the triumphant note in her voice. 'I knew it wouldn't be.'

'All the same, I'll keep this – just in case.'

He folded the paper and thrust it into his coat pocket, noting as he did so the tired look in her eyes and strained expression of her mouth.

'You took a risk in coming to my flat last night,' he said quietly. 'You know that, don't you?'

'I've got to take a risk sometime. I can't go on like this,' she replied in some agitation.

'I quite appreciate that,' he nodded. 'But there is a chance that someone saw you come . . . and there may be . . . well, reprisals!'

She caught her breath.

'And if you want to get in touch with me again, I shouldn't advise you to come round without letting me know first. You can always telephone me—'

'It's a relief to know that, Mr. Temple. Would you give me the number?'

He scribbled on a visiting-card . . . 'This is a private number,' he informed her. 'You won't find it in the book.'

'Thank you,' said Mrs. Trevelyan gratefully, taking the card.

'And watch your step,' advised Temple. 'I shall be out of town tonight, but I'll be back first thing in the morning. If anything should crop up during that time – I don't suppose there will – but if there did, I should advise you to telephone the Yard and ask for Sir Graham Forbes or Inspector Crane.'

'I'll remember,' she nodded. 'Are you going far?'

'Only to Canterbury.'

'Canterbury?' she repeated in a surprised voice.

'Yes,' he murmured deliberately. 'To the Royal Falcon Hotel.'

On the drive down to Canterbury, Steve did her utmost to discover what her husband expected to find there, but he was in a thoughtful mood, and answered mainly in monosyllables, concentrating his attention on the road ahead. Temple did not admit as much to Steve, but he was still not quite sure about Mrs. Trevelyan. There was just a remote chance that she had still been acting under instructions from Rex when she paid them that visit in the small hours of the morning. The possibility that Mrs. Trevelyan herself was Rex hardly appeared as likely now in view of recent events, but this case had abounded in strange and diabolical surprises.

And then there was the question of Doctor Kohima, who might quite easily be working in association with Mrs. Trevelyan, and who had been unable to supply any satisfactory explanation as to how his car had left the garage on the evening when it had collided with Temple's. It was difficult to arrive at a detached estimate of Doctor Kohima; there was something faintly mysterious about him, which may have been traceable to his dark skin or to the peculiar profession which he practised. Accustomed as he was to meeting all sorts of people, even Temple had to admit that he was not altogether comfortable when facing the mesmeric glare of Doctor Kohima.

Nevertheless, Temple still felt it would be a mistake to arrest either the doctor or Mrs. Trevelyan, though when he had called at the Yard that morning to see the report on the bomb attack, Sir Graham had seemed somewhat guarded when questioned about his plans regarding Mrs. Trevelyan.

He could, of course, appreciate the Assistant Commissioner's point of view that Mrs. Trevelyan was the perpetrator of this outrage in one sense, for she had lured the Temples to Marshall House Terrace, even if she had done so unwillingly and under pressure of blackmail. Sir Graham was determined to leave no avenue unexplored, and Temple knew that, if in the Assistant Commissioner's opinion, Mrs. Trevelyan was safer under arrest, then he would immediately have her taken into custody. And this, to Temple's way of thinking, would at once throw a spanner in the machine!

However, worrying about it served no useful purpose, and Temple dismissed it from his mind as they came into Canterbury and made for the Royal Falcon Hotel, which was invariably described in the guide-books as 'an ancient hostelry, dating back to the coaching days'. They discovered it in the centre of the town, and after registering and taking their cases up to their room, had barely time for a wash before dinner.

In the low-ceilinged dining-room, which was only half-full they found a table in a corner, and an elderly waiter with lugubrious expression advanced upon them.

'Are you staying here, sir?' he asked by way of greeting.

'We are,' replied Temple.

'Oh,' grunted the waiter in a tone which implied that they had his deepest sympathy. Temple looked across at Steve and exchanged a meaningful smile. The old waiter shuffled off and presently returned with a menu, muttering something to himself. Temple began to study it, only to find that the waiter had disappeared.

'He's making sure that everything's off,' laughed Steve.

'Anyhow, here's bread without asking for it, so the place may not be as bad as all that after all,' said Temple, reaching for a piece of bread out of the basket on the service table, and passing one to Steve.

'I wonder who runs this place?' she said. 'It isn't owned by a company, is it?'

'I don't think so. The manager was in the office when I registered – a fellow named Chester. He may be the proprietor too. Slightly sinister looking individual, with a scar across his left cheek.'

'Did he seem surprised to see you?'

'No, I can't say he did. I watched him pretty carefully, but he has a poker face.'

'And you didn't mention the mysterious Miss Smith?'

'No. I'll have a chat with Mr. Chester after dinner – that's if we're getting any dinner.'

'Sh! Here's the old man of the sea coming back!' whispered Steve as the waiter came plodding across to them again. She favoured him with her pleasantest smile, and said brightly: 'Gosh! I'm hungry!'

'Well – there's the menu,' replied the waiter dubiously, bestowing a few perfunctory flicks with his napkin on the table. Temple studied it for a moment, then announced;

'Roast duck! What do you say, Steve?'

'Will a duck swim!' she was beginning, when the waiter interposed.

'The duck's off, sir.'

'Off colour, or off the menu?'

'Both, sir.'

Steve leaned over to see the menu and frowned thoughtfully.

'What about the roast lamb?' she asked. 'That ought to be good in Canterbury.'

'I'm afraid it's the wrong Canterbury, darling,' smiled Temple.

'Very tasty, the lamb,' murmured the waiter reflectively. 'Very tasty indeed – while it lasted.'

'But of course it's off!' nodded Temple, suddenly starting to examine the menu much more closely, as if he were seeking some elusive item which had been overlooked. Then he let it fall to the table, with a thoughtful look in his eyes.

'I might be able to do something in the fish line,' the waiter was saying dolefully. 'That's if you fancy a nice bit of fish.'

His voice seemed to have receded into the distance. Noticing Temple's faraway expression, Steve jogged his elbow.

'The fish, darling,' she prompted.

'Oh yes,' replied Temple, coming back to earth. 'That will do splendidly, if it's all right with you, Steve.'

Steve nodded to the waiter.

'The fish!' announced that gentleman, sounding more dubious than ever, as he made his way in the direction of the service hatch.

Temple picked up the menu again, turned it over, put it down beside him, then he took a small magnifying glass from his pocket. Looking round to see if they were observed, he began to examine the menu closely.

'Darling, I'm afraid you won't discover the missing duck!' smiled Steve. 'What is there that's so remarkable about that menu?'

He did not speak for a few moments, then slowly pocketed the glass and passed the menu over to her.

'Have a good look at it,' he advised.

She held it at varying distances, but only succeeded in looking more puzzled than ever.

'It looks just like any other menu to me,' she confessed.

'Don't you think it's typed rather nicely?' he suggested.

'Why yes, of course. Nothing very remarkable about that, is there? Lots of menus are typed and – 'She suddenly caught her breath and began to look at it more closely.

'Why, Paul – it was typed on the same machine – the one that typed the notes sent to Mrs. Trevelyan by Rex!'

'Your eyesight's pretty good, Steve,' he complimented her.

'But this is astonishing! Really astonishing!' she cried in complete amazement.

'Yes,' he mused thoughtfully, 'I suppose it is in a way . . . as long as we don't go leaping to conclusions.'

'But there's no doubt about it, Paul. Look at the a's and d's . . . they're identical.'

'All the same,' said Temple slowly, 'it doesn't follow necessarily that Rex has his headquarters here. Guests staying at a hotel could quite easily borrow the hotel machine for half an hour to answer some private letters. I've done it myself – you know I can work more quickly on a typewriter.'

'But it means that *someone* stayed here – someone very closely connected with Rex – or maybe Rex in person—'

'I think we might be safe in assuming that,' he nodded. 'But we've got to move carefully, Steve – it's a tricky business. Rex must have a pretty good idea that we're fairly close on his heels, and he'll be out to take advantage of the least slip on our part. His next coup will be very carefully planned, and he'll probably take elaborate precautions to throw suspicion on some likely person.'

His mention of a forthcoming possible coup brought to Steve's mind the thought of the list of Rex's victims.

'I meant to ask you last night, Paul,' she said, 'about those two names on the list – before Mrs. Trevelyan—'

'James Barton and Norman Steele?' he queried.

'Yes. Had you heard of them before?'

'I'd heard of James Barton,' he told her. 'He's a director of Meriden-Overland Airways; he invented a patent refuelling apparatus that was used a good deal during the war. I've never met him, but he sounds an intelligent sort of person.'

'What would Rex know about a man like that?'

Temple shrugged. 'Search me! We all have a past of some sort, you know, Steve. The most innocent of us has—' He broke off as the door opened. 'Talking of innocents,' he murmured, 'look who's here.'

A thick-set little man with very dark hair was walking towards them. Steve at once recognised Wilfred Davis, their Welsh acquaintance of the Twisted Keys. He came straight over to their table.

'Hello, Mr. Temple,' he said pleasantly. 'Now whatever would you be doing in Canterbury?'

'I might ask you the same question, Mr . . .'

'Lordy, now I don't suppose I properly introduced myself. My name is Davis, Wilfred Davis – look, here is my card.'

Temple took the card and read: 'Longford Utilities Limited, 16 Queensgate, Manchester. Presented by Wilfred Davis.'

'So that's what brings you to Canterbury, Mr. Davis,' he smiled, pushing the card in his pocket.

'That's right, Mr. Temple. I am a traveller.'

'Well, Canterbury has certainly been visited by travellers for quite a number of years.' Temple pulled out a chair and Davis sat down.

'Are you still reading your detective novels, Mr. Davis?' asked Steve.

His eyes positively glowed.

'Just you try to stop me, Mrs. Temple! I am an absolute glutton for crime and criminology.' He began to play with a

107

fork on the table. Temple noticed that he had very muscular hands, covered with a down of black hair.

'By the way, Mr. Temple,' he said suddenly, 'this Rex affair is a most extraordinary business, is it not?'

'Most extraordinary,' said Temple in a noncommittal tone.

'The newspapers are always full of the most gruesome details,' continued Davis, an eager light in his eyes. He adopted a very confidential tone and leaning forward said: 'I am most intrigued, Mr. Temple. Tell me, is it true that you are sort of investigating the case?'

'Sort of,' replied Temple with a whimsical smile.

'Well now, that must be most interesting. Of course, naturally I am particularly interested in this Rex affair.'

'Oh,' said Temple, rather surprised. 'Why?'

'Well, you see, I suppose in a manner of speaking I am almost part and parcel of it, as you might say.'

'You are, Mr. Davis?' queried Steve incredulously.

'Yes indeed, Mrs. Temple,' he eagerly assured her. 'I have read about hundreds and thousands of murders in books, but never before have I been mixed up with one. You see I was on the train when they found the body of Norma Rice.'

'Good Lord!' exclaimed Temple softly.

'Yes,' continued Davis with avidity, 'I was actually asleep in the next compartment.'

'Did you see Miss Rice?' asked Temple.

'Lordy, yes! A fine woman she was too, Mr. Temple. The ticket inspector found her, then he dragged me into her compartment – he was so upset, you see. My, it was a strange sight, I can tell you. She was kind of propped up in a corner, and there scrawled across the window was the word "Rex" . . . I can see it now. I tell you something though,

Mr. Temple – it is one thing to read about such things and quite another when you are faced with them.'

'Yes,' nodded Temple in some amusement, 'you're right there, Mr. Davis. Do you often come here?'

'About every six months. I am very fond of Canterbury and all those historical places, cathedral towns and such like. The tradespeople are very conservative, you know, but once you are accepted, the orders are very regular.'

'And you always stay at this hotel?' asked Temple.

'Yes. I know it is not as good as it was in the old days. But my customers know where to find me, you see,' he explained almost apologetically. 'In the old days, this was the leading hotel in the town.'

He appeared to be about to embark upon further similar observations, but was interrupted by the arrival of the waiter, who very deliberately deposited two plates of greasy-looking soup on the table, then turned to the novelist and asked: 'Is your name Temple?'

Temple nodded.

'There's a personal call for you from London, sir. You'll see the box just along the corridor on the right.'

Temple excused himself, and Steve began to drink her soup.

Having found the box and made himself known to the operator who was holding the call, Temple was very surprised to hear the somewhat dour tones of Inspector Crane at the other end the line.

'I'm speaking for Sir Graham, Mr. Temple,' the inspector informed him. 'We tried to get you at the flat, but your man said you were in Canterbury – he told me the name of the hotel—'

'Oh, he did,' murmured Temple, wondering if Steve had given Ricky this piece of information or otherwise. 'Is there anything wrong?'

'Sir Graham would rather like you to come back to town, sir, If you can possibly manage it.'

'Tonight?' queried Temple.

'That's right, sir.'

'What's happened, Crane? You'd better tell me now – it just possibly link up with one or two things I've discovered down here.'

There was an appreciable pause, then Crane said flatly: 'A man named James Barton has been murdered.'

Temple whistled softly.

'How was he killed, Inspector?'

'Bullet through the head,' came the laconic reply.

'Did you find the revolver?'

'No, sir. We haven't even found the bullet – can't make it out. But there was something we did find. Came across it myself – right by the body.'

'Oh . . . what was that?'

'A silver pencil,' replied Crane impressively. 'A silver pencil with the initials—'

'The initials C. K. engraved on it,' Temple quickly informed him.

'Yes, sir, that's right. How the devil did you—'

'Tell Sir Graham I'll start back right away,' said Temple briskly. 'Is there anything else?'

'Er – well – no, sir—' came the slightly bewildered tones of the inspector. 'You don't seem very surprised about that pencil, Mr. Temple.'

Temple smiled.

'I should have been very surprised if you hadn't found it, Inspector!' he said.

CHAPTER VII

Cyanide is No Tonic!

HAVING replaced the receiver, Temple stood for a moment deep in thought. Then he pushed open the door of the box somewhat suddenly and heard a stifled exclamation. Turning, he saw Frank Chester, the manager.

'I'm sorry,' he apologised hastily.

'My fault,' said Chester politely. 'That box is in an awkward place – I should have been on the look-out for the door to open, I've been banged often enough . . . did you get your call, Mr. Temple?'

'Oh yes, thanks,' murmured Temple, wondering if it were possible for Chester to have overheard it. Dismissing the thought for the moment, he said: 'Excuse me, but are you the manager?'

'Officially, yes,' nodded Chester. 'Though just at the moment I seem to be head cook and bottle washer. Not to mention pageboy.'

He allowed his somewhat stern features to relax for a moment, then asked: 'Is there anything I can do for you, Mr. Temple?'

Temple pursed his lips in thought for a moment, then said: 'I'm afraid we're going to put you to a little trouble, Mr. Chester. You see my wife and I have received an urgent call back to Town.'

'You mean you have to go tonight?' asked Chester imperturbably.

'Yes, I'm afraid so.'

'I'm sorry about that,' said Chester. 'I'll tell them at the office. You appreciate we have to make a nominal charge for the room—'

'That's perfectly all right,' Temple quickly assured him.

'Then I'll let them know in the office right away.' He turned to go, but Temple laid a hand on his arm.

'Just a minute, Mr. Chester. There's another little matter – if you could help me—'

'Of course. Anything I can do—'

His face was as impassive as ever, but Temple imagined he saw a momentary gleam of discomfort in his grey-green eyes.

'It concerns a friend of mine who stayed here three months ago. Unfortunately, I have mislaid her address, and I was wondering if you would have any record.'

'I expect so,' replied Chester quite pleasantly. 'When did you say she was here?'

'I should say possibly somewhere round the first fortnight in July.'

'And the name?'

Temple hesitated a moment, then watching Chester very shrewdly he said: 'Smith is the name. Miss Judy Smith.'

During the second's silence that followed, Chester's poker face remained set as inflexibly as ever, but when he spoke there was just a slight thickness in his voice, as he said:

'I'll do the best I can for you, Mr. Temple.'

'Thank you,' replied Temple more politely than ever. 'I should be extremely obliged. You'll find me in the dining-room.'

Chester hurried off, and Temple strolled back to the dining-room, where he found Steve still listening to Wilfred Davis and toying with some very unpalatable-looking steamed fish.

'– and then we motored down to Naples,' Davis was saying. 'I don't ever remember seeing a more glorious view. They say "See Naples and die," and I tell you, Mrs. Temple—'

He caught sight of Temple and suddenly became self-conscious of his over-exuberant manner.

'Oh, here is Mr. Temple,' he murmured in some confusion.

'Oh yes,' said Steve with a certain amount of relief.

Temple slid into his chair and smiled at them.

'Sorry to have kept you waiting like this,' he apologised.

'I should imagine your soup is stone-cold by now,' said Steve.

'It was probably stone-cold to start with, if I know anything about the Royal Falcon!' remarked the little Welshman. 'Well I will be off now, Mr. Temple. Perhaps you will join me later in the lounge for a cup of coffee. I have an idea for a story which I am sure would interest you.'

Temple sighed inwardly – he had heard that sentence so many times.

'I am afraid we have to go back to Town almost at once, Mr. Davis,' he announced, hoping that he had disguised the note of relief in his voice.

'Oh,' said Davis flatly, then added somewhat suspiciously, 'I thought you said you were staying the night?'

Steve looked up at her husband.

'Aren't we staying the night?' she asked, wondering if he was serious or merely being politely evasive to Mr. Davis.

'No,' replied Temple quietly, so that there was no mistaking his meaning. Steve looked very puzzled, but said nothing.

'Oh well,' murmured Davis, faintly embarrassed and conscious that his presence was somewhat superfluous, 'I will be making a move. Nice to have seen you again, anyway. Good-bye.'

'Good-bye, Mr. Davis,' replied Temple absently. Steve waited until the little Welshman was outside the door, then demanded in an anxious voice: 'Paul – what is it?'

'Finish your dinner, dear. I want to get back to Town as soon as we can.'

'What's happened?' she asked.

'It's James Barton – the man we were talking about,' he told her. 'He's dead.'

'Oh no!' cried Steve with a look of horror.

'I'm afraid so, Steve. Not much use getting upset about it now. We've got to get moving, and there's no time to lose!'

'First Richard East . . . then Norma Rice . . . Sir Ernest Cranbury . . . Hans Muller . . . and now James Barton . . .' Steve whispered softly. 'You're right, Paul. We've got to do something! If I could only—'

'You can,' he whispered urgently. 'Listen to me – listen carefully.' He laid his cigarette-case on the corner of the table. 'Now, Steve, when I give you the nod, I want you to knock this case on the floor, make it appear quite accidental – have you got that?'

'But why?' she asked in a puzzled voice.

'Never mind now. Do as I tell you.'

She looked up and saw Frank Chester coming quickly in their direction, so she leaned on the table with her elbow conveniently near the cigarette-case.

'Oh, there you are, Mr. Temple,' said Chester as he approached. 'I'm afraid I haven't been able to help you.

I've been through the books and the registration forms for the entire month, but I can't find any trace of your friend. Are you quite sure she was here at that time?'

Temple lifted his eyes in Steve's direction, and she obediently edged the cigarette-case off the table with a casual gesture. Chester stooped and retrieved the case, which he politely handed back to Steve. Temple then introduced them, keeping one eye on the cigarette-case all the time.

'I'm awfully sorry you have to rush away like this, Mrs. Temple,' said Chester politely.

'Yes, it is a nuisance,' agreed Steve. 'I was so looking forward to staying the night in Canterbury – it's so peaceful.'

'Business is business,' murmured Temple cryptically.

'Of course,' nodded Chester. 'And about that little matter of your friend – Miss – er—' he looked hesitatingly in Steve's direction.

'It's all right,' smiled Temple. 'Miss Smith is my wife's friend, too!'

'Are you quite sure she stayed here?' asked Chester.

Temple wrinkled his forehead.

'I could have sworn she said the Royal Falcon . . . or was it the Royal Fountain?'

'In that case, I'm afraid I can't help you,' smiled Chester. 'Though I'm sure if you went along there, Mr. Condale would—'

'Oh, it isn't as important as all that,' smiled Temple. 'In fact I feel a bit guilty at putting you to all this trouble.'

'That's perfectly all right,' Chester assured him. 'I'll tell them to get your car ready.'

As soon as Chester had disappeared, Temple said quietly: 'Wrap the cigarette-case in your handkerchief and put it in your handbag.'

115

She looked down at the case on the table.

'If it's the fingerprints you're after, Paul, I'm afraid I handled it—'

'That's all right,' he nodded. 'I know exactly where the prints I want are to be found. Put it away, Steve.'

Handling the case very gingerly, she stowed it away in her bag.

'These fingerprints,' she said presently, 'you don't think they belong to Rex?'

He shrugged.

'Any prize offered?'

'No, but seriously, Paul, who is Rex?'

'Don't be silly, Steve,' he smiled. 'You know as well as I do that it's Ricky! You've read your Edgar Wallace, and you ought to know that you can't have a mysterious Chinese floating around without—'

'I keep telling you he's not Chinese!' interrupted Steve, laughing in spite of herself. 'He's a Siamese!'

'Well, there you are!' he grinned. 'He's not even a Chinese!'

But Steve could see that Temple was by no means as lightened as he would have had her believe. A tiny nerve near his left temple twitched spasmodically, and she knew this was a sign that he was extremely worried. He seemed to welcome the opportunity to light a cigarette. He slowly expelled a stream of smoke and murmured thoughtfully: 'You know, it's like working on a gigantic jigsaw, Steve, with half the pieces missing and the picture torn to shreds. I keep asking myself the same questions over and over again, in the light of every fresh bit of evidence. Why did Mrs. Trevelyan ask us to meet her at that place in Marshall House Terrace? If she paid Rex three thousand pounds, then where exactly did she get the money? Does Mr. Carl Lathom really believe that he suffered from hallucinations? And if they were not hallucinations, then who is the girl in brown?'

'At any rate, she isn't Mrs. Trevelyan,' interposed Steve.

'Is she the same girl – the one who followed you that night? And then there's the silver pencil belonging to Doctor Kohima.'

'What's that?' asked Steve.

'A silver pencil bearing the initials C. K. – presumably for Charles Kohima – was found beside the body of James Barton. Curiously enough, while I was in the doctor's office, he told Mrs. Trevelyan that he mislaid his silver pencil, the one with his initials on it.'

'Good gracious!' exclaimed Steve. 'That makes things look pretty black against Doctor Kohima.'

'That's just it – the whole thing's too obvious. Rex isn't the type of murderer to leave silver pencils lying around by accident.'

'Then you think it was deliberate?'

'I can't be sure without knowing more facts. But I can't help feeling very suspicious. It makes the jig-saw fit together much too easily.'

'Jig-saws often do as one goes on,' Steve reminded him. 'But remember you said that Rex would lay his plans very carefully for his next coup. This may be part of the plan.'

'Yes,' nodded Temple, 'on the face of that evidence, Sir Graham is almost certain to arrest the doctor, and maybe Mrs Trevelyan, too.'

'Mr. Davis suspects Mrs. Trevelyan,' Steve informed him.

'Davis does?'

'Oh yes, he has quite a theory. The man's mind seems to run upon crime and criminals every spare minute he has.'

'How does he know Mrs. Trevelyan, anyway?'

'It was mentioned in one paper – about the name being found on Norma Rice. Rex Bryant got the story somehow and did his best with it.'

'Oh yes, I remember. All the same, I don't quite know what to make of our Welsh friend. Does he really spend *all* his time reading detective novels?'

'Seems he has a certain amount of business to transact.'

Temple took the card Davis had given him and carelessly examined it. Obviously, it must be genuine, yet a commercial traveller's job would be an ideal cloak for the activities of a person like Rex.

Temple did not know quite what to make of Mr. Wilfred Davis.

'This case seems so complicated,' Steve was saying, 'that I am really beginning to wonder whether we shall ever get to the bottom of it. I'm half afraid that it will go into the Scotland Yard files with all the other unsolved murders – there have been nine so far this year, I was reading this morning.'

'Don't worry, Steve,' he smiled. 'Something will turn up.'

'That's just it,' she retorted. 'Something is always turning up. I have never known a case so full of surprises.'

'Life's full of surprises, darling,' he gently reminded her. 'Take this soup! It says tomato soup on the menu, and it looks like tomato soup. But the question is, does it taste of tomatoes?'

He stubbed out his cigarette and took a spoonful of soup. An expression of blank amazement swept over his face.

'By Timothy, it does!' he exclaimed. Then he recovered and said with a smile: 'There you are, you see. Didn't I say life was full of surprises?'

When they passed the lounge on their way upstairs a quarter of an hour later, they saw Wilfred Davis and Frank Chester, the manager, in close conversation. The little Welshman was expounding at some length in his typically Celtic fashion, and Chester was nodding politely and putting in an occasional word of agreement. When he caught sight of Temple and Steve, Chester excused himself and came over to them.

'I had your cases brought down, Mr. Temple,' he said. 'They're in your car.'

'Good,' said Temple. 'We'll just get our coats and see that we haven't left anything behind.'

'And the next time you visit us, I hope we shall have the pleasure of seeing you for some days at least,' said Chester, as they moved away.

It was very dark when they started on their homeward journey, and there were a few stray patches of mist at intervals along the road, so they were unable to make the progress Temple would have liked, and he chafed impatiently as he dropped into second gear time after time.

'I hope to goodness this doesn't turn into a fog in the Thames Valley,' said Steve, straining her eyes to make out the road ahead.

'Let's not meet any more troubles,' he murmured grimly as he deftly steered the car past a heavy lorry. Switching on the dashboard light, he noted that it was already after nine-thirty, and he put his foot down on the accelerator as they came to a clear stretch of road.

'Did you speak to Sir Graham on the 'phone?' asked Steve presently.

'No, it was Crane.'

'Was he as abrupt as ever?'

'He'd had plenty to upset him,' said Temple.

'I dare say. All the same, I don't know quite what to make of Crane.'

'He has an unfortunate manner as far as polite society is concerned,' smiled Temple. 'Though I should imagine it has its advantage in dealing with the criminal classes.'

Steve frowned pensively.

'It's not only his manner,' she said. 'He always seems to have an air of mystery about him. I don't know how it is, but I always get a feeling that he might be leading some sort of double life – that he might even—'

'He might turn out to be Rex?' suggested Temple, switching off his headlights as a motor coach came towards them.

Steve laughed without very much conviction.

'But he couldn't very well turn out to be Rex, now could he?' she insisted.

'Why not?' he asked. 'A man from Scotland Yard would be a pretty formidable master criminal. He could always keep one jump ahead with very little difficulty.'

'Then you think that Crane might—'

'I didn't say so, Steve. At least, not in so many words! But there's always a chance. Remember the inspector in that first case we tackled together soon after we met?'

'Do I remember?' echoed Steve. 'My heart was in my mouth for days on end! And if you think Crane is – well – suspicious, shouldn't you have a word with Sir Graham?'

Temple dexterously extracted a cigarette from his case, and Steve lit it for him.

'No,' he said at length. 'I think Sir Graham will have quite enough on his plate for the time being.'

'But if Crane were an accomplice of Rex, you would be able to go straight to—'

'To the fox's lair?' he suggested. 'No, I don't think it would be quite as straightforward as that. All the same, I think we can keep a watchful eye on Inspector Crane.'

With a stifled imprecation he reached over for the hand-brake as they came unexpectedly into a patch of mist which slowed them down to a comparative crawl. As they emerged about five minutes later, he asked, quite casually: 'Have you made up your mind about Mrs. Trevelyan yet, Steve?'

She turned quickly and looked at him, but his face was immobile.

'Why do you ask?' she demanded.

'I thought a woman's point of view might be useful. She's a pretty complex character.'

'She's certainly a woman with a past in more senses than one, if that's what you mean,' Steve nodded. 'All the same, I like her. I feel there's something human about her, even though there are times when she may not exactly tell the truth. I should say a lot of men have considered her very fascinating,' she added shrewdly.

'I wonder who Mr. Trevelyan was?' he speculated. 'Sounds rather like a penniless member of the Cornish aristocracy.'

'What interests me more is her dark secret,' said Steve. 'It must be pretty something drastic if she's prepared to pay three thousand to keep it quiet.'

'Unfortunately, that three thousand is only a first instalment. Blackmail always works that way. I think she realises that. She's a clever woman, and she sees her only chance is to come in on our side and help to bring Rex to book. But there's another complication somewhere, and she has to keep on playing for time. Of course, all this is only my theory . . .' His voice trailed away as a red lamp loomed up out of the darkness. Their headlamps picked up the figure of the man who held it. Temple stopped the car almost level with him.

The man, who looked very much like a policeman in plain clothes, came round to Temple.

'I'm afraid you'll have to make a detour, sir,' he said. 'There's a bit of a hold-up farther on down the road.'

'What's happened?'

'Oh, nothing much. One of those big Army lorries bumped into a farm-cart and overturned when it skidded.'

'Was anyone hurt?' demanded Steve anxiously.

'No, ma'am – the driver had a bruise or two. But it'll take an hour or so to get the lorry right side up. If you take the first lane on your right, then keep bearing left, you'll be back on the main road in no time. Brings you out about a couple of miles farther on.'

'Right,' nodded Temple. 'Thanks for the tip.'

He turned into the lane indicated, which immediately narrowed so that there was barely room for two fair-sized cars to pass each other. Again, he had to drop into second, and the high banks seemed to make the road darker than ever. The surface was very rough, and matters did not improve when they ran into another belt of fog.

'Damn!' exclaimed Temple softly, and leaned forward to switch on the fog lamp, which sent out an orange beam that helped a little.

'It's a pretty long lane,' muttered Steve after they had jolted along in this fashion for over a mile.

'Cheer up, darling. We ought to be back on the main road soon,' he said with an attempt to take a lighthearted view of the detour.

Just then the mist cleared a little, and Steve suddenly clutched his arm.

'Paul – stop! That rope!'

'Get down, Steve!' he yelled, and grabbed the handbrake. They were only the length of the car from a steel rope which was stretched across the road between two trees. He managed to reduce the speed of the car to a mere crawl by the time the rope sliced into the windscreen, but they felt a considerable jolt. By this time they were both crouching on the floor, and escaped without any injury apart from the fact that Temple jarred his left wrist and Steve's new hat was badly knocked out of shape. The engine stalled and for a moment there was complete silence.

'Phew!' gasped Temple. 'Are you okay, Steve?'

She felt herself gingerly and slowly returned to the seat.

'A bit shaken,' she said, 'but no bones broken.' She took of the damaged hat and eyed it ruefully. 'Oh well, it's time I had a new one anyway,' she added.

'Yes, you must have had it quite a fortnight!' he grinned, opening the car door and getting out to inspect the damage.

The steel rope had forced the windscreen back through an angle of at least thirty degrees. It was going to be distinctly uncomfortable driving back to Town, unless they could get the windscreen repaired at a garage. Temple took out his torch and examined the rope, which had been very firmly secured to a tree on either side of the road.

'Lucky the fog slowed us down, Steve . . . and that you caught sight of the rope . . . If we'd smacked into it even at twenty—'

Steve covered her face with her hands. Presently, she whispered: 'Paul, whoever fixed that rope must have known we were due this way—'

'Yes,' he nodded, 'it was quite deliberate, of course. I expect the man with the lamp might know something about it.'

'Then couldn't we go back and see—'

'Not much chance of finding him there now,' he replied. 'All the same, it looks as if we shall have to go back. This rope is fastened pretty firmly, and I've nothing to cut it with.

I'll have to back the car till we come to a gateway or an opening of some sort. Are you sure you feel up to it now?'

'Oh yes, I'm all right, Paul. We mustn't lose any more time if we can help it.'

'Righto then.' He climbed into the car and pressed the self-starter, which whirred for some seconds without producing any response from the engine.

'H'm . . . not so good,' murmured Temple, groping in the back of the car in search of the handle. 'It's no use running the battery right down.'

Suddenly, he straightened himself and listened intently.

'I thought I heard something,' said Steve in a whisper.

'So did I.'

They sat and listened and presently heard a strange strangled moan which obviously came from someone in considerable pain.

'Where is it?' cried Steve.

'Over there, I think,' replied Temple curtly, nodding in the direction of one of the trees to which the rope was fastened. Steve took the torch from a side pocket in the car and quietly opened the door, his ears on the alert for the slightest sound. Once again, he heard the queer agonised gasp and unhesitatingly moved towards the tree. For a moment or two, his light revealed nothing, until the beam swung over to a neighbouring tree from which a dark object was dangling.

He quickly pointed the torch downwards, but not before he had heard a cry of horror from Steve.

'Stay where you are, Steve!' he ordered brusquely. 'Don't move from the car!' But as he went forward, he heard the car door open and presently the sound of Steve's footsteps behind him. There was no time to argue, and without further ado he pushed his way through the hedge at the side of the road and crashed through the undergrowth towards his objective. Steve came up with him as he was looking up at the body of a man, whose feet were level with his shoulder.

'I told you to stay in the car, Steve,' he snapped.

'What are you going to do, Paul?' she cried breathlessly.

He shone his torch along the branch of the tree to which the body was fastened, and noticed that the man's weight had already fractured it near the trunk.

'I'll try to break down that bough. It'll be quicker,' he decided at once. 'Hold the torch, Steve.' He ran to the end of the branch, leapt up and caught it. Then he swung his feet off the ground and presently there was a sound of splintering wood. In another moment the branch came crashing to the ground. Temple rushed to lift it clear of the man's body.

'Get the flask of brandy out of my suitcase in the back of the car,' he called to Steve, who scrambled back through the hedge to the further detriment of her stockings. When she returned, she found that he had managed to straighten out the man, who had fallen in a crumpled heap, and was busily applying artificial respiration.

She gave him the flask, and directed the beam of the torch upon the man on the ground.

'Paul!' she cried, suddenly recognising the distorted features. 'This is the man we met in the Twisted Keys, the man you spoke to about the car—'

'That's right,' he agreed somewhat breathlessly. 'It's Spider Williams.'

Then Steve remembered that she had some particularly strong smelling-salts in her bag and hurried back to get them. Temple loosened the rope from round Williams' throat and began to massage it. He judged that it would be no use trying to make him swallow anything just yet. From time to time,

Williams moaned feebly. His breath came in spasmodical gasps. Then after a minute or two he opened his eyes . . .

'Take it easy, Spider,' whispered Temple encouragingly.

'It's you, Mr. Temple!' said Spider weakly. 'I – I heard a car – and I thought – then it all went black—'

'Don't worry about that now, Spider. Lie back and try to breathe easily.'

'But I got to tell you, Mr. Temple. I came down here with the money. I did exactly as I was told . . . then at the last minute—'

'Who sent you down here?' asked Temple.

'Lord Stanwyck. He offered me two hundred quid to bring the money . . . it looked easy . . .' His voice trailed away, but he lifted his head with a nervous start as Steve approached.

'It's all right,' Temple reassured him. 'It's only my wife.'

He took the smelling-salts from Steve, lifted the stopper and held the bottle under Williams' nose. The little man continued to gasp, but the colour had drained from his face.

'Take your time, Spider,' said Temple, still massaging the badly bruised throat.

'You were just in time, Mr. Temple,' the little man whispered. 'Another two minutes and I'd have been a goner!'

'Don't think about it,' repeated Temple, unscrewing the top of the brandy flask Steve had brought.

'I'll be all right, Mr. Temple, once I can get on my feet.'

'You'll do nothing of the sort. Have a drink of this brandy and then we'll carry you down to the car.' He passed the flask over to Spider, lifting his head and holding an arm round his shoulders. The little man took the flask eagerly and tilted it into his mouth.

A second later he gave a sudden cry of anguish and dropped the flask. Temple was so startled that he let Spider's head fall back, and was horrified to see the features contorted in excruciating agony.

'Paul! What's wrong?' cried Steve.

'I don't know,' he snapped, looking down at Spider in complete mystification.

'Perhaps his throat is injured internally. Maybe we shouldn't have given him spirits . . . oh, look—' She indicated the body of Spider Williams which had doubled in its agony, and now lay very still.

'He's dead!' she cried hysterically. 'We shouldn't have given him brandy—'

'Brandy?' echoed Temple, a thought striking him. He picked up the flask and sniffed it cautiously.

'My God! Cyanide!' he murmured softly.

CHAPTER VIII

Carl Lathom is Perturbed

AT ten o'clock the next morning, the Assistant Commissioner was holding an informal conference in his office overlooking the Embankment. It was a pleasant, sunny morning, and the sounds of traffic came up from the road below, while there was a constant stream of shipping up and down the river, slowly lowering their funnels to negotiate the bridge at Charing Cross. In fact, a casual observer might have been forgiven for thinking that all was very well with the world.

But Forbes was pacing up and down the office with the distracted air of a statesman facing yet another European crisis. Crane sat bolt upright on a chair, looking very irritable as if he were chafing at some delay. The calmest person present, to all outward appearances, was Paul Temple, who was perched on a corner of the Commissioner's desk, slowly smoking a cigarette and throwing in an occasional remark when Forbes' harangue dried up. An onlooker would have found it hard to believe that Temple had enjoyed exactly three hours sleep on the previous night.

'It's not a bit of use arguing, Crane,' Sir Graham barked emphatically. 'You saw exactly what happened.'

'Yes, we know what happened,' replied Crane irritably, 'but the point is what the devil are we going to do about it?'

Temple knocked the ash from the end of his cigarette.

'There's only one thing we can do in my opinion,' he announced.

'And that is?' asked Forbes, turning on him suddenly.

'Sit tight,' replied Temple simply.

Forbes struck his fist into the palm of his other hand.

'It's all very well your saying sit tight, Temple,' he snorted. 'You've no idea what I'm up against here at the Yard. I had Lord Flexdale on the 'phone first thing. He is threatening to make another of his damned broadcasts to the nation.'

Temple could not restrain a smile, then after a moment he said: 'You still haven't found the bullet that killed Barton?'

Forbes shook his head.

'No sign of a revolver either.'

'And you say the murder took place in his office – at Overland Airways?'

'That's so. His secretary happened to come back for some papers late in the evening, and found him.'

Temple thoughtfully stubbed out his cigarette.

'Didn't I read something about this new office building of Overland Airways a little time back?'

'I shouldn't wonder,' nodded Forbes. 'It's all prefabricated, you know, almost built overnight – the very last word—'

'And if I remember,' went on Temple, 'it was constructed – windows as well – from a new plastic, discovered during the war, that happens to be bullet-proof.'

'What are you getting at, Temple?' asked Sir Graham curiously.

'Well,' murmured Temple, 'it's rather difficult for me to theorise without seeing the place, but the murderer might have shot Barton, and as the bullet could not penetrate the walls or windows, he should have been able to retrieve it.'

'H'mph!' grunted Forbes. 'I suppose it is possible.'

'Not that it gets us very far,' put in Crane.

'Of course not,' smiled Temple. 'But it does help to dispose of the impression that Rex's powers verge on the uncanny.'

'Oh, as to that—' Forbes was beginning scornfully, when the door opened and revealed the rubicund features of a middle-aged sergeant.

'What is it, Smith?' snapped Sir Graham, annoyed at the interruption.

'Begging your pardon, sir. I heard that Mr. Temple was here, and I thought he would like to see the report on the cigarette-case he sent round last night.'

'Any good, Sergeant?' asked Temple.

'Oh yes,' nodded Smith, looking very pleased with himself. 'That was a lovely print you got, Mr. Temple. It came up a treat.'

Well,' snapped Forbes, 'have you checked it?'

'To be sure, sir,' replied Smith, quite unruffled. 'It's in the record all right.' He paused for a moment, then inquired, 'And what did you say the gentleman calls himself nowadays, Mr. Temple?'

'He goes by the name of Chester – Frank Chester. He's manager of the Royal Falcon Hotel at Canterbury.'

'Imagine that now!' exclaimed Smith. 'And they say crime doesn't pay!'

'That'll do, Sergeant,' snapped Forbes. What do the records say?'

'This print,' began Smith impressively, 'belongs to a man named Michael David Richard Mulberry. Served a term in '34 for robbery with violence – came out in '36 – back again

131

in '38 for a similar offence—released in '42. Since then we've lost track of him – some talk of his having got away to America. Simpson says he thinks he was suspected of being mixed up in a big black market case, but he can't be certain. No conviction against him in that respect, anyway.'

'I see,' nodded Temple. 'This is most interesting, Sergeant. Thanks for all the trouble you've taken.'

'Not at all, sir. A pleasure to work on a print like that. Wish they were all as clear.'

When the sergeant had gone, Crane turned and said: 'Well, there you are, Temple. You can see where the cyanide came from. Chester put it in the flask while you and Mrs. Temple were having dinner.'

'Seems plain enough,' agreed Forbes. 'He felt sure that if the rope across the road didn't quite do the trick, you'd be pretty badly shaken and sample the brandy.'

'On the face of it, it seemed a fairly safe bet too,' agreed Temple. 'I was just going to suggest a nip when we heard Spider moaning.'

'You've had a damned lucky escape, Temple,' said Forbes quietly. 'But it was a pity about Spider Williams – another two minutes and he could have told us practically all we want to know.'

'I wonder,' mused Temple.

'But you said yourself the fellow claimed to have seen Rex.'

'He saw someone, certainly. But we're not to know that it was not just another of Rex's accomplices – and he seems to have plenty of them – voluntary and otherwise!'

Crane reached for the telephone.

'I reckon it's about time we acted.' He asked for a number, then said curtly: 'Stevens? Get a warrant for the arrest of Michael David Richard Mulberry, alias Frank Chester—'

'Wait!' said Temple.

'All right – hold it!' snapped Crane into the telephone and slammed down the receiver. 'Well?' he said challengingly.

'I wouldn't do that, Inspector, not just at the moment,' said Temple in a soothing tone. 'After all, we're not interested in Mr. Mulberry, are we? The person we are after is Rex. Once we get Rex, the others fall into our lap.'

'But supposing Mulberry or Chester or whatever his name is turns out to be Rex?' cried Crane in some annoyance.

'That,' replied Temple with a faint smile, 'would be most intriguing – in fact, it would involve supernatural power on the part of Mr. Mulberry.'

'How do you mean?' asked Crane.

Temple lighted another cigarette.

'Just what I say, Inspector. It would mean one man being in two places at the same time.'

'But I don't see how—' broke in Crane.

Temple held up his hand and started to explain.

'Three days ago,' he said, 'Lord Stanwyck received a letter from Rex demanding four thousand pounds, with orders to deliver the money personally last night at a small place called Lenford. He decided to pay up, but instead of going himself he sent Spider Williams. When we found Spider, presumably Rex had just left him. Yet Steve and I had seen Chester at the Royal Falcon well over half an hour previously.'

'He might have passed you on the road,' Crane pointed out.

Temple shook his head.

'He might have, but he didn't. Nothing passed us.'

'He could have taken a short cut maybe.'

'I don't think so, Inspector. In any case, there were patches of fog which would have held him up just as they did us.

133

And there's another interesting point, Inspector, that doesn't seem to have entered your calculations.'

'Oh?' said Crane suspiciously.

'It doesn't necessarily follow that Chester put the cyanide in the flask,' said Temple slowly. 'So I wouldn't want you to make an arrest you couldn't substantiate. Remember, there were no fingerprints on that flask except mine and Steve's.'

'The fellow wore gloves, of course,' growled Crane. 'Anyhow, who else could have done it except Chester?'

'Wilfred Davis,' said Temple quietly.

'Good lord!' ejaculated Forbes softly. 'I'd forgotten about him. Who the devil is this little Welsh fellow, anyway?'

'I told you,' replied Temple. 'He's a commercial traveller, and a student of criminology in his spare time.'

Crane sniffed. 'Sounds fishy to me,' he ventured.

'So you see, Inspector, it would be a trifle unpleasant if you got yourself mixed up in a case of wrongful arrest.'

'You're right there, Temple,' agreed Forbes, walking over to the window and pensively watching a tug churn its way under the bridge. 'I think we can afford to wait in this Chester business, Crane,' he decided. 'Better telephone the local chief to have him kept under observation – report by 'phone at once if they notice anything unusual.'

'Very good, sir,' nodded Crane, and gave the instructions over the telephone. He was just replacing the receiver when the dictograph buzzed and a voice announced: 'Doctor Kohima to see you, sir.'

Forbes went over and pressed the switch.

'Bring him up right away,' he ordered.

Temple looked from Crane to Forbes for a moment, slightly puzzled by this new move, then asked:

'Did you send for Doctor Kohima, Sir Graham?'

'I did,' put in Crane.

'Any special reason?'

'Well,' replied Crane bluntly, 'for one thing, I want to make sure about that pencil – I want to be quite certain it belongs to Doctor Kohima.'

'Then you didn't believe me last night when I told you on the 'phone that—'

'It isn't a question of not believing you, Mr. Temple,' interrupted Crane. 'We've got to check every detail.'

'Of course, Inspector,' said Temple politely. 'I quite understand.' At that the door opened, and the doctor came in. He was obviously a little surprised to see Temple, whom he nevertheless greeted very affably, as if it were a pleasant surprise. Temple introduced the others.

Forbes invited the doctor to sit in the most comfortable armchair reserved for visitors. Then he nodded to Crane, who began: 'We're very sorry to drag you down here, Doctor, but the fact is we are hoping you might be of some considerable help to us.'

Kohima inclined his head politely.

'This sounds interesting,' he murmured. 'Are you referring to my professional services? Because if it is a question of using—'

'No, no,' interposed Crane. 'This is quite another matter. A personal matter relating to yourself. I understand that you recently lost a silver pencil bearing your initials.' Kohima looked up in some surprise.

'Why, yes,' he admitted. 'How did you—' Then his expression changed. 'But of course – Mr. Temple was there when I mentioned it to my secretary.'

'That's true,' nodded Temple. 'But I didn't ask the question, you know, Doctor.'

Kohima looked slightly puzzled for a moment, and seemed

135

to be about to make some remark when Crane broke in once more: 'When did you lose the pencil?'

The doctor considered for a moment, then said: 'Well, I first realised that it had disappeared yesterday morning. I am quite sure I had it the night before last – yes, absolutely positive, because I remember taking it out of my pocket to mark a passage in a new text-book.'

He paused and a flicker of amusement spread over his handsome features.

'But, Inspector, you surely did not get me down here just to talk about a missing silver pencil? I had not even considered reporting the loss at my local police station.'

Crane fumbled in his pocket and said abruptly:

'Is this your pencil?'

A silver pencil lay in the palm of his hand.

The doctor turned over the pencil by the broad end, looked at the initials for a moment, then calmly shook his head.

'No,' he replied in an even tone. 'That is not my pencil.'

'It isn't?' gasped Crane, open-mouthed.

Once more the doctor shook his head.

'You're quite sure?' demanded Forbes incredulously.

'Quite,' was the cool reply.

Temple was the only one of the three who showed no sign of surprise. He leaned over and pointed to the end of the pencil. 'These are your initials, I believe, Doctor,' he murmured imperturbably.

'Oh yes,' agreed Kohima quite readily. 'But it is not my pencil, Mr. Temple.'

He rested his hands on the silver knob of his walking-stick and looked each speaker straight in the eyes as he answered their questions. Temple was secretly amused to note the complete bewilderment of Crane and Forbes.

'You really mean to tell us that this is not your pencil?' reiterated Forbes deliberately.

Kohima looked round the little group.

'I admit my pencil was worth a few pounds, but surely you are rather exaggerating its importance. I fail to see how—'

'The point is, Doctor Kohima,' interrupted Crane, 'that this pencil was discovered under rather exceptional circumstances.'

'Oh, I see,' murmured the doctor slowly. 'Am I permitted to know where it was found?'

'Yes,' replied Crane. 'You may have read in the papers of the murder of James Barton—'

'You mean the big airways director. Of course.'

'You knew James Barton?'

'Fairly well.'

'Indeed?' said Forbes quickly. 'How did you come to know him?'

'The way I meet most people. He was a patient of mine about two years ago. He was sent on to me by a Harley Street man after he'd had a bad nervous breakdown.'

Temple was interested at once.

'Would you say that Barton was in any way an exceptional case?' he asked.

Kohima frowned in an effort to remember.

'You must understand I get so many people through my hands – and they tell me so many things.' He pursed his lips as he sat deep in thought, then said presently:

'No . . . I wouldn't say Barton was exceptional. Just the usual hallucinations from what I remember.'

'You couldn't recall the nature of those hallucinations, I suppose?' asked Temple.

Kohima rubbed his chin pensively. 'Now let me see . . . yes . . . I am fairly sure it was Barton who was troubled with the fear of being shot in the back by some mysterious woman. H'm I recollect now . . . we had quite a little trouble in getting rid of her.'

'It looks to me as if you didn't get rid of her,' said Crane bluntly.

'But I thought he was supposed to have been killed by this fellow Rex,' said the doctor.

'Quite so,' agreed Temple. 'But we have yet to establish whether Rex is a man or a woman.'

'Oh, I see,' murmured Doctor Kohima in an expressionless voice, as if he were not greatly interested.

'Supposing,' began Temple, 'this mysterious gunwoman who troubled Barton was not an hallucination. Suppose he actually seen her before he came to you – supposing she had threatened him. Would you still be able to erase her from his mind?'

'That would depend entirely on the nature of the patient's mind,' replied the doctor slowly.

'But such things have been done?' insisted Temple. 'Surely I read a book by Hellmann a little while ago—'

'Ah yes, yes,' agreed Kohima readily. 'Hellmann has quite a lot to say about it, and I am told he has achieved some remarkable results. With the mind, of course, almost anything is possible under suitable conditions. But I fail to see the connection between these theories and my silver pencil.'

'There is, perhaps, a certain association,' said Temple. 'You see, that pencil the inspector is holding was found beside the dead body of James Barton.'

Doctor Kohima slowly nodded his head several times.

'So!' he murmured. 'Now I understand your curiosity.'

Then he shook his head and added in a definite tone:

'But it still isn't my pencil.'

Crane looked openly sceptical, and was about to make some remark, but the telephone buzzed and Forbes took the call.

'It's for you, Temple,' he announced, handing him the receiver.

There was no mistaking the familiar inflections of Ricky at the other end of the line.

'So sorry to disturb you, sir, but there is a gentleman here to see you. He insisted that I should telephone at once. He says it is very urgent.'

'What's his name?' asked Temple.

'It is a Mr. Lathom, sir. Mr. Carl Lathom.'

'Oh. Well, where is Mrs. Temple?'

'She is out shopping, I believe, sir. She will not be back until before lunch.'

'I see.' Temple hesitated a moment, then made up his mind.

'All right, Ricky,' he said. 'Ask Mr. Lathom to wait – I shan't be more than ten minutes.'

'Yes, sir – very good,' came the soft Oriental voice, which dropped slightly to add: 'The gentleman seems most perturbed, sir.'

Temple grinned.

'You will get used to receiving visitors who are a little perturbed, Ricky. We have quite a lot of them.'

'Yes, Mr. Temple. I quite understand.'

'That's all right then, Ricky. Offer him a drink and some Chinese philosophy. I shan't be long.'

He rang off, and turned to the others.

'Well, if you'll excuse me, Sir Graham, I have rather an urgent appointment – and I don't think there's much more I can do here just at the moment.'

'But about this pencil—' began Crane.

'I'm afraid we can hardly dispute the doctor's word if

139

he insists that it is not his property,' said Temple smoothly. 'After all, the initials "C. K." must apply to hundreds of people who own silver pencils.'

Crane looked baffled and sullen, but appreciated the force of Temple's argument.

'I'm sure Doctor Kohima must be very busy, and it's good of him to spare the time to come down here,' continued Temple smoothly, exchanging a look with Sir Graham. 'Perhaps I can give you a lift back, Doctor?'

'Thank you, Mr. Temple. I have my car outside,' replied Kohima urbanely.

'Good. Then I'll see you down. These corridors are rather confusing.' At the door, Temple turned and said:

'I'll telephone you, Sir Graham, the minute anything turns up.'

'But this pencil—' stammered Crane helplessly.

'I suggest that it will make an interesting exhibit for the Black Museum,' said Temple with a shrug, as he held open the door for Doctor Kohima.

Temple let himself quietly into the flat, and stood at the door of the lounge as he took off his gloves. Inside, he could hear Ricky saying: 'Is there anything else I can get you, sir?'

'No, no,' came Lathom's voice. 'Nothing else, thanks.'

'Perhaps another glass of sherry, sir?'

Lathom said: 'No, really, I'm quite all right.'

'Mr. Temple should be here any moment now, sir. It is just ten minutes since I telephoned, and he is extremely reliable in such matters.'

'How long have you been with him?' inquired Lathom.

'About forty-eight hours, sir.'

'Then surely you haven't had much opportunity—'

'To certain insects, forty-eight hours is double the length of a lifetime,' murmured Ricky.

Temple smiled to himself and opened the door.

'Well, Lathom, what seems to be the trouble?' he asked as Ricky discreetly withdrew.

Lathom had risen to his feet, then sank back on to the settee. His face was drawn and haggard, and he seemed to be under a considerable nervous strain.

'I'm terribly sorry to drag you away from Scotland Yard, Temple,' he began apologetically.

'That's all right. You didn't drag me away. Anyhow, the Yard isn't exactly my idea of an ideal spot for a busman's holiday. Have a glass of sherry?' smiled Temple.

'I've just had one, thanks.'

'Well, have another. It's quite harmless,' urged Temple.

'Well . . . thanks.'

Temple carefully poured out two glasses and handed one to Lathom.

For a minute or two, they sipped it without speaking. Then Temple said: 'You look worried. Anything wrong?'

'I am worried, Temple. Hellishly worried.' Lathom set down his glass. Temple noticed that his hand shook slightly.

'Suppose you start your story at the beginning,' suggested Temple quietly. 'Take your time – there's no hurry.'

'I wish I could start at the beginning!' exclaimed Lathom somewhat dramatically. 'If only I could! That's just the point, Temple. Where *is* the beginning? If I knew that I might be able to see things much more clearly.'

'All right,' nodded Temple equably. 'Start wherever you please.'

Lathom's face worked spasmodically, and at last he burst forth.

'Temple, when I met you in the doctor's waiting-room yesterday morning, you said rather a strange thing. I haven't forgotten it. You advised me to consult you if by any chance my hallucination returned.'

'Did I say that, Mr. Lathom?' asked Temple amiably, taking his cigarette-case.

'Of course you did!'

'Then,' murmured Temple, lighting a cigarette, 'I must have had a very good reason.'

'Your reason is quite obvious to me now,' replied Lathom tensely. He leaned forward and added: 'You don't think it is an hallucination, do you?'

'Do *you*?' stalled Temple.

'No!' retorted Lathom fiercely. 'No, I don't! Every day – every night – wherever I go there's someone following me! I feel it! I feel it instinctively!'

'But you felt it before – and Doctor Kohima convinced you that it was purely imagination,' Temple reminded him, taking another sip at his sherry.

'I tell you I'm being followed!' cried Lathom almost hysterically.

'All right,' said Temple quietly. 'You're being followed. So are dozens of other people. I have been myself quite a number of times. The world isn't coming to an end yet, Mr. Lathom. Let's try to view the matter objectively. Have you caught sight of this person who is following you?'

'Yes, yes, of course,' replied Lathom impatiently. 'It's the girl in brown – the one I told you about. Last night she followed me all the way from Hyde Park Corner to Shaftesbury Avenue. At first I thought I was seeing things. I just couldn't believe my eyes. Then I tried to lose her – I turned into the back-streets near Shepherd Market – but I couldn't shake her off.'

'You've never actually spoken to this girl?' asked Temple, eyeing him curiously.

'Spoken to her!' echoed Lathom. 'Goodness knows I've tried. When I couldn't get rid of her last night, I tried to confront her – but she disappears like lightning! I tell you I did my damnedest to corner her . . . I even turned and ran after her full tilt, but she vanished—'

The telephone rang abruptly and Temple picked up the receiver.

'Is that you, darling?' came Steve's voice rather breathlessly.

'Hello, Steve,' replied Temple, a little surprised. 'Where are you?'

'Paul – listen!' she begged urgently. 'I had an appointment at the hairdresser's for this morning, and when I left the flat I had an uncanny feeling that someone was following me.'

'Good Lord!' murmured Temple.

'It was that girl, darling – the girl in brown who followed me the other night. When I left the hairdresser's about ten minutes ago, she was still waiting for me. She's followed me here—'

'Where are you speaking from?' said Temple quickly.

'I'm in a call-box in Derry and Toms,' replied Steve softly. 'She's hanging about at the main entrance. What am I to do, Paul?'

'Keep her waiting,' replied Temple promptly. 'Hang on for another five minutes, Steve.'

He slammed down the receiver.

'Get your hat, Mr. Lathom,' he ordered. 'We've got a date.'

'A date?' repeated Lathom, who had listened to the conversation with growing curiosity.

'Yes!' snapped Temple. 'With an hallucination!'

CHAPTER IX

The Girl in Brown

WHEN they arrived at the store a few minutes later, they saw Steve standing in the entrance and anxiously scanning the passing traffic. She was tapping one foot impatiently, and appeared to be trying to make up her mind to some course of action. As soon as Temple's car drew in to the kerb, she ran across to him.

'Paul!' she cried breathlessly. 'I'm terribly sorry, but you're too late!'

He looked up quickly.

'You mean she's gone?'

Steve nodded. 'I was in the telephone booth, and I was watching her carefully all the time I was talking to you—'

'Then how the devil did she give you the slip?' demanded Temple in a slightly exasperated tone.

'It was when I put down the receiver. I took my eyes off her – only for a second. But she vanished completely. I can't think how she does it.'

'That woman's as clever as Maskelyne and Houdini rolled into one,' commented Lathom. 'She obviously got wise to the fact that you were talking about her, Mrs. Temple. She has an uncanny instinct . . . simply uncanny.'

Steve looked questioningly at Lathom, and Temple recollected that he had not introduced them, so proceeded to remedy the omission. Steve instantly recalled Carl Lathom's name as he politely acknowledged the introduction. Then he said: 'Could you describe this girl, Mrs. Temple? Would you say she was about twenty-eight or -nine? Attractive. Dressed completely in brown . . . brown handbag . . . silk stockings that looked as if they came from America . . .' He spoke quickly with more than a hint of nervousness.

'Yes,' answered Steve, 'that seems a fair description.'

'Then it must be the same girl, by George!' declared Lathom emphatically slapping his thigh.

'Oh yes,' said Steve. 'My husband told me that you had seen her too.'

'I certainly have! She's given me no peace for days. But I can't make head or tail of this. Why should she first of all follow me and then Mrs. Temple? Have you any theories about that, Temple?'

Temple shook his head.

'Better get in the car, Steve,' he advised. 'We'll go back to the flat.'

'Why not come round to my place?' suggested Lathom. 'It's only just round the corner. I can promise you a good cup of coffee to steady your nerves, Mrs. Temple. And by jove, I could do with one myself!'

Steve was rather surprised to hear Temple accept the invitation, and presently they drew up outside a large mansion of modern flats in a quiet side street.

Steve shrewdly assessed the rentals as being somewhere in the region of eight hundred a year, and was duly impressed by the atmosphere of unobtrusive luxury in the thickly carpeted entrance lounge to which Lathom admitted them.

Lathom went into the kitchen to give some instructions to his housekeeper, and returned a minute or two later to find Temple examining a set of unusual little brass images which presumably represented some Oriental idols.

'Not worth very much, I'm afraid,' Lathom informed him. 'I got 'em in Cairo, so they were probably made in Birmingham. But I couldn't resist the saturnine expression on their brass faces.'

'It is rather quaint,' smiled Steve, picking up one of the images.

'When were you in Cairo?' asked Temple.

'Let's see . . . I left there in '37 – that's right, June, '37,' he estimated thoughtfully. 'I was only there eighteen months, but I rather liked it. In fact, I've often toyed with the idea of going back.'

'Why don't you?'

Lathom shrugged, 'I don't know. I suppose there's no particular reason why I shouldn't.'

'Were you there on business?'

'Yes, I told you I was in the advertising racket for some years, the firm had the idea of opening up fresh territory all over the world – and they allotted me Cairo. It was pretty stiff going too, I can tell you. I found they were an exclusive sort of community out there. Though once I was in I began to enjoy myself. It was quite a good life, with all expenses paid!'

'You seem to have knocked around quite a bit,' murmured Temple.

'I say, you must think I'm something of a mysterious character!' exclaimed Lathom with a disarming laugh. 'First of all, I meet you at a psychiatrist's, then I tell you that I am suffering from hallucinations, and now you learn I've actually spent eighteen months in the shadow of the Sphinx!'

The entrance of Lathom's housekeeper carrying a large tray interrupted the conversation. Steve poured out the coffee, which was quite up to their expectations. Presently, Temple asked:

'When did you write that play of yours – the one Norma Rice was in?'

'Oh, that was years ago – just after I left the Varsity. They say we've all got one good play in us. So I got mine out of my system, and I may say that nobody was more surprised than I was when it clicked! Of course, it was Norma's acting, really,' he added modestly.

'And you have never written anything since?'

'Not a word – except advertising copy. I don't really consider myself a professional writer, you know. I'm more a sort of – well, a dilettante. When I came back from Egypt I inherited a fair-sized fortune, so I have an adequate private income, and I'm afraid I fell into the habit of doing less and less—'

'But you can't just do nothing all day long,' protested Steve with a smile.

'You'd be surprised,' he told her. 'I read a bit, play a spot of golf, stroll along Piccadilly . . . lunch at the Club . . . or sometimes I go for a drive in the country. I'm rather fond of getting around. Not abroad so much as within fairly easy reach of Town . . . I love exploring old places . . . historical towns . . .' He passed round the cigarettes.

'Have you,' said Temple, casually lighting a match, 'ever been to Canterbury?'

He was watching Lathom very carefully without betraying any sign of doing so.

'Good heavens, yes!' exclaimed the other, his face lighting up with eager interest. 'It's quite a haunt of mine. I spend hours wandering round the back streets, poking in nooks and crannies, in and out of the cathedral, nosing around those funny antique shops – yes, I always get a kick out of Canterbury. I stay at a nice old pub called the Royal Falcon. It's not what it was ten years ago, but it still has some of the genuine old atmosphere.'

'The Royal Falcon?' repeated Temple noncommittally, 'I must remember that. Steve and I had some thought of running down to the coast one week-end and staying a night at Canterbury.'

'Well, if you care to mention my name at the Royal Falcon, I'm sure they'll do their best for you. Ask the manager, a man named Chester. He's not a bad sort of fellow, goes out of his way to make you feel at home.'

'We must remember that,' said Steve, sipping her coffee.

'Of course, it's not exactly to be compared with Shepheard's, Mrs. Temple,' smiled Lathom, 'but the beds are comfortable, and if you're lucky you get a decent meal.'

'Have you been there recently?' asked Temple.

Lathom shook his head.

'I've been down to Canterbury for the day, of course, but it must be about a year now since I stayed at the Royal Falcon.'

He paused to urge Steve to try the cakes which his house-keeper had brought in with the coffee. She could not help reflecting that Carl Lathom seemed very much at his ease now, and indeed looked the typical man about town, the last sort of person who would suffer from hallucinations or need to consult a psychiatrist.

Then she glanced up at a small bookcase near her left shoulder and noticed that all the books dealt with the subject of black magic. She told herself that there were more aspects to the character of Carl Lathom than met the eye of the casual acquaintance. She was about to make some inquiry about this varied selection of volumes when the door opened and the housekeeper came in with a jug of hot milk and two letters which had apparently arrived by the midday post.

He did not look at the letters immediately, but pressed Steve and Temple to take a second cup of coffee.

'There was one thing I wanted to ask you, Temple, about this girl in brown business,' he said suddenly.

'Oh – what's that?' asked Temple.

'Well, it now appears to be fairly definitely established that this girl *is* a creature of substance; not just a figment of my imagination.'

'We can't both have imagined exactly the same girl,' smiled Steve.

'Exactly.' Lathom leaned forward in his chair and demanded earnestly, 'Then why should Doctor Kohima take all that trouble to convince me that the girl in brown was an hallucination?'

Temple stirred his coffee and laid the spoon in the saucer.

'That,' he conceded, 'is quite a nice point. Of course, the doctor may have believed quite genuinely that your girl in brown was an hallucination. How could he know there was such a person?'

'He might,' replied Lathom slowly, 'if he were in touch with certain people.'

'What do you mean, exactly?' asked Temple.

Lathom shrugged.

'Oh well, we all have our enemies, I suppose,' he parried lightly.

'And why should an eminent psychiatrist be in league with any enemies of yours?' demanded Temple shrewdly.

Lathom smiled and lighted a cigarette.

'Yes, I admit that is where one has to start guessing,' he murmured disarmingly. 'The only answer would seem to be that Kohima is something more than an eminent psychiatrist. You realise, of course, Mr. Temple, that men like him are in a very powerful position in relation to their patients' private lives. They discover a tremendous number of secrets.'

'But you repeatedly assured me that Kohima was a first-class man,' Temple reminded him.

'Yes, I know. I thought that at the time. Now, I'm not so sure. You see, I really believed then that the girl in brown had been an hallucination. Now I find she wasn't, I naturally become a trifle sceptical about the doctor who persuaded me that she was.'

'At the same time,' said Temple. 'Doctor Kohima's intentions may have been of the best. After all, Lathom, you were probably in a highly strung frame of mind, and he really treated you as a genuine case.'

Lathom rose and placed his empty cup on a side table.

'All the same, I've a sort of feeling that there's more in this affair than meets the eye. Though why anyone should pick on me . . .'

He took the two letters which the housekeeper had placed on the table, and with a murmured apology opened the first one, which was an official envelope.

'I say,' he commented as he scanned it, 'these Income Tax people are optimists, if nothing else.'

He flung it down on the table and picked up the smaller envelope which he carelessly tore open, then began reading

151

the letter in a very casual manner. Suddenly, his expression changed, and he quickly turned the page to see the signature.

'My God!' he ejaculated, letting the envelope fall to the floor.

Temple and Steve looked at each other in some embarrassment.

'Is anything the matter, Mr. Lathom?' asked Steve a little uncertainly, for she had observed that his face seemed suddenly drawn and much older.

'This letter,' said Lathom hoarsely. 'Read it . . .'

He passed it over to Temple and sank into a chair. Temple began to read aloud for Steve's benefit:

You are requested to obey the following instructions without fail. On the evening of Tuesday next, October the 9th, you will drive your car down to the village of Haybourne. On the north side of the village you will find a small country lane, known as Fallow-end. Park your car at the point where Fallow-end joins the main Haybourne road. The car should be there not later than 10.15. Then walk back to the village and stay there until eleven o'clock.

On the back seat of the car you will leave an attache case; containing two thousand one pound notes, which must not be numbered consecutively. If you do not obey these instructions, a letter will be forwarded to certain newspapers explaining the real reasons for your visit to Cairo in the autumn of 1935. No further explanation should be needed, Mr. Lathom. 'Rex.'

For some seconds no one spoke. Lathom had sunk his head in his hands, and looked desperately miserable.

'Of course,' said Steve softly, 'if he wrote those letters to the papers, it doesn't follow they would be printed. They're pretty scared of libel in Fleet Street.'

'No!' cried Lathom, waking to life. 'Whatever happens, he mustn't send those letters! He mustn't do that, Temple!'

'Two thousand pounds,' replied Temple quietly, 'sounds a lot of money.'

'I'll have to find it somehow,' said Lathom desperately. 'I daren't take any chances.'

Temple picked up the envelope from the floor and studied it thoughtfully.

'It's rather difficult to advise you in this matter, Lathom,' he murmured, 'as of course I have no idea what happened in Cairo.'

For a moment it seemed that Lathom was going to take them into his confidence. Then his face hardened again. He shook his head.

'I don't see that it would serve any useful purpose, Temple,' he muttered.

'Then the only thing I can recommend is that you put Scotland Yard wise to the blackmail threat, and leave them to work out a plan.'

Lathom pondered over this for a while, but appeared unable to make up his mind.

'You don't think this business is linked up with the girl in brown, do you?' he asked presently.

'Yes,' nodded Temple. 'I think it probably has quite a lot to do with the girl in brown. In fact, there appears to me to be one very significant factor in the whole set-up.'

'Oh?' queried Lathom eagerly, his face lighting up once more. 'What's that?'

'You haven't noticed it?' queried Temple diffidently.

'Why, no,' replied the other in a puzzled voice. 'Have you, Mrs. Temple?'

'I can't say I have,' admitted Steve, 'but my mind goes woolgathering so much lately.'

'Hence the knitting,' put in her husband with a faint smile. 'Well, I may be wrong. Perhaps the factor isn't so significant after all.'

He examined the postmark on the envelope.

'This appears to have been posted from Hampstead,' he mused. 'Afraid that doesn't help us very much—'

'But have you noticed the letter?' put in Steve quickly, who had been reading it for the second time. 'It's been typed on the same machine, Paul.'

'What do you mean?' interrupted Lathom quickly in an astonished tone. 'What machine are you referring to?' His mouth was twitching spasmodically. Temple did not reply immediately and Lathom persisted: 'Have you seen a letter like this before?'

'Oh yes,' replied Temple after a pause. 'I saw one sent to Mrs. Trevelyan.'

'You mean Doctor Kohima's secretary?' queried Lathom in patent amazement. 'This gets more and more involved. You mean that Mrs. Trevelyan actually received a note from Rex?'

'Typed on this very same machine,' nodded Temple.

'But this is amazing!' cried Lathom. 'There must be some connection between Rex and Doctor Kohima, Temple. There must be! First, the doctor treats me for hallucinations—'

'By the way, how did you come to consult Doctor Kohima?' interrupted Temple.

'Didn't I tell you? I was recommended quite a while ago. I quite thought I told you that.'

'And who sent you to him?'

'I could have sworn I told you.' Lathom hesitated a moment, then said simply, 'It was Norma Rice.'

Temple nodded, but did not speak.

'I saw her at a cocktail party just after she got back from America,' continued Lathom. 'She said I was drinking too much – and of course I was. So I told her I'd been rather jittery during the past few months . . . and so on. That was when she recommended me to try the doctor. Said he'd done a friend of hers a lot of good. But about this letter,' he went on impatiently, 'have you found out which machine it was typed on?'

Temple shook his head.

'We have eliminated one or two, that's all.'

'Mr. Lathom, if I were you, I should be inclined to call Rex's bluff,' suggested Steve. 'I've worked on a newspaper, and I know they get dozens of silly letters making all sorts of charges against people. They never take them seriously unless there is some pretty substantial evidence and the writer is ready to come forward and—'

'No, no, I tell you I daren't take the risk!' he reiterated. 'It would ruin me completely. Haven't you anything at all to suggest, Mr. Temple?'

'I have told you what I should do in your place,' replied Temple. 'I should notify Scotland Yard. That gives you a double chance. If the Yard doesn't get Rex, well, he'll probably give you a second "life", though the stakes will be raised if I know anything about blackmail. If you pay up without a murmur, you may depend it's only a first instalment. So it's up to you to take a gamble on the Yard getting Rex when he comes to collect.'

'But he may not collect it himself,' Steve pointed out.

'Quite likely. But if the Yard managed to pull in one of his associates, that would be something,' argued Temple, then added lightly: 'You never know, Lathom. It might even be the girl in brown!'

CHAPTER X

Ordeal for Mrs. Trevelyan

IN the Assistant Commissioner's room at New Scotland Yard, the telephone gave a discreet buzz, and Forbes picked up the receiver. He recognised the voice of Detective-Inspector Bradley, one of his most reliable lieutenants, who had just returned to the Yard after a spell with the Special Branch in Lisbon.

'We're just about to leave, sir,' said Bradley in his customary brisk fashion. 'I've got three of the new Harmans – the fast model. Don't imagine there are many cars on the road going to pass us tonight.'

'No fancy business, mind,' adjured Forbes gruffly, for he knew Bradley's love of speed. 'You understand the layout of the village?'

'Perfectly, sir. Perhaps Inspector Crane would like to check over the details before we start.'

'I'm afraid Crane isn't here at the moment. I'll check them. All right, you can go ahead.'

Bradley proceeded to read out rapidly a list of names of the men and their positions in the cordon around the little village of Haybourne. For the date calendar on Forbes' desk

157

showed Tuesday, October 9th, and New Scotland Yard was on its toes to round up Rex at last.

Forbes ticked off the names on a list near the telephone. 'Right!' he said eventually. 'Now you understand, Bradley, that whatever happens once Rex has reached that car, he must not get back through the cordon. He's got to be stopped – alive or dead! You understand that?'

'I've got it, sir.'

Forbes replaced the receiver with a thoughtful air, and turned to Temple who was smoking a cigarette and glancing through the evening paper, in which for once in a way there was no reference to the Rex case. He realised that Forbes was feeling the strain of events more than he cared to admit, and was doing his utmost to appear casual and completely at ease.

Temple had had to induce Carl Lathom to show the letter to the police and allow them to take the matter in hand. It had then taken Sir Graham the better part of a whole morning to persuade Lathom to follow the instructions of the letter himself and he had had to promise that the police escort would be so formidable that any organisation that Rex might produce for the occasion was certain to be overwhelmed.

Temple glanced at the clock on the mantelpiece, which pointed to ten minutes to nine. It was an hour's run to Haybourne even in a fast car.

'Crane's cutting it fine, isn't he?' he asked.

'Can't understand it. The fellow's generally too damn punctual,' growled Forbes. 'He moved out to Golder's Green a few days ago, and maybe he doesn't allow himself enough time—'

At that the door opened and Crane appeared, very red in the face and considerably out of breath.

'I'm very sorry, sir,' he apologised. 'My confounded car broke down and the nearest garage was closed. Had to shove it half a mile and then walk to Hampstead to pick up a taxi.'

'Hard luck, Inspector,' sympathised Temple.

'Bradley was on the 'phone checking up just now,' said Forbes.

'Yes, I had a word with him on my way up here. We're all set now.' He rapidly scanned the list Forbes had passed over to him, then said:

'You've spoken to Mr. Lathom, sir?'

'I had a final word with him this afternoon,' interposed Temple.

'I expect he's nervous,' said Crane.

'He isn't exactly the rock of Gibraltar, but he'll go through with it all right. I assured him that there was practically no danger as far as he was concerned.'

'And we've got to make sure of that,' insisted Forbes. 'I have impressed upon Bradley that under no circumstances must Rex get through that cordon. If he makes a dash for it, then we've got to be right on our toes.'

'You can leave that to me, sir,' said Crane quietly, with a determined ring in his voice.

'Right!' said Forbes briskly. 'You'd better get started right away then, Crane. Take your time stationing your men.'

'I'll see to it, sir.'

'Come along then, Temple,' nodded Forbes. 'We'll have to hurry. Lathom will be waiting for us at the garage.'

'I'm ready, Sir Graham,' replied Temple. 'Cheerio, Inspector, and good luck.'

'And keep your eyes peeled, Crane,' adjured Sir Graham. 'There must be no slip-up this time.'

They found Lathom nervously pacing up and down the concrete floor of a large garage near his flat. As they came in he was just lighting a fresh cigarette from the butt of an old one, and his hand was shaking noticeably. He seemed relieved to see them, as if the spell of inaction had been getting on his nerves.

He led them over to an expensive light blue Hesketh sports saloon, with a long bonnet and low chassis. Temple looked round to see if they were alone before saying: 'Have you got the money, Lathom?'

Lathom nodded.

'Yes, I went round to the bank immediately after seeing you.'

'Is that the attache-case in the front?'

'That's it.'

'Good. Then that protects you. At least, you've fulfilled your side of the bargain.'

'Has Mr. Temple explained the layout to you, Mr. Lathom?' asked Forbes.

'I think I've got it fairly clear, Sir Graham.'

'We'll just run through it once again. You park the car in the lane at Fallow-end, leaving the attache-case just as it is, and walk straight to the village. Inspector Crane will be waiting for you at the Red Lion. You may be stopped by one or two of my men, but they can all identify you, so there should be no difficulty.'

'You've nothing to worry about, Lathom,' said Temple reassuringly.

Lathom puffed nervously at his cigarette.

'I can't help thinking about that poor devil who was hanged by Rex when he delivered the money,' he said with a worried air.

'Yes, but he had no escort,' Temple reminded him. 'Come on, let's not waste any more time. You'll feel better when you're driving and have something to occupy your mind.'

'I put the cushions on the floor of the car as you suggested, Temple,' Lathom told him.

'D'you mean we have to sit on the floor of the car?' asked Forbes in some surprise.

'That was the idea, Sir Graham,' said Temple. 'The car may be tailed from the minute we leave here, and we can't take any chances.'

'H'm . . . you may be right,' conceded Sir Graham, as he proceeded to squeeze into the narrowish space between the seats. Temple joined him, and Lathom got in the front and started the engine. Suddenly, he turned and said: 'There's just one point, Sir Graham. Supposing you catch Rex this evening, and he decides to talk.'

'Well?'

'You have seen the letter Rex sent me – the one that refers to Cairo. It's a little difficult to explain, but—'

'I think I understand, Lathom,' interposed Forbes. 'Didn't you hear the broadcast by Lord Flexdale the other night?'

'No.'

'Lord Flexdale promised that a free pardon would be given to any person, other than one guilty of actual murder, providing that person would furnish information leading to the arrest and conviction of Rex.'

There was a short pause. Then Lathom put his foot on the accelerator. 'That's all I wanted to know,' he said. The engine roared and the car nosed its way out of the garage.

'Remember what I told you, Lathom,' said Temple, raising his voice. 'Don't look back, and follow the instructions in that letter down to the last detail.'

'Don't worry, Temple,' replied Lathom in a more determined tone. 'I'll go through with it all right.'

'That's the style, Mr. Lathom!' applauded Forbes. The car negotiated the Marble Arch roundabout, and headed West at a good pace. Forbes was already beginning to wonder if it was really necessary to occupy this cramped position, particularly as it was now very dark.

'I say, couldn't we draw the back blind?' he suggested to Temple, but the novelist shook his head.

'Better not risk it,' he advised.

They were soon on an arterial road, and the car was roaring along at seventy miles an hour. Temple noticed Sir Graham's head drop forward once or twice as if he were dozing.

After a time they left the arterial road and encountered a somewhat rougher surface, but Lathom drove on without slackening speed. Presently, he drew up at some crossroads so that the beam from the headlamps could pick up the directions from a signpost; then the car roared on once more. Temple locked his hands around his knees and silently reviewed the recent events in the Rex case. The most sinister aspect of the whole affair, he decided, was the fact that Rex seemed to have so many people utterly in his power and was liable to make use of them in so many ways to distract suspicion from himself. He would sacrifice them quite relentlessly . . . which made Temple wonder if Rex could be a woman after all. Surely no woman could be as callous as that. Even Iris Archer[1], that glittering actress with the cruel mouth and completely amoral outlook on life, would have drawn the line somewhere . . .

Temple was suddenly conscious that the car was slowly coming to a standstill, and looking up he could see trees overhanging the road. Lathom applied the handbrake and then switched off the engine.

---

[1] See *News of Paul Temple*

'This is the place,' he said, in a voice which was almost a whisper. There was a further clicking of switches and the car lights were extinguished. Then they heard him fumble for the attache-case in the front seat. The car door opened and he got out, closing the door after him. Then he opened the back door somewhat ostentatiously, placed the case on the seat and slammed the door noisily. They heard his footsteps receding into the distance.

'Well, that's that!' muttered Forbes in a low tone. 'He's certainly seen it through so far.'

Temple shifted into a slightly more comfortable position, and Forbes followed suit. His left foot was badly cramped and felt quite numb. 'What time do you make it?' he whispered.

Temple glanced at the luminous dial of his wrist-watch.

'Nearly half past ten.'

After the continuous noise of the journey, the silence now seemed intense. They could even hear an occasional leaf falling from the trees overhead and the swish of wings as a bat dived through the air above them.

'What wouldn't I give for a cigarette!' sighed Forbes.

'We daren't risk it,' replied Temple.

Forbes fingered his silver cigarette-case, snapping it open and shut. Suddenly he sat up with a jerk and clutched Temple's arm.

'Listen!'

Very faintly in the distance they could hear the throbbing of an approaching car engine.

'It's coming up from the village,' whispered Temple. 'It couldn't be one of your men, I suppose?'

'No, they were ordered to park in the side lane half a mile away. They were to keep off this road till I gave the

163

signal.' The car was much nearer now. Temple and Forbes were almost holding their breath when it passed the turning into the lane. But it gave no sign of stopping, and the beat of the engine faded into the night.

'One of the farmers been down to the local,' guessed Temple.

'No,' snapped Forbes. 'Wait!'

Again they sat in silence for some seconds. Presently they heard a very soft whistle, which was repeated twice.

'One of Bradley's men,' said Forbes quickly. 'That was the signal we arranged.'

'Then the car must have stopped further along,' murmured Temple.

Again the whistle came clearly through the night. This time only once.

'That means stand by for immediate action,' muttered Forbes. 'But I can't hear anything.'

'The leaves would probably deaden anyone's footsteps,' Temple pointed out.

Forbes carefully took his revolver from his hip-pocket, and Temple followed suit. Temple also placed his pencil-torch in his outside coat pocket, so that he could snatch it easily. Once more they listened, and this time managed to detect the steady rustle of leaves. Then a small twig snapped.

'Keep down – right down,' advised Temple. 'Don't move till the door opens.'

They crouched in silence while the stealthy footsteps drew nearer. Suddenly they stopped. Again there was no sound except an occasional falling leaf and the distant bark of a dog.

Just when Temple and Forbes felt they could bear the suspense no longer, they heard the handle of the back door of the car gently turning. As the door opened, the whole landscape seemed to change as dramatically as the *denouement* in a sensational film.

Police whistles sounded, the beams of four powerful torches picked out the car, there was a trampling of heavy men in the undergrowth.

'Don't move!' shouted Forbes, levelling his revolver at the figure by the car.

'Steady, Sir Graham!' exclaimed Temple, restraining him.

At that moment, the beams from the torches focused up the figure of a woman.

'Don't shoot!' she cried in terror, looking round like a trapped animal as the circle of men relentlessly closed upon her.

'What the devil—' Forbes was beginning, when Temple interposed smoothly.

'Sir Graham, I don't think you've met this lady. Allow me to introduce Mrs. Trevelyan!'

Subsequent events proved that it was one thing to arrest Mrs. Trevelyan, but quite another to persuade her to give any lucid explanation of her recent actions. She was obviously in a highly emotional state, bordering on hysteria, and the Yard men were somewhat bewildered by her extravagant statements which seemed more than a trifle improbable.

'Leave me alone! Please – please leave me alone!' she begged for the twentieth time, and with a helpless shrug Forbes nodded to Temple to see if he could make any further headway.

The novelist pulled up a chair next to hers and said very earnestly:

'Mrs. Trevelyan, I've been very patient with you up to now, and you must realise that we only want to help you.

We have brought you to Scotland Yard as much for your own safety as—'

'Leave me alone!' she cried again. 'I've told you all I know!'

'You have told us practically nothing!' retorted Temple in a firmer tone. 'If you would only come out into the open, I'm sure you could give us enough information to enable us to arrest Rex – and what's more you would get a free pardon for any—'

'I tell you I am Rex!' she screamed at him. 'Now will you leave me alone!'

'You make that statement before five witnesses, Mrs. Trevelyan,' Forbes reminded her.

'I don't care. It's true, I tell you!'

'That's all we want to know, Temple,' said Forbes briskly. He went across and spoke into the telephone. 'Put me through to Lord Flexdale's private number,' he ordered.

'Just a minute, Sir Graham,' interrupted Temple. Forbes recalled the operator and cancelled the call. 'What is it now, Temple?' he demanded impatiently.

'There are several things I want Mrs. Trevelyan to clear up,' said Temple in an even tone. He turned to the woman crouching in the armchair.

'You say you're Rex, Mrs. Trevelyan,' he began.

'How many more times!' she almost screamed. 'I'm Rex – Rex – Rex!'

'Very well,' replied Temple smoothly. 'Then perhaps you can tell me why you came to my flat that night and confessed about the affair in Marshall House Terrace. Why did you tell me about the Royal Falcon Hotel at Canterbury? And why did you—'

'Oh, please!' she broke in tearfully. 'Please don't ask me any more questions.' Deep despairing sobs shook her slight frame.

166

But Temple was not to be denied.

'I know you are desperately distressed about this matter,' he continued gently. 'But you've got to pull yourself together, and you must tell us the whole truth. Otherwise, you know what will happen. You will be tried and found guilty. And then one morning they'll take you out into a small, dark courtyard. And he'll be waiting for you, Mrs. Trevelyan – the public hangman.'

She shuddered and could not conceal the expression of sheer terror in her eyes. Then she gripped the arms of her chair.

'You can't frighten me!' she cried defiantly. 'You can't frighten me, Mr. Temple. I tell you I'm Rex! I'm Rex! I'm Rex!'

Temple looked at Sir Graham with a helpless gesture.

'Very well, Mrs. Trevelyan,' said Forbes quietly. 'We shall require you to sign a statement to that effect if it's really true.'

'Yes, yes, I'll sign it!' she replied wildly.

Forbes was about to lift the receiver to telephone Lord Flexdale when the door opened and a sergeant announced: 'There's a Doctor Kohima to see you, sir.'

Mrs. Trevelyan leapt to her feet.

'I don't want to see him!' she cried urgently. 'Don't let him in here!'

But it was obvious that Doctor Kohima was already at the door. He dodged neatly under the outstretched arm of the sergeant, and exclaimed angrily:

'What is the meaning of this? What are you doing with my secretary?'

The sergeant grabbed him by the shoulder, but at a nod from Forbes let him go. Mrs. Trevelyan cowered in her chair sobbing.

Sir Graham eyed his visitor with considerable curiosity, and said:

'Now Doctor Kohima, what seems to be the trouble?'

'You may well ask, sir!' snorted the doctor. 'Why is my secretary being detained in this manner here at Scotland Yard?'

'How did you know you would find her here?' put in Temple quite calmly.

Kohima swung round on him. 'If you please, Mr. Temple,' he snapped, 'for once *I* will ask the questions.'

'Certainly, Doctor,' replied Temple imperturbably, 'but I'm not guaranteeing you'll get the right answers!'

'Doctor—I beg of you, please don't interfere!' cried Mrs. Trevelyan tearfully.

Kohima went over to her chair and stood looking down at her for some seconds without speaking. Then he said slowly: 'You look ill, my dear. What has happened to you?' His voice was gentle and full of solicitude.

'It's not surprising that Mrs. Trevelyan looks ill,' Temple informed him. 'Apart from spending last night in gaol, she insists upon defying us at every turn.'

'In gaol!' repeated Doctor Kohima in a horrified tone. 'Are you joking?'

'Not that we're aware of,' replied Forbes drily.

'But what does this mean?' protested Kohima.

'To the best of our knowledge,' growled Forbes, 'it means that Mrs. Trevelyan is Rex.'

'What!' exclaimed Kohima in complete astonishment. 'Are you all mad?'

'Better ask Mrs. Trevelyan,' said Temple.

'But I've known her all my life. She's no more Rex than I am!'

'That may be so, Doctor Kohima,' replied Temple politely. 'But she tells us she is willing to make a statement to that effect, and to sign such a statement, so what possible reply can there be to that?'

'A very simple reply,' retorted the doctor. 'Mrs. Trevelyan is not in a fit state of health to sign any such statement at the moment.'

Forbes looked across at Temple with an expression of exasperation.

'Now look here, Doctor,' he snapped, 'there's nothing wrong with Mrs. Trevelyan, apart from a guilty conscience.'

'And I say there is very much that is wrong,' insisted Kohima, his light accent becoming much more noticeable in his excitement. 'Mrs. Trevelyan is tired and exhausted and emotionally unbalanced. Under such circumstances, cross-questioning broaches upon third-degree methods, and is grossly unfair upon Mrs. Trevelyan.'

'I resent that implication,' said Forbes angrily.

'Do not misunderstand me, Sir Graham,' said Kohima quickly. 'I am not accusing you of deliberately taking advantage of Mrs. Trevelyan's condition. I am merely trying to tell you that in this state she is liable to confess to anything.'

'Doctor, please leave me alone!' begged Mrs. Trevelyan once more, as distressed as ever.

But Doctor Kohima was not to be deterred.

'You must further understand, Sir Graham, that Mrs. Trevelyan is not only my secretary; she is also a patient of mine, and as her medical adviser I must insist—'

'You insist on what, Doctor Kohima?' demanded Forbes in a faintly irritated tone.

'I insist that she rests – if only for an hour. Obviously, she had very little sleep last night, her nerves are completely upset.'

'I have no objection to Mrs. Trevelyan resting,' replied Forbes bluntly, 'after she has made her statement—and signed it!'

'No!' snapped Kohima. 'I must insist that she makes no statement unless she is allowed to rest for at least two hours.'

Forbes sighed.

'Very well,' he agreed at last. 'I've never forced anybody to sign a statement without every opportunity to think it over.'

'But there's nothing to think over,' protested Mrs. Trevelyan. 'I can't rest! I didn't get a wink of sleep last night and I'm more wide awake than ever. I'll sign anything if you'll only leave me alone.'

Kohima went and stood over her, resting a hand on either shoulder and looking down into her eyes. After a while, he took her elbow and led her without speaking over to the settee near the window.

'Why did you come here?' she whispered tensely. 'You know they suspect—'

'Look at me,' he interrupted in a quiet but compelling tone, as he passed his finger tips lightly across her forehead. 'Look at me, Barbara . . . poor girl, you're worn out—'

'Yes,' she murmured, 'I am tired . . . so tired . . .'

She tried ineffectually to avoid his piercing dark eyes.

'You are not afraid of me,' he murmured soothingly. 'There is no need—'

She was breathing a little more easily, but there was still the look of terror in her eyes.

'No questions, please Charles,' she whispered imploringly.

'No questions, my dear,' he replied reassuringly, his eyes still focused intently upon hers.

'It was good of you to come, Charles,' she murmured in a relieved tone. 'But you mustn't get mixed up in this – don't let them drag you into it . . . promise!'

'Don't talk . . . don't excite yourself,' he ordered. 'Just let yourself relax completely.' He continued to smooth her forehead with his right hand.

'You are still tired?' he asked presently, noticing that the muscles of her face were sagging a little.

'Very tired.'

'But everything is going to be all right now,' he declared very slowly, as if he were talking to a child.

'Everything is going to be all right,' she repeated mechanically as if she were already half asleep.

'There is no need to worry about anything,' he continued in the same deliberate tones, and again she repeated the words after him. He placed a cushion for her head, and slowly allowed her to sink back upon it. In a very low voice, he murmured:

'Gently, Barbara . . . you can close your eyes now . . . you're almost asleep . . . that's it . . .'

Her left arm fell lifelessly to her side and she was apparently asleep. But Kohima watched her for quite five minutes before he turned to Temple and Forbes, who had been talking in very low tones.

'So!' said Kohima almost to himself, and looked up at Temple, who had been watching him with the merest flicker of a smile.

'Is this so amusing, my friend?' asked the doctor.

'I was just thinking, Doctor,' said Temple quietly, 'that you can lead a horse to the water, but you cannot make him drink.'

'Now what do you mean by that, Mr. Temple?' asked Kohima.

'I think you have a pretty good idea, Doctor Kohima,' replied Temple significantly.

It was the doctor's turn to smile.

'Perhaps I have, Mr. Temple,' he said softly. 'I must go now, if you will permit. I have several patients waiting for me – but you know my address if I am wanted. In any case, I should like to be present when Mrs. Trevelyan is questioned again.'

'I'm sure that can be arranged, Doctor,' agreed Temple pleasantly, rather to Forbes' surprise.

After the doctor had gone, Forbes asked:

'What was the idea, Temple?'

Temple lighted a cigarette.

'I don't see that Kohima can do much harm if he's here when Mrs. Trevelyan talks—'

'But supposing he's implicated,' suggested Forbes.

'That gives us a better chance of catching him.'

'He might even be Rex,' persisted Forbes.

'Then if he comes to us, it saves us the trouble of going out after him.'

'H'm, may be something in that,' conceded Forbes. 'What are we going to do about her?' He indicated the sleeping figure on the settee.

'I suggest you leave her just where she is. My guess is that she'll probably sleep till Kohima comes back. I think we should hold everything till then. Meanwhile, I'll go home for lunch, I think. What about coming along?'

Forbes reluctantly shook his head.

'I'd like to, Temple, but I've a feeling I should be here just in case anything else breaks, or that damn fool Flexdale rings up and wants to arrange another broadcast.'

Temple grinned.

'All right, Sir Graham. I'll see you later. Give me a ring at the flat if anything sensational develops.'

When Temple got back he found Steve was beginning to worry at his prolonged absence. Also, it appeared there was a visitor patiently waiting for him.

'Anyone we know?' he asked.

'Yes, darling, it's that little Welshman again.'

'Good lord! Davis!' murmured Temple. 'What is it this time?'

'I don't know,' replied Steve. 'He's in the lounge. I gave him your new book to read.'

'Then he's probably asleep by now!'

'He might have seen something in the papers,' speculated Steve. 'They're making an awful fuss about Mrs. Trevelyan. I suppose you saw the *Evening Graphic*?'

Temple nodded.

'If it hadn't been for Crane, the papers wouldn't have got hold of the story. The damn fool opened his mouth a yard wide the moment we got back.'

'But it's true, isn't it, Paul?' asked Steve, slightly perplexed.

'Darling, you ask a question like that—you, an ex-reporter!'

'Hasn't Mrs. Trevelyan confessed then?'

'Oh yes,' he shrugged, 'she confessed until she was practically blue in the face. But it didn't enlighten us very much.'

'She's a very strange person,' commented Steve thoughtfully, 'and I find it hard to believe she's Rex. But she says she's Rex—'

'And the papers say she's Rex,' put in Temple lightly.

'And after all, she was caught red-handed.' Steve hesitated, then added quietly: 'But you don't think she's Rex, do you, Paul?'

'I'm always open to conviction,' he temporised. 'However, let's see what our Welsh friend has to say for himself. Has he been here very long?'

'About half an hour I should think.'

Temple went into the lounge and found Davis deep in his book.

'Hello, Mr. Davis – what can I do for you?' he asked.

The Welshman looked up quickly.

173

'Well, I don't know that you can do anything, Mr. Temple,' he replied with his air of faint bewilderment. 'I suppose it is sheer impertinence on my part to trouble you like this.'

'Not at all,' replied Temple politely. 'Let's hear all about it.'

Davis shifted uncomfortably in his seat, hesitated, and finally blurted out: 'It's about that night I saw you at the Royal Falcon, Mr. Temple. You remember that?'

'Of course. Nothing wrong that night, was there?'

Davis leaned forward and spoke in a confidential tone.

'Something very peculiar happened that night, Mr. Temple. I do not like to make a mountain out of a molehill, as they say, but I could not help noticing what went on.'

'This is very interesting,' said Temple, offering him a cigarette. 'What happened exactly?'

Davis wrinkled his forehead thoughtfully, then began: 'Well, you remember after I left your table I went upstairs to my room.'

'I didn't know that – but go on.'

'My room was number twenty-six, and that was next door to the one you and Mrs. Temple were to have occupied. When I turned into the corridor I saw someone trying the door of your room. I had barely turned the corner when he opened the door and went in. He didn't see me.'

'Of course, he might have been going in to see that our cases were ready to be taken down,' Temple pointed out.

'That is true, Mr. Temple. But he was acting in such a furtive way that my suspicions were aroused and I tiptoed up to the door. It was shut. Now if he had been there just to take a look at your cases, he would hardly have troubled to close the door after him.'

At this point, the little Welshman showed signs of visible embarrassment, but eventually added somewhat awkwardly:

'I could not resist the temptation, Mr. Temple. I stooped and looked through the keyhole.'

With difficulty, Temple repressed a smile.

'I suppose it was rather wicked of me,' went on Davis deprecatingly, 'but I had a feeling that something was wrong.'

'I appreciate that, Mr. Davis,' said Temple seriously. 'Did you manage to see anything through the keyhole?'

'Yes, indeed, Mr. Temple!' cried Davis. 'I saw this man opening your suitcase. He took out a silver flask – then he turned his back on me, but I thought I heard something poured out – I could not be sure. Then he put the flask back in the suitcase.'

'Did you recognise this man?'

'Well, to be quite truthful, Mr. Temple, I think it was Mr. Chester, the man who runs the hotel – I have always thought he was a nasty piece of work ever since he took over the place.'

'Did he see you, d'you think?' asked Temple.

'Oh no, indeed. As soon as he moved towards the door I was inside my own room like a shot.'

'Then why didn't you tell me this at the time?'

'I tried to, Mr. Temple,' Davis earnestly assured him. 'But I waited until the coast was clear, and when I came downstairs again you had left.'

'Oh well,' said Temple. 'I'm afraid we can't do very much about it now, except perhaps keep an eye on Mr. Chester. Was that all you wanted to tell me, Mr. Davis?'

The Welshman leapt to his feet.

'Lordy, no!' he exclaimed excitedly. 'Not by a long chalk! Later on that night, I went into the bar for a glass of ale, and put my hand in my pocket to pay for the drink. I took

out what I thought at first was a pound note, but it turned
out to be this—'

He produced his wallet and extracted a folded piece of
paper which he passed over to Temple.

On it was scrawled in pencil:

No matter what happens, Mrs. Trevelyan is not Rex.
Rex is the girl in brown.

CHAPTER XI

Doctor Kohima Intervenes

OPENING the door of the lounge just as Temple had finished reading the note, Steve was amazed to hear him burst into prolonged laughter.

'Paul!' she cried in astonishment, noting the Welshman's bewildered expression. 'Paul, what on earth is the joke?'

'Oh dear!' gasped Temple, 'there are some aspects of this case which remind me of the Marx Brothers!'

Wilfred Davis looked even more surprised.

'Have I said something very funny?' he asked in rather a pathetic tone.

'No, no!' Temple assured him. 'Please forgive me, Mr. Davis. I don't know what made me go off like that.'

'Do you mind if I have a look at that note?' asked Steve.

Temple passed it over and Steve took it gingerly by the top left-hand corner.

'This one isn't typed, Paul,' she exclaimed, slightly surprised.

'No, it's just a pencil scrawl,' he nodded. 'So unlike the other artistic efforts from Rex.'

'It may have been that he was in a hurry,' pointed out Davis earnestly.

'There is always that possibility,' conceded Temple gravely. 'He may not have had the time to open his portable typewriter and dash off a little note.' Steve looked up and caught a twinkle in his eye. But Mr. Davis was not to be denied.

'I was wondering if we could have the handwriting tested at all,' he speculated. 'Isn't there some sort of system, rather like the fingerprint method?'

'Only as a means of comparison,' Temple informed him. 'I'm afraid that wouldn't get us very far.'

Davis eyed him shrewdly and then said:

'You don't think this note was written by Rex?'

Temple shrugged.

'Since you ask me point-blank, Mr. Davis,' he replied, 'I'm afraid I don't. We can test it for fingerprints if you like, but that would involve taking yours and those of anyone else who had handled it. Quite frankly, I don't think it's worth the trouble.'

'But why don't you think it was written by Rex?' asked Davis eagerly.

'Well, in the first place the other notes were typewritten, and secondly, well, I just don't think it's Rex's handiwork.'

Davis sighed.

'I am sure it's all very confusing,' he murmured. 'Not at all like such affairs happen in books.' He was unconsciously turning the broad gold signet ring on the little finger of his left hand. Steve could not help feeling sorry for the little man, who had the appearance of someone in a very strange land with no knowledge of the language.

'If the note wasn't written by Rex, darling, then who did it?' she asked.

'Your guess is as good as mine,' replied Temple.

'But how did it come to be in my pocket?' persisted Davis. 'That's what I want to know.'

'It was obviously put there by the person who wrote it,' said Temple urbanely. 'But in my humble opinion that wasn't Rex.'

'I see,' mused Davis, patently more puzzled than ever. 'At least, I think I see, though I cannot think why this person should pick on me. I'm not a detective; I'm just a commercial traveller.'

'The person who slipped it in your pocket may have seen you talking to me,' Temple reminded him, 'and concluded that you were implicated in this Rex case. After all, you were present when Norma Rice's body was discovered.'

Davis looked a little frightened.

'Mr. Temple, you do not think that note was meant as some sort of warning to me not to interfere?' His sing-song accent was more pronounced than ever now.

Temple smiled.

'I think it was put in your pocket because the writer thought you would pass it on to me or to the police,' he said calmly.

'Oh well,' murmured Davis, obviously reassured, 'I had better be getting along. I am sorry to have made such a nuisance of myself.'

'On the contrary,' replied Temple courteously, 'you have been most helpful.'

'Thank you, Mr. Temple,' he answered gratefully. 'As a matter of fact, I have to go down to Canterbury again in two or three days time to investigate a complaint from one of our biggest customers there. Now, if you would like me to keep an eye on Mr. Chester—'

He broke off abruptly as the door opened and Ricky came in.

179

'Why, Ricky, I thought you were out,' said Steve.

Ricky said: 'Only for a little while, madam. So sorry if you were inconvenienced.'

'Well, I must be off,' said Davis, getting to his feet.

'Did you bring a hat or coat, Mr. Cortwright?' demanded Ricky politely.

Temple looked up quickly.

'You've met Ricky before, Mr. Davis?' he asked.

The little Welshman shook his head.

'I don't think so,' he said.

It was Ricky's turn to appear surprised.

'You do not remember me, sir?' he asked. 'You do not remember Ricky? Hotel Nevada – Twenty-third Street – New York – I was lift boy.'

Davis shook his head in a definite negative.

'I'm afraid you are making a mistake. I have never been to New York, though I have always wanted to visit that wonderful city.'

'But, Mr. Cortwright—' Ricky began to protest.

'My name is Davis, Wilfred Davis,' asserted the Welshman, a trifle irritated. 'You must be confusing me with someone else. They say we all have a double.'

Ricky inclined his head, his face now inscrutable.

'So sorry,' he murmured. 'I see many people in the hotel. I ask pardon.'

Davis patted him on the shoulder.

'Oh lordy, that's all right,' he exclaimed heartily. 'We all make mistakes.'

Ricky bowed slightly again, and conducted Davis to the front door, after he had taken a hearty farewell of Temple and Steve, who were both a little intrigued by the meeting with Ricky. Presently, the Siamese returned and addressed himself to Steve.

'Would you like me to start the silver before lunch, madam?' he asked politely.

Temple went over to him and asked: 'Ricky, why did you call Mr. Davis, Cortwright?'

Ricky smiled as blandly as ever and murmured:

'Why did you call Mr. Cortwright, Davis?' He folded his hands and looked innocently into Temple's eyes.

'But we know him as Mr. Davis,' replied Steve,

'I knew him as Mr. Cortwright,' said Ricky indifferently.

'You heard him say he couldn't possibly be Mr. Cortwright,' said Steve patiently.

Ricky looked from Temple to Steve and back again, his almond eyes narrowing the merest trifle. Then he said:

'I made a mistake. I am so sorry.'

He was about to turn away, but Temple detained him.

'No!' he exclaimed softly. 'You did not make a mistake, Ricky, and you know you didn't! You still believe it was Davis that you met at the Hotel Nevada, and that he was calling himself Cortwright then.'

'My memory is always very good,' replied the servant evasively. 'I notice Cortwright – er – Davis – still wear same ring.'

'I see,' nodded Temple. 'I must congratulate you on such a remarkable memory, Ricky.'

Ricky beamed at him but did not speak.

'Well now,' went on Temple, 'perhaps you can tell us when all this happened?'

'Last year,' replied Ricky promptly. 'January – February – March I work in the hotel. Mr. Cortwright – he has an apartment on the second floor – goes up and down in the lift a good deal. Mr. Cortwright – Mr. Davis – same face – must be the same person. I don't make mistake. When I was in America, I took course of memory training—'

'Quite so, Ricky,' interposed Temple, smiling inwardly. 'It must have been a very excellent course.'

'Cost me thirty dollars,' replied Ricky laconically. 'Would there be anything else, sir?'

'That's all, Ricky,' said Steve. 'You can leave the silver until after lunch.'

Ricky had only just gone when the telephone rang, and Crane came through to ask if Temple could go down to the Yard that evening, when Forbes proposed to interrogate Mrs. Trevelyan further. After some hesitation, Temple agreed and rang off. He experienced a vaguely disturbed feeling whenever his mind switched back to Mrs. Trevelyan. Things looked very black against her; indeed Forbes appeared to have compiled a cast-iron case, she was even willing to sign a confession which would send her to the gallows, and yet . . . Mrs. Trevelyan was an enigmatical type capable of strange deeds. If she was so willing to confess to being Rex, why should she not be anxious to tell the full story? But Temple found it difficult to believe that Mrs. Trevelyan could be guilty of this long series of callous crimes, each planned to the last detail and executed without a trace of mercy.

As Steve was going out to see about lunch, he called to her.

'Darling, I've arranged to meet an old friend of mine at Luigi's in the Haymarket at nine-fifteen. A man named Leo Brent.'

'I seem to remember your mentioning him,' said Steve.

'That's right – he was a friend of Maisie's[2] in the old days in Chicago,' explained Temple hastily. 'Knows his way around, and was very good to me out there. So I want you to entertain him.'

---

[2] See *Paul Temple Intervenes*

'Me?' queried Steve in some surprise.

'That's right, darling. I may be detained round at the Yard, so if you could contrive to keep Brent amused till I turn up—'

'But couldn't you telephone and put him off?' she suggested.

'No, no, I particularly want to see him. And now I come to think of it, darling, you have met him. He was at Juan when we were there seven years ago.'

'Oh, *that* American,' mused Steve. 'The tall, fair man – rather good-looking?'

'That's the fellow.'

'He was rather good fun,' she recalled. 'D'you remember how he took us right into the Casino as if he was one of the directors of the place? And then we had to lend him the taxi fare back?'

'I remember,' he grinned. 'Maybe he's sobered down since the war. Anyhow, you'll be able to find out.'

'I don't think finding out about Americans could be described as my favourite hobby,' she smiled, 'but as you seem so anxious to see him again, I'll try to oblige.'

He patted her shoulder. 'That's fine. Now have we got time for sherry before lunch?'

'I should think so,' said Steve, 'though you always drink too much when you're on a case.'

'No, darling, it's when I'm writing a book. And as I'm trying to do both at the moment—'

He turned to get the sherry decanter.

As she sipped the wine, she said thoughtfully: 'I can't make out that business of the note Davis found in his pocket. D'you still think it didn't come from Rex?'

'I think it came from Mr. Wilfred Davis,' replied Temple calmly. 'And what's more, I think he wrote it and slipped it into his own pocket.'

'Then don't you think he was telling the truth about seeing Chester take the flask out of your case?'

'I'm quite positive he wasn't.'

'What makes you so certain?'

'It's quite simple. If you just take your mind back to the key they gave us to our room in the hotel at Canterbury.'

'But I never saw the key, darling. You had it.'

'So I did,' he nodded. 'Well, there was nothing very remarkable about it. It was pretty much the same as any other Yale key.'

'A Yale key!' she repeated thoughtfully. 'That means it was impossible to see through the keyhole. Why didn't you mention that when he was telling you?'

'I just wanted to hear the end of the story, darling. You know how I always like to do that.'

'There is one point you've forgotten,' she said.

'Well?'

'There was a Yale lock on the door, of course. But I seem to remember that the old lock was still there, too, lower down. So it's just possible—'

'I believe you've got a soft spot for that little Welshman!' grinned Temple.

'Well, after all, he is one of your most devoted admirers,' she parried.

'Anyhow, I don't think it's worth another journey to Canterbury just yet, simply to discover whether he was telling the truth,' said Temple, draining his glass. 'Shall we go and see what Ricky has managed to contrive for lunch?'

At the door, he added lightly: 'And you'll be nice to Brent this evening, won't you, darling? Not too nice, of course!'

Temple spent the whole of the afternoon wrestling with his new novel, but he found that his mental picture of the heroine was continually getting confused with the pale, drawn features of Mrs. Trevelyan, the tense, shapely mouth, the rather deep-set eyes, the broad forehead . . .

Resolutely, he shut the image from his mind and tried to concentrate upon the chapter he was writing. Temple always smoked a pipe while he was working, though as often as not it was out. But he seemed to gain some measure of inspiration from biting hard upon the stem. Twice, Steve brought him a cup of tea which he thankfully accepted.

'I can't see myself finishing this book to schedule,' he mused as he stirred the second cup.

'Never mind, darling,' said Steve cheerfully, 'you know you always worry them out in the end. Why don't you try dictating it – that might be a lot quicker.'

He shook his head.

'My brain doesn't work out loud that way,' he replied rather regretfully.

'I'm sure it's only a matter of practice,' she told him.

'All right,' he smiled, 'you get back to your knitting and leave me to work this out my own way.'

He picked up his silver pencil again and tried to concentrate once more. But it only brought to mind the silver pencil discovered beside the body of Rex's recent victim. His thoughts wandered to Doctor Kohima and psychiatrists in general. Temple estimated that the rent of Kohima's house would be in the region of £700 a year. Why should a man who achieved comparative eminence in his own sphere be mixed up in a case of this type? Such men were invariably far too immersed in their job to allow themselves a second string of such an alarming nature.

Temple dismissed the doctor from his mind and started to plan the next chapter, which was to be set in and around an old fishing hut in one of the many lovely bays in North Wales. And this brought to mind the strange personality of Mr. Wilfred Davis, whose timely appearances at critical moments had proved an unusual feature of the Rex case. Was he really just a commercial traveller? And if he had not seen Chester pour the cyanide into the flask, why should he say that he had? More intriguing still, why should he write himself a note to the effect that Rex was the girl in brown? It just didn't add up.

Once again, Temple made an effort, and began to plod away at the fresh chapter, but he was not sorry when the door opened and Ricky appeared with a silver tray on which was tea and a plate of his favourite muffins. Steve came in and joined him, but did not seem very much inclined for conversation. Secretly, he was glad of this, for it gave a chance to turn over in his mind the events of the chapter on which he was working. Steve's mind, had he but known it, was busy with the problem of the girl in brown.

'Paul,' she said suddenly. 'I've just thought of something.'

'Yes?' he murmured, with his mouth full of muffin.

'There's been nothing about the girl in brown in the papers, has there?'

He shook his head. 'And you haven't discussed her with anyone but Carl Lathom?'

'Why, no—'

'Then if you suspect that Wilfred Davis wrote that note himself, how does it come about that he had heard of the girl in brown?'

Paul Temple added a generous spoonful of sugar to his tea and stirred it thoughtfully.

'Yes, that's quite a point,' he admitted. 'Quite a nice point.'

'Of course, I can't imagine a funny little man like that being Rex,' reflected Steve, passing the muffins to him.

'Is there anyone involved in this case whom you can imagine as Rex?' demanded her husband with a wry smile.

'Oh yes,' she replied promptly. 'Inspector Crane. I never did like the man.'

Temple burst out laughing. When he had recovered a little, he said:

'I suppose that's what's meant by feminine intuition. All I can say is thank the Lord I don't write colourful romances for a living. Female psychology is a mystery to me.'

'Oh, I don't know,' smiled Steve, 'you seem to handle Mrs. Trevelyan pretty well. And there was Iris Archer and of course Maisie—'

'All right,' he said hastily, 'maybe I've got a certain amount of intuition, too. But don't go classing me as a ladies' man, Steve.'

She laughed.

'Well, you certainly know most of the answers, Mr. Temple. Have another muffin.'

After tea, Temple tried vainly to get back to work, but found it almost impossible to concentrate, and finally went for a walk in the park. He was beginning to feel the loss of sleep the previous night and other nights during the past week or two, but he found it difficult to make up for this in the daytime.

When he had walked for over two miles, he decided that he had better move in the direction of New Scotland Yard, so he made his way towards the Mall.

At the Yard, the sergeant at the door said that Inspector Crane 'phoned down to say that Temple was to go straight to his room as soon as he arrived. Somewhat mystified, Temple obeyed.

In Sir Graham Forbes' room, the Commissioner was pacing to and fro in a considerable state of agitation, while Doctor

Kohima and Mrs. Trevelyan were now comparatively composed.

'This is preposterous!' Forbes exclaimed, but Mrs. Trevelyan sat in an upright chair with her hands folded in her lap and murmured quietly:

'Surely I've made myself perfectly clear, Sir Graham. I am simply refusing to make or sign any statement.'

'But dammit, earlier today you screamed at me that you were Rex and that you'd sign anything to that effect,' replied the bewildered Assistant Commissioner.

Doctor Kohima placed a protective arm across her shoulder.

'Earlier today, Mrs. Trevelyan was in an extremely over-wrought, one might almost say unbalanced frame of mind,' he declared in a level tone. 'I told you so at the time, Sir Graham.'

'You told us several things at the time,' snapped Forbes. 'I'm fully aware of that. But Mrs. Trevelyan insisted that she was Rex, a statement which incidentally agrees with a number of facts we have marshalled in evidence—'

'You know perfectly well, Sir Graham, that Mrs. Trevelyan's not Rex,' said Kohima slowly and with some emphasis. 'If you really thought for a moment that she was, you wouldn't be wasting your time like this.'

'You will permit me to employ my own methods of procedure,' retorted Forbes frigidly as he turned to Mrs. Trevelyan.

'Why did you go to Haybourne last night, Mrs. Trevelyan?' he demanded forcefully. She made no reply.

'How did you know about Carl Lathom and the two thousand pounds?' insisted Forbes.

'Don't answer him, Barbara,' said the doctor quietly.

Forbes was on the verge of losing his temper.

'Why did you go to Haybourne?' he repeated, raising his voice.

After a pause, Doctor Kohima said softly: 'Perhaps you will allow me to answer that. Mrs. Trevelyan went to Haybourne because she was sent there.'

There was a stifled exclamation from Mrs. Trevelyan.

'Charles, please!'

'I'm afraid I cannot accept your answer, Doctor Kohima,' said Forbes. 'Everything points to the fact that Mrs. Trevelyan ordered Carl Lathom to deliver the two thousand pounds, and arranged to pick up the money herself. In a word, that Mrs. Trevelyan—'

'Sir Graham,' interrupted Kohima with forceful sincerity, 'I give you my word that Mrs. Trevelyan is not Rex!'

Sir Graham shrugged.

'I don't see that gets us very much further.'

At that the door opened, and Inspector Crane appeared, to inform the Assistant Commissioner that Temple had arrived. Forbes excused himself, telling Mrs. Trevelyan that he would be back in a few moments.

Forbes and Crane went into the inspector's office just along the corridor and found Temple gazing thoughtfully out of the window. He turned and smiled at Forbes.

'Well, Sir Graham, what goes on now?'

'I think you've got a pretty good idea, Temple,' replied Forbes shrewdly.

'You've been cross-questioning Mrs. Trevelyan?'

'I've certainly been asking her some questions,' admitted Sir Graham with a slightly rueful expression.

'And she won't talk,' nodded Temple. 'Woman's privilege of changing her mind, eh, Sir Graham?'

'H'mph!' grunted Forbes. 'Seems like it.'

'Is the doctor still with her?'

Forbes nodded.

'Well, whether she talks or not,' continued Temple, 'the fact remains that she turned up at Haybourne to collect that money.'

Sir Graham looked very worried.

'Yes, I've been thinking about that, Temple. But there are other factors to be taken into consideration.'

'You mean there's a doubt in your mind?'

'Quite frankly, yes. Up till last night, I was pretty certain that Mrs. Trevelyan was Rex. But somehow, ever since she turned up at Haybourne – well, I haven't been so sure.'

'You thought that set-up was a shade too obvious?' queried Temple.

'Don't you?'

'I'd sooner hear your theory,' said Temple.

'Well it seems to me that in Rex we're dealing with a man, or woman of course, who works on quite an unprecedented scale. We know, for instance, that attempts were made to blackmail Norma Rice, Richard East, Carl Lathom, and poor old Cranbury. And blackmail's a tricky thing, Temple. For every case that comes to light, there are several hundred where the victim pays up – and goes on paying till he hasn't a penny left. But I can't say I've ever come across blackmail on such a large scale as this before.'

'And you're beginning to think that Mrs. Trevelyan was coerced into turning up at Haybourne and confessing that she was Rex?' asked Temple.

'It looks like it to me,' admitted Forbes.

'And you don't think Mrs. Trevelyan is Rex?'

'I'm damned if I do!'

'Well,' smiled Temple, taking out his cigarette-case, 'now we're starting to get somewhere!' He glanced across at Crane, who had been following the conversation closely. 'And what's your opinion, Inspector?'

Crane shook his head slowly.

'I wouldn't like to be as downright as all that, Mr. Temple,' he said cautiously. 'Though I must say I agree with Sir Graham about Mrs. Trevelyan. I've been watching her pretty carefully, and I'd lay fifty to one she isn't Rex. But if you want my frank opinion – of course it's only a theory—'

'Yes, Inspector?' said Temple curiously.

'Well, I think Doctor Kohima is the man we're looking for. He's the mastermind all right. Look how he keeps giving her orders and laying the law down. She seems to do exactly as he tells her. First of all, he sends her down to Haybourne to play the part of Rex, then he comes here and finds she isn't putting up a very good show, so he cancels the idea and tells her she's not to talk. And another thing—'

'Yes?' said Temple.

'There was the car accident,' Crane reminded him. 'It was the doctor's car that crashed into you the night Sir Ernest was murdered, and don't forget he's never been able to give us a satisfactory explanation of how it came to be out of the garage.'

'That's true enough,' agreed Temple.

'And of course,' Crane continued, 'we have to keep in mind that we found Doctor Kohima's silver pencil beside the dead body of James Barton.'

'But he insists that it wasn't his pencil,' Temple pointed out.

'Now I ask you! Do you think that pencil belongs to the doctor, or don't you?'

'I think it does, Inspector,' smiled Temple.

'And yet,' interrupted Forbes, 'you don't think that Kohima is Rex?'

'I didn't say so, Sir Graham,' replied Temple in an enigmatical tone.

'But you have decided that Kohima was lying about the pencil?'

'That doesn't necessarily imply he was Rex. Blackmail brings a whole crop of lies in its train – look at Mrs. Trevelyan, for instance. We can never be quite certain when she is telling the truth; but we have agreed that she can't be Rex.'

'All the same, I'm seriously thinking of detaining Kohima on the Barton murder,' said Forbes thoughtfully. 'By the way, Temple, I've been meaning to ask you what you were doing in Canterbury the night Barton was murdered.'

'I told you what happened at Canterbury – about Frank Chester and the little Welshman,' replied Temple evasively.

'Yes, Mr. Temple, you told us that,' put in Crane, 'but what you haven't told is why you went to Canterbury.'

'I – er – went to see an old friend of mine,' stalled Temple.

'M . . .' grunted Crane dubiously. 'I see.' But it was obvious to Temple that the inspector was far from satisfied, and he began to feel that Crane's grip on this case was beginning to penetrate into many places where it was least expected.

Sir Graham began pacing up and down once more.

'I don't know what to do about Mrs. Trevelyan, Temple,' he confessed in a worried tone.

'The main thing,' Temple assured him, 'is to keep an eye on her.'

'Then you think she's in danger?' queried Crane curiously.

'Yes, Inspector,' replied Temple, 'outside Scotland Yard I think she is in considerable danger.'

'But you can't suggest any way to make her talk – it would be for her own good,' said Forbes.

Temple shook his head.

'I can think of no way to convince her that it would be for her own good,' he admitted. 'You must appreciate that Rex has a considerable hold over Mrs. Trevelyan, and he's continually putting the screw on. In fact, he has so played on her nerves that the prospect of being hanged seems like a picnic to her compared with what he threatens.'

Forbes rubbed his chin.

'This business seems to get more and more involved,' he growled. 'You don't want to see Mrs. Trevelyan then, Temple?'

'Not just now; I don't think it would help very much. Besides, I must dash off. I should be at Luigi's by now.'

'Luigi's in the Haymarket?' asked Crane, slightly surprised.

'Yes – know it?'

'I know Luigi very well. Used to see a lot of him when I was a dress clothes detective. As a matter of fact, I'm meeting a friend there later this evening.'

'Good!' smiled Temple. 'If we're still there I'll buy you a drink.'

'That's a bet,' agreed Crane.

'Cheer up, Sir Graham,' said Temple as he moved over to the door, 'things will begin to sort themselves out soon.'

'I'm sure I hope so,' muttered Forbes doubtfully.

Feeling slightly guilty at leaving Forbes without offering any further support, Temple made his way downstairs and was lucky enough to get a taxi outside.

He found Luigi's crowded as usual, and Luigi himself as effusive as ever. He made his way to a table in a far corner where he could see Steve talking vivaciously to Leo Brent.

CHAPTER XII

Enter Leo Brent

STEVE had enjoyed renewing her acquaintance with Leo Brent, and he, too, had appeared quite overjoyed to see her again. He was as young and irresponsible as ever and wore a well-fitting dress suit which enhanced his Nordic good looks. His fund of stories, personal and otherwise, seemed inexhaustible, and Steve was enjoying the evening so much that she did not realise her husband was nearly half an hour late. It was only when she saw Brent take a sly glance at his wrist-watch that she discovered the time.

'Gee, is it as late as that?' he murmured. 'I ought to be making a move.'

'I'm sure Paul will be here almost any minute now,' she hastily assured him.

'That guy was always the same in the old days,' murmured Brent. 'You haven't broken him of his bad habits, Mrs. Temple. He was always rushing in anything up to an hour late on account of meeting some crazy adventure.'

'But he really did have some important business, and he most particularly wanted to see you.'

'That's too bad,' said Brent. 'I think I'd better go down-stairs and 'phone. I got a date round at the Green Curtain Club, and it's kinda awkward.' Then an idea struck him.

'Say, why don't you come, too? We could leave a message with Luigi and Paul could follow us.'

'I think we ought to give him another ten minutes,' answered Steve. 'Why don't you go down and 'phone anyway? He'll probably be here when you get back.'

'All right, I'll do that,' he decided. 'I won't be more than five minutes.' She watched his lithe figure threading its way among the tables, and in a few seconds he had disappeared. She was silently castigating her husband for his unpunctuality when a familiar voice at her elbow said, 'Can I get you a drink, Mrs. Temple?'

She turned to see Carl Lathom sitting at the next table. There was a large brandy in front of him, and he had apparently only just arrived, but she had been so absorbed in her conversation with Brent that she had not noticed him before.

'Well, perhaps a small martini,' she replied in answer to his invitation.

'Won't you join me, that is if you're alone now?' he asked after he had given the order.

'As a matter of fact, I'm waiting for my husband,' she informed him. He chuckled.

'I say, that's a new slant on things! Man bites dog – wife waits for husband – sounds like a headline in the *Daily Reflector.*'

'Why don't you come and join in the vigil?' smiled Steve, 'that is if you're on your own.'

'That's very nice of you.'

He came and sat in Brent's empty chair.

When the drinks had arrived and the waiter had left them, Lathom leaned forward and said: 'I suppose you know all about what happened last night?'

'Mrs. Trevelyan?'

'Yes.'

Steve sipped her drink.

'It must have been quite an ordeal for you,' she said presently.

'Oh, it wasn't as bad as all that,' he said deprecatingly. 'They got me safely out of the way before the fun began.'

'All the same, I wouldn't have liked to be in your place,' said Steve with a slight shudder.

'It was an extraordinary business altogether,' he went on in a puzzled voice. 'I really can't believe it even now. D'you know, when I woke up this morning and realised what had happened last night—'

'It seemed like a bad dream?' queried Steve.

'Yes, it did – quite honestly!' he declared fervently.

'Even worse than the affair at Cairo?' she suggested.

'Oh, that!' He made a grimace. 'I thought that was forgotten. I wish to God I knew how Rex—' He broke off and seemed anxious to dismiss the subject.

'You knew Mrs. Trevelyan fairly well, didn't you?' asked Steve.

'I suppose you might say that,' he nodded thoughtfully. 'We generally used to chat when I called to see Doctor Kohima. Nothing very personal, of course.'

'But you must have told the doctor himself quite a lot about your – er – past?'

Lathom looked somewhat startled.

'Mrs. Temple – you – don't suggest that Doctor Kohima . . .' His voice trailed away.

'I don't know Doctor Kohima,' said Steve, 'but I have heard quite a lot about him, and after all it's a psychiatrist's job to sort of – well – worm out one's past.'

'Well, yes, I suppose it is essential for the practitioner to know as much as possible if he's to get at the root of the trouble. Incidentally, my hallucinations had no connection with Cairo, but you never can tell, of course.'

Steve sipped her drink but made no comment.

'This last week had made me very confused,' he went on. 'First of all, there was the girl in brown coming to life – you seeing her and proving she wasn't an hallucination. Then, before I could get over that, there came the note from Rex. I say—'

His expression changed. 'I say, Mrs. Temple, you don't think there could be any connection between the two—'

'Could be,' said Steve pensively.

He thumped his fist on the table.

'It's an idea!' he said. 'But that would mean that Doctor Kohima is somehow in league with the girl in brown.'

'Could be,' said Steve again.

'But – but this is staggering. He couldn't have deliberately set about dispelling that hallucination knowing the girl in brown was real, could he? I mean it all seems so fantastic!'

Steve accepted one of his cigarettes which he lighted for her.

'There are so many things in this case that appear quite unconnected with the main problem,' she murmured, 'until one suddenly hits upon the link.'

'But Mrs. Trevelyan seemed such a nice sort of person,' he murmured in some perplexity.

'So many people appear outwardly pleasant and normal, but we know nothing of their private lives,' answered Steve, unconsciously quoting her husband.

'It's all very difficult,' he mused. 'Somehow, I don't think I'd have been much good as a detective.'

'Cheer up, you two!' said a voice behind them, and they turned to see Temple standing there.

'Paul – at last!' said Steve. 'Where on earth have you been?'

'I have always been told that that is a question a woman should never ask,' smiled Lathom.

'Steve breaks all the rules,' said Temple. Then he went on to ask: 'Where's Leo? Don't tell me you let him go.'

'He's downstairs 'phoning,' answered Steve.

'Oh, good. I was afraid he'd cleared off.'

He found another chair and sat down.

'Well, how are you this evening after yesterday's ordeal, Lathom?'

'Rather better than I felt this morning,' replied Carl. 'I was just telling Mrs. Temple that it all seemed like a bad dream.'

'As unpleasant as that?'

'I still can't believe it.'

'You can't believe what, Mr. Lathom?'

'That Mrs. Trevelyan is Rex. I know that, according to the papers, she has already confessed, but I can't believe that. We aren't living in the pages of a detective story, Mr. Temple. It isn't feasible that a doctor's secretary should be such a master-criminal.'

'Stranger things have happened in the underworld,' Temple told him.

'Yes, I dare say. Even so, I can't believe it. I mean—Mrs. Trevelyan – of all people – have you seen her, Temple, since—'

'I've seen her,' nodded Temple.

'Then is it true about her having confessed?'

'Yes and no,' was the enigmatic reply, and before Lathom could ask any further questions, the voice of Leo Brent boomed in on their conversation. Temple apologised for being late and introduced Brent and Lathom. Carl Lathom refused their invitation to take another drink, saying that he was meeting a friend for supper at a nearby night club.

'Can't think where I've seen that bird before,' mused Brent, watching Lathom's retreating figure. 'I've got an idea that it was somewhere I wouldn't take my best girl. Now let me think—'

But his memory failed him. They went over to a corner which had just been vacated, and Temple talked to Brent in a low voice for about ten minutes. First of all, the American seemed amused, then intrigued. Finally, his expression became rather more serious.

'Well, there you are, Leo. That's the proposition,' said Temple at last. The American locked his hands round his left knee and gazed thoughtfully across the room.

'How long would you want me to stay in Canterbury?' he asked.

'That depends,' replied Temple. 'Three or four days at least, I should think.'

Brent considered this for a moment, then said: 'I take it that you don't think this guy Chester – or Mulberry, is really Rex.'

'I'm certain he isn't,' replied Temple quickly. 'But I'm equally positive that Chester is in frequent contact with Rex. That's why I want you to go down there, Leo. You're not known there – you can pass off easily enough as an American tourist doing the sights – you don't look particularly—'

'Intelligent?' suggested Brent with a grin.

'I was going to say "suspicious",' smiled Temple, 'but have it your own way.'

'Yes,' mused Brent, 'it sounds a pretty good set-up. I get the angle now. You want me to be rubberneck number one, complete with camera, Baedeker and the almighty dollar.'

'Not to mention acute dyspepsia?' smiled Steve. 'But don't go overdoing it.'

'You leave that to me, Mrs. Temple. Though there is just one thing,' he added seriously.

'Yes?' said Temple.

'Well, supposing Chester should catch on, and starts to make things unpleasant?'

Temple laughed. 'I think you can handle that sort of situation pretty well, Leo. I seem to remember watching you battle your way through the semi-finals of a welter-weight contest.'

'Oh, sure! I'm not worried about the rough stuff, I can take care of that. But let's just suppose I happen to hit upon something pretty big. I'm strange around here as far as crime's concerned, you know.'

'All right,' nodded Temple. 'What you have to do is telephone me every morning between seven and ten, and every night between nine and midnight. That's very important, Leo,' he said earnestly, 'because if I don't get a call from you I shall be down there in less than two hours.'

'I get you,' said Brent.

'Anything else you want to know?'

'I don't think so.' He leaned back in his corner and relaxed, and the conversation became general, until Brent finally looked at his watch. 'Guess I'd better be moving along,' he announced. 'I've always found redheads get kinda impatient if they're kept waiting.'

He finished his drink and rose to shake hands with Steve. Suddenly, he leaned over and whispered in Temple's ear.

'Just one thing. If, by any chance, you don't hear from me, and I'm not kicking around when you get down to Canterbury, don't forget – it's all done by mirrors!'

'I shan't forget,' laughed Temple.

'Good night, Mrs. Temple,' said Brent, adding gallantly: 'Next time we meet, I hope it'll be "Steve".'

'Good-bye, Leo,' she smiled.

They watched him threading his way blithely through the crowded restaurant.

'He's an awfully nice fellow,' declared Steve after a moment. 'What was all that business about mirrors?'

'Oh, nothing much. It goes back to the days when we used to share a room in Chicago. We had rather an inquisitive landlady, so that if either of us had a private message for the other, he wrote it on a scrap of paper and stuck it behind the mirror on the dressing-table – usually with chewing-gum. We did it occasionally in other places too, outside the house. It got to be a sort of gag between us.'

'I can just imagine you two painting the town red,' smiled Steve.

'Not exactly red, darling,' he assured her. 'But we had to have a little relaxation sometimes.'

His expression changed as he caught sight of Lathom standing behind them.

'Hello, Lathom. I thought you'd gone on somewhere to supper.'

'I found I'd left my umbrella, so I came back for it right away – you know how scarce they are nowadays. And I saw your man, Ricky, downstairs. He seems to be in rather a "flap" about something.'

'Ricky?' repeated Steve in some mystification.

'You'll find him in the vestibule. Apparently he tried to telephone you, but found the line out of order.'

'Did he say if there was something wrong?' asked Temple.

'Well, to be quite frank,' replied Lathom, 'I couldn't make out what he was talking about – he did seem a bit excited and over-voluble. As far as I can gather, it appears that a girl called at your flat and said she particularly wanted to see you. Ricky seems to think it's pretty vital.'

'A girl?' queried Steve. 'Did he say what sort of girl?'

'No,' laughed Lathom. 'I'm not even sure that he knows. He appears quite delightfully vague about the whole business – unless he was being very guarded for my special benefit!'

Lathom seemed to think the matter quite amusing. Then his tone suddenly changed as he said: 'I say, Temple, it couldn't be—it couldn't be the girl in brown?' he whispered.

'You're quite a thought-reader, Lathom,' replied Temple briskly. 'Come along, Steve, we'd better look into this.'

Slightly bewildered still, Lathom watched them go.

'Did you bring the car, Steve?' asked Temple, as they came into the foyer.

'Yes, it's just round the corner in Panton Street Mews,' she replied a little breathlessly, as they discovered Ricky and heard his story.

Two minutes later they had just backed towards the end of the Mews when Temple felt a jar at the steering wheel, and realised that a front tyre had gone flat.

'That would have to happen now!' exclaimed Temple, snatching at the brake to bring the car to a standstill. Ricky leapt out of his seat and presently called out:

'There's a lot of glass in the road, Mr. Temple.'

Temple joined him and discovered the broken bottle which had obviously done the damage.

'That's rather odd, isn't it?' asked Steve, putting her head out of the window.

'A little unusual to say the least,' said Temple, who had never before seen so much glass lying about in this particular district.

'It almost makes one think that it had been dropped there deliberately,' Steve commented.

'Yes,' nodded Temple. 'So that we'd waste time changing the wheel. Which is precisely what we're not going to do. Jump out, Steve – we can walk home in five minutes and I'll 'phone the garage to pick up the car.'

At that moment, however, a taxi pulled up behind them with a screech of brakes, and thinking it was perhaps disengaged Temple went up to the driver. He was startled when the window was lowered and the face of Doctor Kohima appeared.

'Are you in trouble, Mr. Temple?' he asked, quite calmly.

'We certainly are!' cried Temple. 'Is this your taxi?'

'Why, yes – I was just going home—'

'Steve! Ricky!' called Temple, interrupting him. 'Get in this taxi quickly. Kick that glass in the gutter first, Ricky.'

The little man hastened to obey, and a minute later the taxi door slammed.

''Ere, what's the game? This ain't a blinkin' general bus,' said the driver somewhat truculently through the partition.

'That's all right,' said Kohima quickly, noting the urgency in Temple's manner. 'Where do you wish to go, Mr. Temple?'

'Half Moon Street – and step on it!'

'Okay – okay . . .' murmured the driver in a resigned tone as he let in his clutch.

Temple hurriedly introduced Steve to Doctor Kohima, who gravely bowed.

'I had wanted a word with you, Mr. Temple, and the inspector said I would find you at Luigi's, so I was following you—'

At that moment, the taxi drew up outside the Temples' flat and Paul Temple leapt out quickly. He gave the driver a ten-shilling note, and turned to the doctor.

'If you don't mind waiting in the taxi for a few minutes, I'll be right back,' he promised.

'Of course,' agreed Kohima, unable to conceal the slight note of surprise in his voice.

They ran into the entrance hall and into the lift. As it was ascending, Temple felt in his usual pocket for his latchkey, then recalled that he had left it in another suit.

'It's all right, darling,' said Steve as the lift stopped, 'I've got mine somewhere.' She fumbled in her handbag and found it, but Temple had already pushed open the front door of the flat.

'I swear I locked it,' exclaimed Steve. 'Ricky, you were last to leave—'

'Yes, Mrs. Temple. I locked the door, too – I closed it after me and tried it to make sure.'

They stood in the hallway, looking uncertainly at each other and speaking in whispers.

'Did you leave the light on, Ricky?' said Temple, and the little man nodded. Temple moved over to the lounge door and opened it. The room was in darkness. He switched on the light, and Steve, who had come up behind him, said: 'Why, she must have gone.'

Then she caught her breath and gave a cry of horror as she saw a woman's hand on the floor behind the settee.

Temple strode quickly across the room and looked down at the woman's body, from which a trickle of blood was leaving an ugly stain on the green carpet.

'Paul, she's been shot,' cried Steve, noticing the wound in the woman's left temple. Her husband called for Ricky to help him to lift the body.

'It's the girl in brown,' whispered Steve tensely. 'Is she – is she dead?'

'Shall I fetch doctor from outside?' volunteered Ricky, hut Temple stopped him.

'Wait, Ricky. In any case, he couldn't do anything, I'm afraid. It's too late for that.'

He looked quickly round the room for some sign of a weapon, but there was none. Nor did there appear to have been any sort of struggle. As he moved silently round, Temple suddenly stopped and listened intently.

'What is it, Paul?' asked Steve.

'Listen!' he whispered.

The door was slightly open and from the other side of the hall they could hear running water.

'There's somebody in the bathroom – that's the tap over the wash-hand basin,' announced Steve.

Temple stood at the lounge door for a few seconds and listened. Then he crossed over to a bureau in the corner of the room and took a neat automatic from the bottom right-hand drawer.

'Darling, do be careful!' whispered Steve anxiously.

'All right,' he nodded. 'Steve, you stay in here – you, too, Ricky.'

He went across the hall and rapped smartly on the door of the bathroom.

'D'you mind coming out of there – at once!' he called.

There was no reply, but the occupant of the bathroom immediately turned off the tap. After waiting for about five seconds, Temple repeated his demand in a louder voice, taking the precaution of standing against the wall at the side of the door in case it opened suddenly.

'Do you mind coming out of there?'

There was the sound of a drawn bolt and a familiar voice said:

'Not at all, Mr. Temple.'

The door opened. Inspector Crane stood in the doorway carefully wiping his hands on a small towel on which there was an ominous red stain.

CHAPTER XIII

Mr. Lathom Receives a Visitor

CRANE very deliberately finished wiping his hands, then carefully replaced the towel on the rail.

'So you've finally arrived, Mr. Temple,' he said in a noncommittal tone.

Temple looked round the bathroom, then back at Crane.

'I see you've cut your hand, Inspector,' he commented.

'Yes, I'm glad you've come, Temple. I've been making free of your bathroom – hope you don't mind.'

'Of course not.'

'And I was wondering if you have such a thing as a first-aid outfit. A scrap of plaster might stop this bleeding – it's a confounded nuisance.'

'Certainly – here you are.' Temple went to the bathroom cupboard and passed him a small bottle of iodine and some plaster.

'On second thoughts, better let me,' he suggested. 'It's a bit awkward to fix one-handed.'

The inspector agreed and Temple neatly secured a bit of plaster over the gash. Then he suddenly remembered Steve, and put his head round the door and called: 'It's all right, darling, it's only Inspector Crane. You might get us a drink – we'll be out in a minute.'

He turned to Crane once more.

'Now, Inspector – quickly. What happened?'

Crane nursed his injured hand.

'You may well ask that, Mr. Temple,' he murmured ruefully. 'I'm pretty much in the dark myself.'

'But how did you get here?'

'Well, I told you I'd see you at Luigi's, so I went round there. Luigi said you'd left in a hurry, and I got the idea there was something wrong. So I came on here at once.'

'By car?'

'Taxi.'

'Go on, Inspector.'

'Well, as I was coming up in the lift I heard a revolver shot. I couldn't be sure it was this flat, of course, but I found the door open, and – well, this girl was there on the floor.'

'You didn't see anyone else?'

Crane shook his head.

'I rushed into all the other rooms, but there was no sign of anyone, except in the far bedroom. One of the windows was open, and I noticed it led out on to the fire-escape. I didn't touch it – thought we might get some fingerprints.'

'I'll remember,' nodded Temple. 'That wouldn't have been open before. Steve religiously closes all the windows when she goes out.'

'You've no idea when it could have happened?' asked Crane.

'Not so long back. In fact, the murderer had a narrow escape. I should imagine, you almost caught him in the act.' Temple's glance fell on Crane's injured hand once more.

'How's it feel now?' he asked.

'Oh, it's stopped bleeding. Still throbs pretty badly though.'

'How did you manage to cut it so deeply?' asked Temple curiously.

'I caught it on the corner of that fancy cigarette-box in the lounge as I was moving the little table to look at the body. That box has quite a jagged edge.'

Temple nodded, having suffered a similar mishap some months previously.

Crane perched on the edge of the bath and said quietly: 'I suppose you recognise this girl, Mr. Temple?'

'Yes,' replied the novelist. 'I've told you about her. She's the girl who followed my wife the other night – the girl who worried Carl Lathom.'

'You mean – the girl in brown,' said Crane slowly. 'Yes, now I come to think of it, she is wearing brown, of course. Well, it doesn't look as if she'll trouble Mrs. Temple or Mr. Lathom any longer. Did you know she was here waiting for you?'

'Of course. That's why we left Luigi's. Ricky turned up there and told me that there was a woman who wanted to see me urgently.'

'Ricky – your servant – came round specially to tell you?'

'Certainly. He is pretty shrewd, is Ricky. Seemed to guess that this was a matter of life and death.'

'H'm,' grunted Crane. 'Pity he left her all the same. Looks as if he made a big mistake. Can I have a word with this servant of yours?'

'Of course. We'll go to the kitchen – it'll save time. And that reminds me, I've got Doctor Kohima waiting for me downstairs, so I'll pop out while you talk to Ricky.'

'Doctor Kohima?' queried Crane sharply.

'Yes, he gave us a lift home in his taxi. I had some trouble with my car.'

They made their way to the kitchen, where they found Ricky silently busy preparing for the next morning's breakfast.

'This is Inspector Crane, Ricky. He thinks you might be able to help him with one or two little things,' said Temple, and assuring the inspector that he would be back in five minutes, he left them.

'Now, Ricky,' grunted Crane, perching on the edge of the kitchen table.

'Please?' said Ricky suavely, wiping two teaspoons on a towel.

'From what I gather, you appear to have been the last person to see this young lady alive, Ricky.'

'One moment,' interrupted Ricky, carefully placing the spoons in their respective saucers. 'I must make small correction—'

'Eh? What's that?' Crane ejaculated in some surprise.

'Sorry to contradict, Inspector,' said Ricky blandly. 'But I was not the last person to see the lady alive.'

'No?' echoed Crane, still somewhat taken aback. 'Then who was the last person?'

'If you please, Inspector,' replied Ricky imperturbably, 'that would surely be the murderer.'

Crane looked hard at him, but the little man's features remained inscrutable. The inspector coughed, then said: 'And you have no idea who the murderer might be?'

'If I knew I would tell police,' said Ricky quietly. 'I am good British citizen.'

'You realise, of course,' continued Crane slowly, 'that if you had not left the girl this would probably never have happened?'

The little Siamese gave the merest twitch of the shoulders.
'Who knows?'

'Why did you leave her alone?'

'Because she ask me to find Mr. Temple right away. She said she could not wait long.'

'And how did you know he was at Luigi's?'

'Mrs. Temple told me she was meeting him there.'

'Couldn't you have 'phoned?'

'I tried to telephone. One line was out of order and the other was engaged – always engaged. So I thought it quicker to take taxi.'

Inspector Crane seemed slightly baffled.

'Well, Ricky,' he admitted, 'you certainly seem to know all the answers.'

Ricky looked him squarely in the face.

'In a case of murder,' he answered slowly, 'it is necessary to give the truthful answers.'

Inspector Crane decided to leave it at that.

On the way downstairs, Temple decided that he would like to pay another visit to Luigi's to check up one or two details, and when he got down to the taxi he asked Kohima if he would mind accompanying him.

'Is anything wrong, Mr. Temple?' asked the doctor shrewdly.

'No – why?'

'You've come without your hat.'

'I – er – why, so I have. We – er – we had visitors and I told them I was only just popping out. Anyway, I thought we could talk on the way to Luigi's, if you've no objection.'

'None whatever.'

Temple gave the necessary instructions to the driver, and the taxi started. After a moment or two's hesitation, Doctor

Kohima said: 'I think you know why I wanted to see you, Mr. Temple.'

'I have a slight idea,' nodded Temple, offering him a cigarette, which he refused.

Doctor Kohima fidgeted a little with his gloves, then said in a low but distinct voice: 'I have made up my mind that it would be advisable to tell you the whole truth about Mrs. Trevelyan.'

'I see,' said Temple quietly. 'Perhaps you'd prefer to leave it until tomorrow.'

'No,' replied Kohima with decision. 'So many things are happening so quickly that I feel you should have the full facts.'

He paused again. Obviously he was not finding it too easy to begin his story, though his sincerity was apparent. 'I find it difficult to know where to start,' he confessed. 'During the past twenty years I've been listening to other people's troubles, and now for the first time I have to tell my own to another person – well, it isn't easy.'

'Why not tell me the most obvious fact first?' suggested Temple.

'What would you say that was?'

'I should imagine that most of your troubles are due to your being in love with Mrs. Trevelyan,' replied Temple shrewdly.

There was silence for a few seconds. The taxi pulled up with a jerk as the traffic lights flicked from amber to red.

'You're a keen observer of human nature, I can see, Mr. Temple,' said Kohima presently. 'Yes, you're right about Mrs. Trevelyan and I. We met and fell in love at sight several years ago. You would understand it better if you'd known her then, Mr. Temple. She was a wonderful woman in those days – so gay, so distinguished, so full of life.'

'I can well appreciate that,' murmured Temple seriously. 'I expect you found you had quite a lot in common.'

'Yes indeed. She had a keen, but of course an amateurish interest in psychology, and after a time I persuaded her to work for me as my confidential secretary. She agreed very willingly, and settled down to the work with considerable aptitude; in fact she was of great assistance to me. Until one day I had a shock, a very serious shock that threatened to disillusion me completely at the time.'

'You mean you discovered that she was passing on certain information about your patients to a third party,' put in Temple softly.

'It was a great blow to me,' said Kohima heavily. 'I was utterly taken aback – quite horrified. I just didn't know what to do. Of course, as my professional reputation was likely to be at stake, I had to challenge her. When I did so, I expected an indignant denial, but again the unexpected happened. She completely broke down and confessed.'

He sighed, then went on.

'Afterwards, I heard the whole, miserable story. She was being blackmailed into getting this information.' He stopped, then added after a pause, 'She was being black-mailed by Rex.'

'I gathered as much from what she herself told me,' nodded Temple thoughtfully. After a while he added, 'Would you say Mrs. Trevelyan was a wealthy sort of person?'

'Certainly not,' replied Kohima at once. 'I'd say her greatest fault is her complete lack of any sense of values where money is concerned. I gather that is how she came to fall into the hands of Rex.'

'Then I wonder if you can explain where she obtained the three thousand pounds she paid Rex?'

215

'Of course. I gave her the money,' replied Kohima quite simply. 'It was practically all the ready money I had, but there seemed to be no alternative.'

'You could have gone to the police,' Temple reminded him.

'I know,' said Kohima, somewhat distressed. 'I think now that I should have done. But, rightly or wrongly, I didn't. I paid the money. You can trace the transaction in my banking account if you care to do so.'

'I don't think that will be necessary,' said Temple. 'But I must admit I'm a little intrigued to know why you are telling me all this.'

'Because,' replied Kohima with sudden vehemence, 'I want to convince you, Temple, that Mrs. Trevelyan is not Rex. You've got to believe that, Temple. You've got to believe it.'

At that moment the taxi pulled up outside Luigi's, and Temple suggested that Doctor Kohima would be all the better for a double brandy. The doctor accepted the invitation and they dismissed the taxi.

If Luigi was mildly surprised to see Paul Temple for the second time that evening, he gave no sign of it, and they sat in a corner of the small bar. As they settled down with their drinks, Temple said:

'I don't think we can pursue the subject much further this evening – but I'll certainly bear in mind what you say.' Temple finished his drink quickly, then went and had a few words with Luigi. Outside the restaurant he wished Doctor Kohima good night, walked a little way down the Haymarket, crossed the road, and hailed a taxi.

Ten minutes later he was ringing the bell of the front door at Carl Lathom's flat. Presently, it was opened by Lathom himself wearing a dressing-gown. His hair was slightly ruffled

216

and he had a sleepy look, as if he had been interrupted in the middle of a doze.

'Hello, Temple,' he said quite pleasantly, smothering a yawn.

'I hope I haven't disturbed you,' apologised Temple, still a little out of breath from running quickly up the stairs.

'No, no, of course not. Do come in.'

He held the door open, and closed it gently after his visitor. Then he led the way into the lounge, where an armchair was drawn up before the fire, with drinks on a small side-table.

'I have an awful feeling you were just going to bed,' said Temple in a guilty tone.

'Nonsense! Why, the night's young. As a matter of fact, I was having forty winks in front of the fire.' Carl Lathom indicated the considerable array of bottles. 'What would you like to drink? Whisky, sherry, brandy, gin and lime, gin and Italian, dry martini?'

'You wouldn't have such a thing as a small port?' demanded Temple humorously.

Lathom laughed.

'Afraid I'm right out of port at the moment.'

'Then I'll just have a dry ginger if I may. I've drunk rather a lot this evening,' said Temple, settling in the chair Lathom indicated.

As Lathom filled his glass, he asked eagerly: 'Did you see that girl, Temple – the girl in brown?'

'Yes,' replied the novelist quietly, 'I saw her.'

'Good Lord! Then she's run to earth at last! Who is she? Did she explain why—'

'She explained nothing. She was in no position to explain. She was dead.' Temple rapped out the words in a steel-like tone.

'But how on earth could that have happened?'

'Quite simple. She was murdered.' There was no trace of emotion in Temple's voice.

'You mean she was already dead when you got back to the flat?'

'I'm afraid so.'

Lathom whistled softly to himself, then leaned forward to pick up a glowing coal which had fallen from the fire into the hearth. He carefully replaced the tongs, then turned to Temple and inquired slowly: 'Who was she, Temple?'

Temple shook his head. 'We haven't found out yet.'

'You don't know?' queried Lathom incredulously. 'But surely you searched the body.'

'No,' said Temple calmly.

'But good heavens, man, why not!'

'Because,' said Temple, 'I think she had already been searched by Inspector Crane.'

'By Inspector Crane,' repeated Lathom. 'Then he was at the flat when you arrived.'

'He was.'

'Quick work,' commented Lathom.

'He presumably arrived just after the girl was murdered,' Temple informed him.

'Didn't he see anyone?'

'No.'

'And you've no idea what he was doing at your flat?'

'He tells me that he wanted to see me. And that reminds me, I told him I'd be back in five minutes, and he may be still waiting. Would you mind if I use your 'phone?'

Lathom indicated the instrument in a corner of the room. Temple got through to the flat and spoke to Steve, who told him that the Inspector had left with the ambulance which had taken away the girl in brown. He had left a message that he would see Temple the next day.

'Apparently, whatever it was he wanted to see me about can wait,' smiled Temple, as he put down the receiver.

'How long have you known Crane?' asked Lathom, pouring himself two fingers of whisky.

'Oh, I can't quite remember. Why do you ask?'

'Can't say I very much like the looks of him.'

'No more does my wife,' smiled Temple, 'but I'm afraid that doesn't help very much.'

Lathom shifted uneasily in his armchair, then poked the fire rather agitatedly.

'You don't think it could have been Crane who shot the girl?' he said at last in a dubious tone.

'Why should he?' asked Temple. 'What possible motive could a Scotland Yard inspector have for wanting to get rid of a girl he had apparently never set eyes on before?'

'None whatever, of course,' murmured Lathom, 'if he really is just a Scotland Yard inspector. But if he should be an associate of Rex's or even Rex himself, then he might have shot the girl because he thought she knew too much.'

'How did you know she was shot?' asked Temple in a casual tone, but he was watching Lathom closely as he spoke.

'Why, you said so,' replied Lathom, taking a drink from his glass.

'No,' declared Temple flatly, 'I said that she had been murdered.'

Lathom shrugged.

'Well – murdered – shot – it comes to the same thing.'

'Not quite. She might have been strangled or stabbed or even poisoned. The police are inclined to make a fuss about such distinctions, you know.'

Lathom laughed a trifle uneasily.

'Yes, I suppose they are.' He turned and looked Temple full in the eyes. 'I say, Temple, you don't think I had anything to do with this, do you?' he asked.

'Well, had you?'

'Good heavens, no! I'll admit the girl in brown was getting on my nerves – something of a hoodoo, in fact. I paid Kohima a lot to try and rid me of her – when I thought she was an hallucination – but I draw the line at murder.'

'Well, that's nice to know,' parried Temple lightly, offering his cigarette-case. 'All the same, you have to admit, Lathom, that you're rather relieved to hear that the girl in brown won't trouble you any more.'

Lathom was silent for a moment, then said frankly, 'Now I come to think about it, I dare say you're right.'

'In fact,' persisted Temple, 'on the face of it, you have a much stronger motive for wanting to be rid of her than Inspector Crane, for instance. So in your own interests it might be as well if you gave me some idea of your movements after I saw you last evening.'

Lathom considered this for some moments. He drained his glass and examined it thoughtfully. At length he said: 'Well, I'm afraid that won't be too easy, Temple, from the point of view of checking what I tell you. Actually, all that happened was that after leaving you at Luigi's I came back here.'

'I thought you were going on to a club.'

'I changed my mind. When I went round the man I arranged to meet hadn't turned up, so I came back to Luigi's for my umbrella and then came straight on here. But don't ask me to prove that,' he added quickly.

'Why not?'

'Because I can't. No one saw me come in here.'

'I thought you had a housekeeper.'

'Oh yes, but she's away visiting her sister for a few days.'

Then his worried expression suddenly cleared as he said: 'But really, Temple, if you consider the relevant times, it would have been impossible for me to get round to your flat after leaving you at Luigi's and arrive there before you.'

'If I thought that,' said Temple coolly, 'I wouldn't be here. You see, we were delayed rather considerably getting back to the flat, owing to a puncture.'

'I say, what rotten luck!' said Lathom.

'Well, it wasn't exactly bad luck, we ran into quite a quantity of glass which seemed to have been distributed for our special benefit,' Temple informed him.

'You really think it was put there deliberately?'

'I do.'

Lathom set down his glass, rose and paced up and down the room several times. Temple sat where he was without moving a muscle. There was no sound except the noisy ticking of an Oriental wall clock. At last, Lathom said: 'Well, I'm sorry, Temple. I've been trying to think of someone who might have seen me, but I didn't meet a soul who was likely to recognise me. I may as well be frank about that now as later. I shall just have to rely on your good nature to get me out of this if there is any sort of inquiry involving me.'

'I haven't got you into it, yet,' Temple reminded him. 'And I came here for another reason as well as to inquire into the death of the girl in brown.'

Lathom stopped his pacing abruptly.

'You mean there's something else you haven't told me?'

'I think,' said Temple deliberately, 'that you ought to be warned.'

221

'Warned?' repeated Lathom in a puzzled tone. 'Warned about what?'

Temple stubbed out his cigarette and said quietly:

'About Rex.'

Lathom sank on to the arm of a chair.

'But, good heavens, why?' he demanded in bewilderment.

'I have a feeling that Rex may not be very impressed by the fact that you consulted me about that attempt at blackmail.'

'Yes, but I followed his instructions – the notes were there, and Mrs. Trevelyan went to collect—'

'Do you think Mrs. Trevelyan is Rex?'

'No! No!' exclaimed Lathom forcibly. 'I told Mrs. Temple as much earlier on this evening. But you have to admit that the circumstantial evidence against Mrs. Trevelyan is fairly strong. She did turn up at Haybourne, didn't she? I should imagine she'll find it difficult to convince the police that she isn't implicated.'

Temple stood up and leaned against the mantelpiece.

'You can take it from me, Lathom,' he said, 'that Sir Graham Forbes is pretty well convinced that Mrs. Trevelyan is not Rex.'

'Of course,' nodded Lathom excitedly. 'She's not the type. Anyone can see that.'

'Whom would you consider to be the type?'

'Don't ask me. I only know Mrs. Trevelyan isn't.'

He flung himself into his chair and gazed morosely into the fire. Presently, he asked:

'What do you suppose Rex will do, Temple, if he knows that I consulted you about that letter?'

Temple shrugged.

'That's what you meant when you said I ought to be warned, isn't it?' Lathom persisted.

'That's what I meant,' replied Temple in a voice from which all sign of emotion was deliberately suppressed.

Lathom caught his breath.

'You think I'm in danger, don't you?' There was an expression of tautness on his lean features.

'Well,' said Temple reassuringly, 'there's no need to get alarmed, but I should certainly watch your step, Mr. Lathom.'

CHAPTER XIV

No Picnic at Claywood Mill

PAUL TEMPLE accompanied Inspector Crane to the mortuary. The latter exchanged a few words with the attendant in charge, who jerked an expressive thumb towards the distant corner. Temple lifted a corner of the sheet and looked down at the girl who had once worn brown. Her face was waxen, and was thrown into vivid relief by her chestnut red hair. The bullet wound had congealed to a small red daub, partially covered by her hair. Temple noted that she had shapely, well-manicured hands, and both finger- and toe-nails were painted a vivid red. It was obvious, too, that her lips and eyes had been quite generously made-up.

'Queer business, Mr. Temple,' muttered Crane.

Temple slowly replaced the sheet.

'Did they find the bullet?' he asked.

'Yes, it was embedded in the skull. Markham found it when he did the post-mortem. It's just an ordinary bullet from a .33.'

'Fired from a distance, of course; otherwise there would have been powder burns.'

'Yes, I should imagine she heard the murderer come in, turned quickly to see who it was, and he fired right away from the door. The bullet would have entered at about that angle.'

'Which doesn't help us very much, does it, Inspector?' Temple hesitated, then added casually, 'By the way, didn't I hear that the Yard had a new issue of .33s the other week?'

'That's correct, sir,' replied the inspector. 'But they're kept strictly under lock and key in the armoury, and only issued for special jobs.'

'But I suppose they would be available to certain senior officers in case of sudden emergency?'

'I expect so, sir. Can't say that I carry one very often myself, so I don't take very much interest.'

They came out of the mortuary and stood at the top of the steps in the pleasant morning sunshine.

'What about the girl's personal belongings?' queried Temple.

'There's only her handbag of much interest, sir,' replied the inspector. 'Her clothes are American as far as we can trace – her bag, too. No strange fingerprints on it or on any of the contents. You'd better come up to my office and look 'em over.'

They walked across to Crane's office, and Temple apologised for his prolonged absence on the previous evening. Crane explained that he had merely wished to sound Temple a little further concerning the possibility of Mrs. Trevelyan's contacts with Rex, and whether it might not be an idea to release her from custody, keeping her under close observation.

Temple shook his head dubiously.

'I rather doubt it, Inspector,' he replied thoughtfully. 'You see, Rex knows that contact with Mrs. Trevelyan would be rather dangerous just now.'

'Yes, I agree,' said Crane, 'but don't you think he might try to—'

'To add her to the list of victims?' concluded Temple. 'Yes, I think that's more than probable. But knowing Rex's cunning, I don't think we'd be justified in making a stool-pigeon out of her. No matter how you guard her, Rex holds the master card – that of surprise. He can wait for days for the precise second in which to pounce. No, Crane, I don't think we should risk it.'

'I'm rather inclined to agree with you, Mr. Temple. It just occurred to me that it might provide a sort of short cut.'

They had reached Crane's office by this time, and Temple saw the brown handbag lying on the desk.

'Yes, this is American all right,' pronounced Temple, opening the bag, which contained the usual miscellaneous collection of feminine accessories. Mirror, lipsticks, comb, powder compact, cigarette-case and lighter. But there was nothing to afford the slightest clue to the owner's identity. Temple emptied them out on the desk and casually turned them over with his forefinger.

'Nothing much here, Inspector. Just a minute though . . .' He was busily feeling inside the bag. 'There seems to be a card of some sort sewn in the lining,' he told the inspector, who at once produced a penknife. Temple slit the lining and presently extracted a neat little visiting-card on which was printed:

WALTER AYRTON, 77A SOHO SQUARE, W.1.

Temple passed it over to Crane, who whistled softly.

'Ayrton, eh?'

'D'you know him?'

227

'I certainly do.'

'What's his line?'

'Walter Ayrton,' said Crane emphatically, 'is one of the smartest private investigators I've ever come across in his own particular line.'

'And what's that?'

'He specialises almost exclusively in blackmail.'

'Then he manages to keep it pretty dark,' said Temple. 'Can't say I've ever come across him.'

'That's just it, sir. He likes to play a lone hand. Conducts every investigation with great secrecy, and only takes on a very limited number of cases. Keeps out of the way of the police if he can, and there are times when his methods are a bit – well – unorthodox. But Ayrton gets results, Mr. Temple, and his clients pay him well. I happened to come across him in that big Salisbury case a year ago. It isn't often that Ayrton's cases come into court, but this one did, and I was assigned to it.'

'And have you any idea what possible connection he can have with this dead girl?'

Crane shook his head rather ponderously.

'No idea, sir. But I can ring him up and find out.'

'Ask him if we can go round and see him.'

The inspector pulled the telephone towards him and his conversation was short and somewhat cryptic, but he replaced the receiver with a satisfied smile.

'He'll be in his office all morning,' Crane announced.

'Good, then I think we may as well go round right away. My car's outside – nothing like striking while the iron's hot.'

Temple was a little surprised to find that Walter Ayrton was a youngish-looking man, with alert grey eyes, a long, thin nose and a small toothbrush moustache. His office was furnished almost luxuriously, for he appeared to realise that his clients must be placed at their ease and given an impression of the solidarity of the investigator. Temple was very impressed by this genial young man, for he looked the type who would not hesitate to make a quick decision and act upon it. Moreover, there was an air of extreme reliability behind his apparently casual manner.

'This is certainly an honour, Mr. Temple,' he said after Crane had performed the introduction. 'It seems to be an occasion for producing a box of my very best cigars.' And he dived into a drawer in search of the box in question, which he offered to his visitors.

'Well, I've heard enough about you, Mr. Temple, to know that you haven't just dropped in to pass the time of day,' smiled Ayrton when the cigars were drawing satisfactorily.

Temple grinned back.

'From what I've heard about you from the inspector, Mr. Ayrton, I shouldn't presume to trespass upon your valuable time unless the matter was fairly important.'

Ayrton leaned back in his chair and interlaced his fingers. 'Well,' he said, 'what can I do for you?'

Crane passed over the card and told him where they had found it. Ayrton's face at once took on a serious expression. Then the inspector went on to give a short description of the dead girl, but Ayrton stopped him.

'Poor kid,' he murmured quietly. 'It's all right, Inspector, I can tell you who she is.'

'Perhaps you'll tell us first how your card comes to be sewn inside her handbag,' suggested Temple.

'That's soon explained. In New York, Mr. Temple, I have an agent named Myers – Jeff Myers.'

'You mean the F.B.I. man,' said Temple. 'I heard of Myers when I was out there.'

229

'We have a sort of working agreement, Jeff and I,' proceeded Ayrton. 'I help him out if he wants it on this side, and he gets me any information I need from over there. Sometimes we pass on clients to each other. Nothing cut and dried between us – we just give a hand where necessary, and up to now it's worked out pretty well. A few months back, this young lady we're talking about came to see me with a letter of introduction from Jeff. Seems she was one of his best assistants, and a client had specially asked for her to come over on a tricky job.'

'She gave you her name, of course,' said Crane.

'Yes – it was Carol Reagan. She's fairly well-known over there for handling cases of blackmail by women. Myers used to give her a fairly free hand in that line.'

'You've no idea who the client was who asked her to come over here?' queried Temple.

'Yes, indeed. It was Norma Rice, the actress. The one who was murdered. I remember Miss Reagan telling me just afterwards. She was pretty furious that the blackmailer had called her bluff when she advised Norma Rice not to pay up, and she swore she'd find out who it was.'

'Why didn't you give us the tip before?' put in Crane with a slightly injured air. 'We've been chasing this girl in brown high and low – at least Mr. Temple has – under the impression that she was playing in with Rex.'

Ayrton smiled whimsically.

'I've got worries of my own, you know,' he said. 'What's more, I was supposed to keep out of the business except in case of emergency. She said she wouldn't trouble me unless she was completely up against it, and didn't feel she could handle things herself.'

'Then why did she go to Temple?' asked Crane.

'Maybe she thought I knew more about the case, or yet again she may have discovered something that gave her the idea that I was in danger,' suggested Temple.

Ayrton shrugged his shoulders.

'I've told you all I know,' he said. 'You have my sympathy, both of you. This man Rex seems to be a dangerous merchant. It isn't often blackmailers go in for murder; they usually haven't got the guts.'

He knocked the ash off his cigar.

'Of course, if there's anything else I can tell you,' he offered, 'I'll be only too glad. I'm afraid I haven't been able to help you very much.'

'On the contrary,' Temple assured him, 'you've been a great help, Mr. Ayrton. You've helped me to clear up one side of the case at any rate, and I can't tell you what a relief that is.'

Ayrton accompanied them to the door.

'I should be glad to know if you get any more news about this job,' he said. 'I'll have to telephone Jeff Myers, and I expect he'll want the lowdown. Of course, it's just possible that Myers may know something about the case, but I very much doubt it. The Reagan girl gave me the impression that she was playing a lone hand.'

'I'll let you know, Ayrton, if anything breaks,' promised Crane. 'See you at the inquest.'

'He seems a competent fellow,' commented Temple as they sat in the car on their way back to the Yard.

'That's the sort of job I fancy when I retire,' Crane confided. 'I've always found blackmail more interesting than any other form of crime.'

'There are occasions, like the present, when it's inclined to be just a little worrying, too!' Temple grimly reminded him.

'Anyhow, it's well paid – the investigation I mean,' declared Crane. 'When a man's being blackmailed for thousands, he's only too relieved to pay up a few hundred to get out of the mess. I sometimes think it must be a bit of a temptation to fellows like Ayrton not to go in for a bit of quiet blackmail themselves.'

'Ayrton certainly knows the ropes,' agreed Temple.

At the Yard they bumped into Sir Graham Forbes, and Temple took the opportunity to invite him to dinner the following evening.

That afternoon, Temple gave evidence at the inquest on Carol Reagan, the verdict after the very brief proceedings being: 'Murder by a person or persons unknown.' The only other witnesses were Inspector Crane and Walter Ayrton, who identified the dead woman.

Temple was working on his novel that evening when Steve came to tell him that Doctor Kohima wanted to speak to him on the telephone.

'What can I do for you, Doctor?' asked Temple politely, as he picked up the receiver.

'It's about my secretary – she is still being detained,' came the doctor's voice in which there was a note of anxiety, despite his guarded manner.

'I can assure you that it's for the best, Doctor,' said Temple. 'At the most, it shouldn't be for more than a few days now.'

'But it's so miserable for her,' protested Kohima. 'She is a freedom-loving sort of person, and she's cooped up there—'

'She has quite a nice room, and a certain number of luxuries,' Temple informed him. 'This should be a good opportunity for her to rest and relax. She's been under quite a big strain—'

'I know, I know,' broke in Kohima impatiently, 'but Scotland Yard is hardly the environment for relaxation. I'm sure she'd be quite safe here at my house—'

'I'm not so sure,' replied Temple grimly.

'There is such a thing as Habeas Corpus, you know, Mr. Temple.'

'So there is, Doctor. And you'll find it still operates, but by the time you get the warrant I'm pretty certain Mrs. Trevelyan will be free once more.'

'I hope you're right,' said Doctor Kohima rather abruptly, and rang off.

Steve, who had heard half the conversation and guessed the remainder, asked, 'Paul, is Mrs. Trevelyan still—'

'Still under lock and key,' he nodded. 'She seemed quite indifferent about it when I saw her this morning. And it serves more purposes than one. Of course, it's natural for Kohima to be a bit agitated.'

'D'you think he's upset because he's in love with her – or because he is Rex?' demanded Steve suddenly. 'All this business about lending her that money and being in love with her might be part of a cleverly worked out piece of bluff.'

Temple grinned.

'Darling, don't tell me you've lost all faith in human nature, too!'

'I wouldn't say that, Paul. But it becomes increasingly obvious that Rex is a person with a degree of low cunning that's simply Machiavellian, and it isn't easy to—'

Temple patted her shoulder.

'All right, darling, you get on with your knitting. I've a feeling that Rex is going to make the traditional fatal mistake any day now. We're all set ready to take advantage of it.'

233

'I've an awful feeling that he'll do something very desperate before he throws in his hand,' said Steve in some trepidation. 'I very much doubt if he'll let you take him alive.'

'That's his lookout, surely,' said Temple blandly.

'Don't be so confident, darling. Remember what a narrow escape we had when *The Marquis* set fire to the October Hotel[3].'

Temple smiled pleasantly.

'Kindly concentrate on your knitting, Steve – it looks even more shapeless than ever!'

And he went back to his study.

The following morning, Temple collected his mail from the usual table in the hall. Running rapidly through them, he stopped and looked again at an envelope that bore the Hampstead postmark and a typewritten address. He paused to examine the typed characters, then quickly thrust the letter into his coat pocket, carrying the others with him to read at the breakfast table. It was not until he was alone in his study after breakfast that he read the typewritten letter. Then he refolded it very carefully and replaced it in his pocket. Whatever its contents, they did not seem to interfere with his day's work, for he typed industriously until tea-time, with only a short break for lunch.

Sir Graham Forbes arrived for dinner, looking more worried than ever. Temple guessed that Lord Flexdale had once more been agitating for results. Although the death of Carol Reagan had not been given front-page publicity – the inquest had been held at short notice and only one reporter was present – Lord Flexdale had read the private reports and was pressing his subordinates for tangible results. Forbes said

---

[3] See *Paul Temple Intervenes*

very little during dinner, though he commented favourably on Ricky's cooking.

'Where did you pick up that boy of yours?' he asked Temple. 'Appeared on the scene rather suddenly, didn't he?'

'You'd better ask Steve,' smiled Temple. 'She produced him out of the bag – all I have to do is pay his wages.'

'He makes very good coffee, too,' said Steve, as she rose to go and tell Ricky they were ready for it. Temple and Sir Graham made their way to the lounge and settled in armchairs on either side of the fire. Sir Graham lit his favourite pipe and puffed a huge cloud of smoke towards the fireplace.

'It was a great pity about the girl in brown, Temple,' he said at length. 'A great pity. I was just running through Crane's report before I came. Quite a mysterious affair, that. Pity she didn't come to us sooner. Did you ever actually see her alive?'

Temple shook his head.

'Crane tells me she was quite well-known in the States – used to work with Jeff Myers. I read about him several times when he was with the F.B.I – one of their star men.'

'Yes,' said Temple, 'I knew of Myers. Rather a queer bird, but he gets a lot of results. Not always by strictly legal means, but then one can't blame him for that until one knows the circumstances.'

'No, I suppose not. All the same, it's a pity this girl tried to take a leaf out of his book. That fanciful idea of hers, trailing people around and all that nonsense. It just doesn't work out over here unless there's police organisation behind it. Have you any theory as to what happened that night she came to see you here?'

'I don't know,' Temple confessed. 'But she obviously had something pretty important to tell me.'

'Any idea what it was?'

'Yes,' replied Temple slowly. 'I think perhaps I have, Sir Graham.'

Sir Graham sat up in his chair and began to look interested.

'But first of all,' continued Temple, 'I want you to take a look at this letter that came by first post this morning. Don't let Steve see it if she comes in.' He passed over the envelope.

Forbes took out his reading glasses and opened the letter.

'It's from Rex!' he ejaculated in a startled voice.

'Yes, he seems to have got round to me at last,' said Temple calmly.

Forbes started to read.

If you value your life, Mr. Temple, stop interfering! This is my first and last warning. Rex.

'Short and to the point,' smiled Temple. Forbes glanced at the envelope.

'Posted in Hampstead, I see,' he commented.

'Yes. But it was typed on the usual machine – the one at Canterbury.'

'That's a very queer set-up down there,' mused Sir Graham. 'I'm glad you decided to tell me why you went in the first place, but I still can't make up my mind as to whether it was a good idea sending your friend down there.'

'You needn't have any qualms, not as far as Leo Brent is concerned,' Temple assured him. 'He knows his way around.'

''M,' murmured Sir Graham somewhat sceptically. 'When did he go down?'

'The day before yesterday.'

Sir Graham considered this thoughtfully for a few moments, then said:

'I have a feeling I ought to send someone reliable from the Yard – Bradley or Crane perhaps. You see, Temple, if this hotel really is Rex's headquarters, he may have quite an organisation there, and your one man couldn't possibly cope with it.'

'Please don't do anything yet,' begged Temple. 'I'm taking this chance with Brent because I want to catch them off their guard if possible. Then if there should be a chance of running Rex to earth, Leo will give us the tip and we can concentrate on Canterbury right away. But if Rex and Co. catch sight of a man who looks the least bit like a police officer, well they'll just transfer their headquarters over-night, and we'll have the devil of a job to track 'em down again.'

'There may be something in that,' Forbes conceded. 'Have you heard from this man of yours?'

'Yes – he 'phoned this morning.'

'Bit risky, isn't it? I mean, how d'you know the wires aren't tapped?'

'He goes to a public call-box.'

'And what's he got to say? Anything happening?'

'Not yet. He seemed a bit dubious, as a matter of fact. Everything appeared so normal at the hotel, he found it hard to believe there could be anything underhand going on there.'

Just then Steve came in with the coffee, and the conversation became general. Presently, the telephone rang, and Temple glanced quickly at his watch.

'That's probably Brent,' he announced. 'If you'd like to listen on the extension, Sir Graham, it's in the study.'

Steve rose to show him the way, but he urged her to sit down again, and went out quietly as Temple lifted the receiver.

'Hello, Paul,' said a distant voice that was somewhat indistinct.

237

'That you, Leo?'

'Yeah, it's me.'

'Well, how's things?'

'Pretty dull,' was the laconic reply. 'Say, don't think I'm fussy, Paul, but does anything ever happen down here?'

'You sound rather pessimistic,' replied Temple. 'Even more so than this morning.'

'Yeah, there's been quite a deep depression set in around here since this morning. This place gives me the willies.'

'You've seen our friend?' asked Temple.

'Sure. I've been tailing him night and day. But he doesn't seem to do anything except play golf and run the hotel. Say, Paul, are you sure you're not barking up the wrong tree?'

'Quite sure,' replied Temple positively. 'All the same, maybe you'd better come back to Town, and I'll make some other arrangements.'

'Suits me,' was the prompt reply. 'I'll see you tomorrow. Give you a ring when I arrive. Good night, Paul.'

There was a very thoughtful expression on Temple's face as he replaced the receiver. Steve noticed it at once.

'What's the matter, darling?' she asked quickly. 'Has anything gone wrong?' The door opened and Forbes came in.

He said: 'I'm afraid I'm not very impressed by your friend Brent, Temple.'

'That,' murmured Temple, 'was not my friend Brent.' He spoke slowly, and his thoughts were obviously elsewhere.

'Here, what's this, Temple?' protested Forbes. 'He said he was Brent, and he certainly had an American accent.'

'That man wasn't Leo Brent,' repeated Temple, his voice becoming rather more tense.

'Well, what's going on?' asked Forbes in a puzzled tone. 'If it wasn't Brent, who the devil was it?'

'I don't know. But I'm sure it wasn't Leo.'

'What makes you so certain, darling?' demanded Steve curiously.

'Because he kept calling me Paul. Leo never does that. Right from the first day I knew him, he has always called me Temple.'

Forbes ventured a mild protest that Temple might be mistaken, but his host waved it aside.

'Steve, tell Ricky to pack me a bag right away,' he continued urgently.

'You—you don't mean you're going to Canterbury?' queried Forbes incredulously.

'I certainly do, Sir Graham.'

'But surely it isn't as important as all that. I mean, you've no definite proof.'

'I'm sorry to disagree, Sir Graham,' said Temple, making for the door, 'but I consider it a matter of life and death!'

An hour later, Temple and Steve were through the outer suburbs and heading for Canterbury at fifty miles an hour.

'I'm afraid Sir Graham thinks this trip rather childish,' said Steve. 'And it was rather rude of us, walking out on him.'

'But we left him the whisky and Ricky for company,' her husband pointed out, straining his eyes to discern the road ahead.

'I hope it doesn't turn out to be a wild-goose chase after all,' said Steve.

'In a way, I should be relieved if it did.'

'But Sir Graham seemed to think—'

'Sir Graham is very tired, darling. This case has worn him down a lot, and he isn't quite as quick on the uptake at this time in the evening as he used to be. That's why I didn't suggest he should come with us. We can always telephone him if we need help. Besides, a whole gang of us might have aroused suspicion – at least more than just the two of us.'

When they arrived at the Royal Falcon, the receptionist gave them the key to the room which Temple had reserved on the telephone before they started. However, when Temple asked if he could see Mr. Chester, the clerk replied rather surprisingly that he was on holiday, having departed that afternoon, and would be away for a few days.

They had just turned to follow the porter to their room when they encountered the familiar stocky figure of Wilfred Davis descending the stairs.

'Why, hallo, Mr. Temple – Mrs. Temple, too – how nice to see you again,' he said. But his voice and manner were rather more subdued than usual. His suit looked somewhat untidy and he was badly needing a shave.

'I thought we might bump into you,' said Temple, leaning against the banisters.

'Yes, of course,' smiled Steve. 'You told us you were coming down here again soon the last time we saw you.'

She hesitated, then asked: 'Have you been ill, Mr. Davis?'

'Yes,' replied Davis quietly. 'I'm afraid I have been a bit under the weather, as the saying goes.'

'I'm sorry to hear that,' said Steve.

'But it's nice to see you down here,' said Davis, brightening perceptibly.

He hesitated for a moment, then asked: 'Will you be staying long?'

'Just for one night, I think,' replied Temple quietly, watching the Welshman's face.

'I see,' he murmured. 'We may meet tomorrow morning at breakfast, perhaps.'

'By all means,' smiled Temple. 'We're in number thirty-two, if you should want to find us.'

Davis acknowledged the information with a polite nod, and wished them good night.

Temple and Steve found their room without much difficulty. As soon as they were inside, Temple closed the door and said in a low voice: 'Wait here, Steve, till the boy comes with the cases. I shan't be long.'

'Where are you going?' she demanded anxiously.

'Down to Leo's room. It's on the next floor.'

'You've got the number?'

'Yes – fourteen. I shouldn't be more than five minutes at the very outside.'

'But the odds are that he won't be there.'

'Yes, I dare say. But I've got to find out.'

'You mean whether he's left a message of some sort?'

'That's right – remember – it's all done by mirrors!'

'Well, I'm glad we came, anyway,' said Steve. 'You were quite right, of course, darling. That couldn't have been Leo Brent on the 'phone. If it had been, he would have told you about Chester going away.'

'That's true,' he nodded. 'Shan't be long.'

He went out quickly and along the corridor. When he came to Brent's room, he found the door locked, but it presented few difficulties, for it was a Yale lock, and he opened it with a strip of mica which he carried for such emergencies. After looking round cautiously to see if he were observed, Temple went in and shut the door. Two minutes later he was back in his own room.

Steve was very startled as he opened the door, but recovered at once.

'Did you get anything?' she asked.

241

'Yes,' he replied, slightly out of breath, 'there was a note behind the mirror. I haven't stopped to read it yet.'

'Did anyone see you?'

'I don't think so. Not many people about just now.'

He tore open the rather grimy envelope which he had found tucked away behind the mirror, where it had picked up a certain amount of dust.

The note had been written very hastily in pencil and it took Temple a little time to decipher the somewhat cryptic scrawl. It said:

Dear Temple,
This is just in case I can't 'phone you tonight, as arranged, things having brisked up a bit since this morning's call. I caught sight of Chester leaving the hotel this morning, and followed him to an unpleasant spot called Claywood Mill. This mill is supposed to be derelict, and it's certainly no place for a picnic! Anyhow, I have a pretty good idea that it's here that Chester meets Rex. The mill is about sixteen miles from Faversham and four from Moondale. It stands by the side of a wood near the cross-roads; you can't miss it. I overheard Chester tell the receptionist that he would be out again this afternoon, so I shall be on the trail. I don't think he's caught sight of me yet. Keep your fingers crossed!
Leo.

Temple passed the paper over to Steve, who tried to decipher the scrawl.

'Claywood Mill,' he repeated thoughtfully. 'Steve, d'you remember that night we found Spider Williams?'

'You mean down that awful lane?'

'That's right. Before we got back on to the main road we passed a wood on the left. The mist cleared a bit I remember, and there was a moon just then. I distinctly recall seeing a very ancient mill with a water wheel.'

'Well, if Leo went to the mill this afternoon, he should have been back hours ago,' said Steve. 'I asked the porter when he brought the luggage if he's seen anything of Mr. Brent, and he said he went out soon after lunch and hadn't returned. So it looks—'

'It does!' said Temple grimly. 'Is the torch in the side pocket of the car?'

'Yes, I put it there myself – and a spare battery.'

'Good. Then you'd better get your coat on, Steve. And change into a thicker pair of shoes if you've brought some.'

'Yes, of course. But, Paul – where are we going?'

'Where d'you think we're going?' he retorted grimly. 'To Claywood Mill!'

It was a brilliant moonlight night when they set out. They were both muffled in overcoats and scarves for the night was frosty. Steve could not repress a shudder as they turned down the lane and passed the spot where they had found Spider Williams.

Temple pulled up in the shadow of some trees which overhung the road. Away to the left they could see the derelict mill silhouetted in the moonlight, and even an unimaginative person might have considered its appearance somewhat uninviting. As they left the car, a church clock was striking midnight, and away in the distance a dog was howling at the moon.

They discovered a rough cart track leading in the direction of the mill, but it was very muddy, so they walked silently on the grass. Temple carried his torch but did not use it, as he did not wish to risk attracting any attention from a possible occupant of the mill. Presently, they could see the tumbledown structure quite distinctly, and then they got a view of the old water wheel which the waters of the small stream now swept past in undisturbed silence. It was the sort of scene favoured by water-colour artists on fine summer days, but on a winter's night it had an eerie aspect to which few visitors could have remained impervious.

'I can't imagine anyone living here,' whispered Steve with a slight shudder.

'It looks as if no one has for quite a while.'

When they came up to the mill, they found that to reach the door they had to cross a decrepit wooden bridge which looked as if it might collapse beneath the next flood. Temple cautiously placed a foot on it to see if it would take his weight.

'Are you sure it's safe, Paul?' asked Steve nervously.

'Well, if the worst comes to the worst, we shall only get a wetting,' he replied. 'I should imagine the water isn't more than four feet deep at the most.'

He extended a hand to her, for the bridge had no handrail of any description. A step at a time they cautiously made their way over, and eventually reached the other side,

'Thank goodness for that!' exclaimed Steve with a tiny sigh of relief.

'Don't look so pleased,' he murmured. 'We've still got to get back!'

They looked up at the gaunt structure which now seemed to tower above them, and they walked slowly round it. When they came to the water-wheel, Temple climbed up on to the little platform at the side of it.

'Looks as if it hasn't been used for centuries,' Steve commented.

'I'm not so sure about that,' he replied, leaning over and examining the wheel closely. Testing his foothold, he edged his way towards the centre, and suddenly producing his torch, shielded the light and focused it beneath his gloved hand.

'This wheel has been used quite recently,' he told Steve when he returned. 'There's oil right across the crankshaft.'

'But what on earth could it have been used for?' demanded Steve in a puzzled tone.

'That's one of the things we have to find out. There seems to be a crude sort of pump at the end of the platform there, the pipe leads inside—'

'Perhaps that's how the previous tenant got his water supply,' Steve suggested as they moved towards the door.

'Well, it seems about time we took a look inside,' said Temple, lifting the latch. At first he thought the door was locked, but it yielded slightly under pressure, and he realised that it was badly warped by the damp.

He managed to open it about a foot, and they squeezed in. The atmosphere was musty, and the moonlight filtering through a small grimy window showed a bare room which they found surprisingly small. There was no furniture of any sort, but there was a pile of sacks in one corner, a couple of boxes in another and a rough ladder which presumably led to a loft or upstairs room. As they walked in there was a tiny scuffling sound and Steve gripped her husband's arm tightly. They stood for a moment or two to get their bearings. Temple grasped his torch in his left hand and his right was closed over his revolver. But he did not use the torch immediately.

Once again there was a scuffling noise, and they held their breath and stood silently in the shadows. Then Temple began to make his way cautiously round the room, moving a foot or two at a time very slowly, in case any of the floorboards were rotten.

'What was that?' exclaimed Steve suddenly.

Once more they stood and listened. Beneath their feet they could hear a queer strangled noise that might have been a man's voice, or yet again might have emanated from an animal in pain.

'It's coming from down below,' said Steve softly.

Temple dropped on to his knees and was presently able to hear what sounded like a cry for help, very faint and muffled.

'By Timothy! I believe it's Brent!' he exclaimed. Once again they heard the cry, this time more distinctly.

'Leo!' he shouted. 'Leo! Where are you?'

'In the cellar,' came the muffled reply. 'Down below in the cellar.'

Temple switched on his torch and a couple of seconds later he located an iron ring in the middle of the floor. He clasped it with both hands and wrenched at it desperately. Then he noticed that the trapdoor was secured by a long bolt at the side. When he had released this, he was able to lift the trap without very much difficulty.

'Is that you, Temple?' came a weak voice from out of the darkness. Temple flashed the torch around the cellar, and located Brent lying in a distant corner. His hair was very dishevelled, his face pale under a coating of grime, and he was lying in a peculiar position as if he was suffering considerable pain.

'All right, Leo, I'm coming down,' said Temple quickly. He started to climb down the narrow ladder which was hooked to the ceiling of the cellar.

'Do be careful, Paul,' urged Steve in some trepidation.

'Are you hurt, Leo?' he asked as he climbed down.

'I'll say!' sighed the weary voice. 'I've caught a packet all right. Busted my right leg. Gee! Am I glad to see you!'

Temple shone his torch on the clammy walls and cobwebbed ceiling as he made his way over to the corner. He bent down and looked at Brent's leg.

'I'm afraid it's broken, old man,' he murmured presently.

'You're telling me!' winced Brent. Temple noticed that perspiration was dripping from his forehead, and had made grotesque streaks through the grime on his face.

'Boy! Am I glad to see you!' he repeated in a hoarse whisper. 'I was just about giving up all hope of ever seeing daylight again.' Then he struggled to prop himself on his elbow, and asked, 'But say, how come you got wise to this place, anyway?'

Temple looked down at him, somewhat surprised.

'I got your note.'

'Note?' queried Brent in some mystification.

'That's right. The one you stuck behind the mirror.'

Brent looked even more bewildered.

'Are you kiddin'?' he asked slowly.

Temple took the paper from his pocket and passed it over, holding the torch so that Brent could read it.

'This isn't my writing,' said the injured man at once. 'You should have known that, Temple.'

'It's years since I saw your writing – I'd forgotten—' Temple admitted. 'All the same, it's just as well—'

He broke off as there came the sound of a woman's scream.

Temple rushed to the foot of the ladder.

'Steve!' He had only climbed a couple of rungs when the trapdoor slammed down heavily and he heard the bolt shot.

There were sounds of struggling, but Steve's screams had obviously been stifled. Temple ran up to the top of the ladder

247

and tried to lift the trapdoor. Time and again he strained frantically but without avail. Brent tried to struggle into an upright position.

'If only I could get up—' he whispered.

Temple continued to beat on the door and shout to Steve, but there was silence in the room above now. Suddenly, Temple's cries were interrupted by the harsh whirring sound of a dynamo.

'Temple! What's that?' called Brent weakly.

Temple came back slowly down the ladder, listening intently.

From the far side of the wall came a gentle swishing sound and a loud rumble.

'It's – it's the wheel!' exclaimed Temple, switching off his torch, and standing at the foot of the ladder.

'The water-wheel!' said Brent. 'Say, what in hell is the big idea? What are those devils up to?'

Temple looked round desperately without replying. He was seeking for something to batter open the trapdoor, but the cellar was bare of any suitable instrument. Presently, Brent called softly: 'Hey, Temple! The floor's wet! There's water coming from somewhere—'

Temple switched on his torch and saw pools of water forming round his feet.

He swung the beam quickly round the walls, and picked out a small grating near the ceiling. Water was pouring through it in a steady stream.

'Temple! They're pumping water into the cellar! They're flooding the place!'

There was a note of terror in Brent's voice now.

Temple leapt to the top of the ladder again and began to beat upon the trapdoor.

'We'll be drowned like rats!' cried Brent. 'It's coming in faster now! There's a couple of inches of water already!'

Once more Temple hammered at the trapdoor.

'My God! They can't leave us like this! They can't . . .' gasped Brent in a dazed voice. Suddenly, his head dropped. Obviously, the pain he had endured and the present ordeal had been too much for him . . .

The grinding of the water-wheel was the only sound which broke the silence.

CHAPTER XV

Forbes to the Rescue

AFTER Paul Temple and Steve had left, Forbes lay back in his armchair and gazed thoughtfully into the fire. To Forbes there was a certain unknown element in Rex's make-up, something which he almost feared as many men approaching old age fear some innovation which may disrupt their daily lives. Forbes had contended with all types in his day, but most of the criminals had been of the more leisurely and casual type. Rex's high pressure methods of dealing in wholesale blackmail were outside Forbes' experience, and he found them almost as terrifying as the advent of the gangsters to Chicago. It was Rex's elusive qualities which baffled Forbes, who was more than capable of dealing with the average criminal mentality by his relentless routine methods. He even welcomed a dangerous situation if it was likely to provide an ultimate solution to a crime. But the manner in which Rex brought off his coups at lightning speed, leaving no clue and no obvious hint of a motive, had Forbes continually groping in the dark, clutching at the slightest clue, which as often as not turned out to have been planted by Rex himself.

One after another, Forbes reviewed his suspects. Mr. Trevelyan, Doctor Kohima. That little Welsh fellow . . . The trouble with these blackmail cases there was so much complicated lying. Forbes knew only too well that even highly respectable people told the most insidious lies under the pressure of the blackmailer. Having achieved a position in society, they strove desperately to maintain it.

Now there was this new complication, reflected Sir Graham. If that had been a faked telephone call from Canterbury as Temple suggested, then Temple and Steve were going down to Canterbury alone, probably to encounter Rex himself. Of course, it may have been only a ruse to draw Temple away from London, but in the light of that letter he'd received it looked as if Rex was out to remove Temple from his path.

Forbes started when he suddenly heard a polite voice inquire if he would like another drink. He turned and saw Ricky, who had entered noiselessly, standing at his side with hands folded and a deferential smile. Forbes levered himself upright.

'No, thanks, Ricky,' he replied, 'I've got to be getting along.'

At the door, he hesitated, then said:

'If Mr. Temple should telephone and you – er – you think it's anything urgent, you had better ring up Scotland Yard at once.'

Ricky inclined his head.

'Very good, Sir Graham. I will see to it,' he replied gravely.

Forbes eyed him dubiously for a moment, then went on his way.

On arrival at the Yard, he went straight to the room where Mrs. Trevelyan was being kept in custody.

It was quite comfortably furnished, and Mrs. Trevelyan was sitting in an armchair reading when Forbes entered.

She looked up anxiously.

'Is he all right?' she demanded eagerly.

For a moment it did not occur to Forbes that she was referring to Doctor Kohima. His thoughts were still on Temple, and he replied mechanically:

'Oh yes – he's just gone to Canterbury.'

Mrs. Trevelyan leapt to her feet.

'No!' she cried. 'Not the Royal Falcon Hotel! You mustn't let him!'

Without enlightening her, Forbes asked quickly: 'What do you know about the Royal Falcon?'

'Nothing except that the letters come from there. The letters from Rex. Sir Graham, why should Doctor Kohima—'

'It's all right, Mrs. Trevelyan,' replied Forbes curtly. 'It isn't Doctor Kohima who's gone down to Canterbury – it's Mr. and Mrs. Temple.'

An obvious look of relief relaxed her tired features.

'Oh well, I daresay Mr. Temple can take care of himself,' she said rather doubtfully.

'Are you quite sure there's nothing else you can tell me about the Royal Falcon?' persisted Sir Graham. She shook her head.

'When are you going to release me?' she asked presently.

Forbes shrugged.

'Very soon, I hope. I hope you appreciate that I am keeping you here chiefly for your own safety.'

'And also because you wish to prevent Rex from blackmailing me again – or trying to?' she suggested.

'Next time, he might not be content with blackmail,' said Forbes.

She shuddered. Then a thought struck her.

'Do you think he might try to contact Doctor Kohima?' she asked nervously.

'I've thought of that,' he answered. 'Two of my best men are keeping a close watch.'

She gripped the arms of her chair until her knuckles showed white.

'I do hope he'll be all right,' she whispered.

'If you two would stop worrying about each other, it might simplify matters quite a lot,' said Forbes, going to the door.

Still feeling vaguely disturbed about Temple and Steve, having been denied the assurance he had actually sought from Mrs. Trevelyan, he went along to Crane's office, where he found the inspector going through some earlier reports connected with the case. After some hesitation, Forbes told Crane what had happened at the Temples' flat that evening.

Crane immediately began to look serious.

'You mean Mr. and Mrs. Temple have gone to Canterbury alone?' he asked at last.

Forbes nodded.

'I don't like the sound of it, sir,' said Crane. 'Think I'd better get through to Mason down there and just check up—'

'No!' replied Forbes with sudden resolution. 'You and I will go down there.'

'You mean now?' queried Crane, a little surprised.

'No time to be lost. Ring down for a car, will you?'

'Certainly,' agreed Crane, picking up the receiver and giving the necessary instructions.

Sir Graham and Crane left the car at a garage near the Royal Falcon Hotel, and walked round to the front entrance. It was dark now, but they could not fail to recognise a familiar figure leaving the hotel.

'It's that Welsh fellow,' exclaimed Forbes, gripping the inspector's arm. They watched Davis get into a small touring car.

'He's heading for the Faversham road,' said Crane.

'Come on, Crane, we'll follow him,' said Forbes, making a snap decision. 'I've a feeling he's up to something.'

They surprised the garage attendant by demanding their car again.

In a very short time the fast police car had the tourer in sight.

Paul Temple slowly climbed back down the ladder and tried to review the situation, but the throbbing of the water-wheel and a gentle gurgling of incoming waters seemed to prevent him from thinking clearly. If he had been on his own it wouldn't have seemed so bad; but the unconscious form of Brent in the distant corner was an added burden that seemed quite overwhelming. He went over to Brent and managed to prop him upright. As he did so, the American opened his eyes and seemed to recover a little.

'Say, this is one heck of a situation,' he whispered. 'What are we going to do, Temple?'

Temple looked round in desperation, then said: 'I'll have to get you over to that ladder, Leo – the water's rising pretty fast. Think you can manage to hold on?'

'Think you can carry me?' replied Brent with a rueful smile. 'Guess I weigh the best part of hundred and sixty pounds.'

'We'll have a shot, anyhow,' said Temple, stooping down. 'Lock your hands round my neck, Leo, say when you're ready for me to lift.'

It proved to be more of an effort for Brent than for Temple. Brent's leg was agonisingly painful, and he fainted twice and slid back into the water before they finally completed their journey.

At the foot of the ladder, Temple said: 'I'll have to lift you up somehow, Leo, even if it is one rung at a time! I only hope to goodness it holds!'

Temple was about to make his first effort, for the water was over a foot deep by this time, when he imagined he heard a footstep above.

'Did you hear that?' he asked Brent.

'No,' gasped the American, 'I can only hear that damned water!'

Temple listened again, then suddenly shouted at the top of his voice. From the room above there came an answering hail.

'By Timothy! It's Forbes!' cried Temple, lifting his voice once more and calling: 'Sir Graham! Sir Graham!'

He ran to the top of the ladder and beat upon the trap-door. Almost at once, the bolt shot back, and Temple saw Forbes and Crane looking down at them.

'Where's Steve?' was Temple's first question.

'She's all right,' Forbes told him. 'She's out in the fresh air, she fainted—'

'I've got Brent down here! His leg's broken – we'll have to get him up somehow,' explained Temple jerkily.

'It's all right, Mr. Temple,' put in Crane. 'I've got a rope here – I'll come down . . .'

Temple descended the ladder again and Crane joined him, paying out the rope which Sir Graham held from above. Crane tied it neatly under Brent's arms, then with the help of Temple lifted him on to his stocky shoulders. As Crane slowly ascended the ladder, Sir Graham took a good deal of the weight of his burden on the rope. The water was pouring in by this time, and when Temple followed them up the ladder, it was over four feet deep. In another twenty minutes or so they would have been drowned. While they were sitting on the floor recovering from their exertions, Steve came in, walking a trifle uncertainly. She was overcome with relief on seeing her husband, and both she and Temple started talking simultaneously, while Crane began to contrive an amateurish splint for Brent's leg.

'I was watching you go down the cellar, Paul,' explained Steve breathlessly, 'when somebody suddenly came up behind and put their hand over my face.'

'A man's hand?' queried Temple.

'Oh yes – no doubt about that. I nearly screamed myself hoarse . . .'

'We heard you, darling,' he told her with a slight smile.

'You didn't see this man, Steve?' asked Forbes.

'No, I'm afraid I didn't. He put a handkerchief over my face – I think it had chloroform or something on it. The next I remember was Inspector Crane here shaking my shoulder – he carried me outside and I soon came round . . .'

'How did you get here, Inspector?' asked Temple curiously.

Crane paused a moment in his efforts to fashion a splint and said, 'Better ask Sir Graham.'

'Well, Sir Graham?' said Temple.

'It's rather a long story, Temple,' replied Forbes. 'But the person who actually brought us this last stage of the journey was your old friend, Wilfred Davis.'

'Good Lord!' exclaimed Temple softly. 'You mean you followed him here?'

'Yes, and he must be still around somewhere unless he's made a getaway. We lost trace of him just as we found Steve.'

'Sir Graham, d'you think we ought to go and search for him?' began Crane, looking up from the splints.

Forbes waved this aside.

'We can pull him in any time we want him. I've got the number of his car, and we can circulate an accurate description.'

'You don't think Davis is Rex, do you, Mr. Temple?' inquired Crane curiously. 'I had my suspicions of Doctor Kohima, but now I'm not so sure.'

'Shall I help you with the bandage, Inspector?' asked Steve. 'Oh – and here's some smelling-salts, Leo.'

'Thanks, Steve,' said Brent gratefully. He sniffed and seemed much more comfortable. In fact, he began to join in the conversation, and murmured:

'Say, I'm beginning to get pretty interested in this case of yours, Temple. It gets better as it goes on.' He paused, then added softly, 'I suppose, Temple, you wouldn't have any idea who this fellow Rex is?'

'Nobody knows that, Mr. Brent,' snapped Forbes.

'Do you, Temple?' persisted Brent. There was a noticeable pause.

'Yes,' said Temple at last. 'I know.'

It seemed to be a second or two before Sir Graham appreciated the implications of Temple's reply.

'Darling,' said Steve anxiously, 'are you sure you're all right? It isn't like you to make rash statements, and I don't see how you can possibly—'

'Temple, are you serious!' broke in Forbes incredulously.

'This is no time for ribbing,' protested Brent, with a slight gasp as Crane began to apply the splints.

'I hope I'm serious,' Temple declared evenly. 'I never felt more serious than I do at this minute. I've suspected someone for quite a long time. Now I know for certain that I'm right.'

'Say, you've got a nerve, laying the law down to Sir Graham and the inspector,' grinned Brent. 'Go on, you two – why don't you call his bluff?'

'Go on, Mr. Temple,' challenged Crane. 'Who is Rex?'

'Are we ready to go?' said Temple. 'I think the sooner we get Brent to hospital—'

'He can wait five minutes while you tell us who Rex is,' snapped Crane.

'Yes, if you've got anything up your sleeve, Temple,' said Forbes rather anxiously, 'I think you ought to tell us. Time may be valuable.'

'Don't worry, Sir Graham, I shall be only too pleased to introduce you to Rex *in person in the near future*,' Temple assured him. 'Perhaps if you and the inspector dropped into the flat tonight – would eight o'clock be too early?'

'We'll be there, of course,' said Sir Graham, 'but how do you know Rex will?'

'Because,' replied Temple urbanely, '*I propose to invite him!*'

CHAPTER XVI

Appointment with Rex

TEMPLE stood in front of the bedroom mirror brushing his hair and whistling softly to himself, pausing occasionally to puff at the cigarette which lay in the ashtray on his dressing-table.

'You look very pleased with yourself,' commented Steve from the other side of the room, where she was carefully applying lipstick.

'I feel very pleased with myself,' he retorted, brushing away more furiously than ever.

She swung round and looked across at him.

'Your hair looks very nice, darling – there's no need to keep brushing,' she assured him.

'I know, dear, but I like the sensation. And it is supposed to be good for the hair,' he informed her. He laid down a brush and picked up a shapeless bundle of wool which was lying under the mirror.

'Hullo, what's this?' he asked.

'It's my knitting,' said Steve, coming over to claim it.

'Your knitting turns up in the most extraordinary places!'

Temple went to the door and called to Ricky, who came hurrying out of the kitchen.

'Did you get that bottle of gin, Ricky?' asked Temple.

'Yes, sir,' said Ricky blandly. 'And a bottle of sherry, a bottle of port, a bottle of whisky and a bottle of Italian.'

'Good Lord,' exclaimed Temple. 'We could practically open a night club!' He called over his shoulder to Steve, 'Darling, I think Ricky had better do all the shopping!'

'Shall you be wanting anything more this evening, sir?' asked Ricky.

'Anything more? Well, I think we shall do pretty reasonably if we dispose of that little lot.'

'He means can he go now,' explained Steve. 'It's Ricky's night out.'

Temple appeared to be slightly taken aback.

'Did you wish me to stay in tonight, sir, to help with your guests?' asked Ricky politely.

'Well, if you could manage it just this once, Ricky, I'd be extremely grateful.'

'Not at all, sir. I stay with pleasure,' grinned Ricky.

Temple closed the bedroom door and turned to Steve. 'I'm certainly getting some new angles on the servant problem,' he smiled.

'Had you any special reason for wanting Ricky to stay?' she asked. 'I could have managed quite well, you know.'

'Well, Ricky has been a trifle involved in this business from time to time,' said Temple. 'And knowing his interest in such things I thought he might – as a student of criminology—'

'I don't believe you,' broke in Steve. 'Did you spend half an hour getting through to Mr. Davis at the Royal Falcon Hotel this morning to invite him here as a student of criminology?'

'Well, he is. You've heard him say so often enough,' protested Temple stoutly.

'You've got something up your sleeve,' said Steve.

'Yes,' smiled her husband, 'and I shouldn't be surprised if it turns out to be your knitting!'

There was a gentle tap on the door, and Ricky's voice said:

'Sir Graham Forbes and Inspector Crane have arrived with Mr. Lathom.'

'All right, Ricky,' called Temple. 'We'll be out in a moment.'

'Mr. Lathom?' queried Steve. 'Another student of criminology?'

'Now, darling,' said Temple reproachfully, 'you know Lathom has been mixed up in this affair, just as much as Ricky and Davis. Come along, darling, before he finishes the whisky.'

They found the three men in the lounge engaged in animated conversation which ceased rather abruptly as Temple and Steve came in.

After greeting his guests, Temple went over to the sideboard and began to pour out drinks. Forbes went on chatting to Lathom, while Crane, rather surprisingly, inquired as to Steve's health, and whether she had recovered from the effects of her ordeal.

'I've had a 'phone call from Rochester just before we left the Yard,' he told her. 'They've picked up Chester at a lodging-house there. Seems it's an old haunt of his. Seems as if the Royal Falcon will have to look for a new manager.'

'And what about Wilfred Davis?' asked Steve.

'Well, Mrs. Temple, it couldn't have been Davis who attacked you, and we've nothing really definite against him – except that he seemed to know what was going on at Claywood Mill. Mr. Temple seemed to think we should give him a bit more rope in a manner of speaking.'

'We're expecting him here tonight,' said Steve. 'My husband 'phoned him at the Royal Falcon this morning.'

'H'm, so he didn't try to make a getaway,' mused Crane. 'I wonder if he'd be the man who tipped us off about Chester.'

'What do you mean?' asked Steve.

'In the early hours of this morning, the sergeant on duty at the Yard got an anonymous 'phone call – we get dozens of 'em – saying that Frank Chester could be picked up at a certain lodging-house in Rochester.'

'It might have been Rex himself,' Steve suggested. 'After all, he did worse than that with Mrs. Trevelyan, and—'

Crane slapped his knee.

'I never thought of that, Mrs. Temple. And if Davis followed Chester after he got away from the mill . . .' He began to look puzzled again.

'I shouldn't worry about it too much if I were you, Inspector,' said Steve, who was beginning to feel that Inspector Crane wasn't quite as churlish as she had first imagined. Their conversation was interrupted by the front-door buzzer, and Temple called: 'Just finish mixing this cocktail, darling.'

He went to open the door. Steve took the cocktail shaker rather dubiously.

'I'm not very good at this sort of thing,' she said.

'Allow me, Mrs. Temple,' said Lathom, coming over to her. He took the shaker and eyed it critically.

'You seem quite an expert, Mr. Lathom,' said Steve.

'One of the signs of a misspent youth in the roaring 'twenties,' he replied with a smile.

Steve went across to Sir Graham, who was standing on the hearthrug looking faintly perplexed.

'I expect that will be Mrs. Trevelyan and Doctor Kohima,' he told her. 'I've released her for this evening at Temple's

264

special request, Steve. He seemed to think they ought to be here, though I must say I don't altogether like it.'

'Well, whether they're guilty or not, they are implicated in the case, aren't they, Sir Graham?' said Steve brightly, unconsciously using her husband's argument.

Outside in the hall, Temple welcomed Doctor Kohima and Mrs. Trevelyan quite informally, for he noticed that they seemed more than a trifle suspicious and ill at ease.

'What did you want to see us about, Mr. Temple?' asked Mrs. Trevelyan in a nervous voice.

'Now, there's no need to worry,' he reassured her. 'It's just a friendly little party—'

'But I understood that you wanted to have a confidential chat with just the two of us,' interrupted Kohima.

'Well, come and have a drink anyway,' urged Temple, ushering them into the lounge, where Forbes looked up and nodded pleasantly. Steve went over to Mrs. Trevelyan at once, found a chair for her and asked her what she would like to drink.

'Here's your gin, Temple,' called Lathom, who was busily dispensing drinks in his host's absence.

'Thanks, Lathom.'

The front-door buzzer sounded again, and still carrying his glass, Temple went out to answer it. The presence of Doctor Kohima and Mrs. Trevelyan had a depressing effect on the conversation, which began to lag until Kohima said abruptly: 'Sir Graham, why did Mr. Temple send for us like this? What exactly are we doing here?'

Sir Graham shrugged.

'I can only tell you that Temple seems to have a new angle on the Rex case.'

'But what have we got to do with it?' asked Lathom. 'I simply received a note from Temple asking me to call in at eight o'clock this evening as he'd come across something that he thought would interest me.'

'Perhaps it's an idea for a play,' suggested Steve lightly. 'He was saying only the other day that he was surprised you hadn't written another.'

'Well, I know why we're here,' said Crane bluntly, 'and I think you may as well hear the reason now as later. We're here to meet Rex.'

There was a pause. Everyone looked round at the other members of the gathering, but no one spoke, and Crane went on: 'Temple has promised to introduce us to Rex tonight at eight o'clock precisely.'

Outside in the hall, a clock began chiming the hour.

Almost immediately, the door opened and Temple, still carrying his glass, brought in Wilfred Davis, looking very much his old self and obviously as garrulous as ever. He nodded to everybody and smiled at Steve in reply to her pleasant greeting.

'We meet again, Mrs. Temple,' he said. 'Lordy! We always seem to be bumping into each other, don't we?'

Temple introduced the little Welshman to his other guests, several of whom eyed him with considerable suspicion, and it looked as if Crane were going to ask him one or two pertinent questions when Temple drew him away with the remark: 'Before we go any further, you must have a drink, Mr. Davis. I know I could do with one.'

'You've got one, darling, in your hand,' whispered Steve.

'Eh? Oh, so I have,' smiled Temple, passing a glass of port over to Davis. 'Oh well, here's to crime!' He took a gulp at his glass and pulled a wry face. 'Perhaps I shouldn't have said that,' he murmured reflectively. He took another sip, then said, 'No wonder they let Ricky have port and whisky – I hope they're better than this gin.'

'Nothing wrong with the whisky, Temple,' Forbes assured him.

'And this is the nicest drop of port I have tasted for many a day,' declared Davis.

'That's a relief,' smiled Temple. 'All right, let's go into the drawing-room. Bring the drinks, will you, Ricky?' he added to Ricky, who had appeared in answer to his ring. 'And stand by to see all glasses full.'

In the drawing-room they found the chairs disposed in a semi-circle round the blazing fire. Temple saw his guests seated, then leaned against the mantelpiece.

'Ricky, another glass of port for Mr. Davis,' he said.

Ricky obeyed the order, then stood in readiness at the side table by the window.

Temple smiled at them and said quite conversationally: 'Some time ago when I investigated the Marquis affair, I took the liberty of inviting to my flat one evening all the possible suspects in the case – just as I have invited you all here tonight!'

Kohima moved uncomfortably in his chair.

'Does this mean that you think *I* am a possible suspect?' he asked.

'Inspector Crane does, don't you, Inspector?' replied Temple mildly.

'Perhaps I do,' retorted Crane bluffly, 'but you said, Temple, that you were certain you knew who was Rex.'

'Does that mean that Rex is actually here – that he is actually one of us?' queried Mrs. Trevelyan in some bewilderment.

'That's precisely what it means, Mrs. Trevelyan,' Temple calmly informed her. Once again, everybody looked at everybody else.

'Don't you think you owe us an explanation, Mr. Temple?' said Lathom at length.

'Of course I owe you an explanation, and I intend to give you one. But let me begin at the beginning, let me begin, in fact, with suspect number one.'

'Mrs. Trevelyan?' suggested Davis with his familiar rising inflection.

'Oh no,' said Temple with an amused smile. 'Suspect number one happens to be the gentleman present when Norma Rice's body was found – Mr. Wilfred Davis.' He paused for a second, then added softly: 'Alias Mr. Cortwright, alias . . .' once again he hesitated, then declared firmly, 'Jeff Myers.'

'Jeff Myers!' echoed Forbes in amazement.

'You seem surprised, Sir Graham,' said Davis in a voice which betrayed hardly any sign of accent. 'It's true enough,' he went on. 'Since this seems to be the showdown, my name is Jeff Myers, late of the Federal Bureau of Investigation. I came over here about three months ago at the personal request of Sir Ernest Cranbury.'

'The man who was killed in the Brains Trust,' murmured Lathom thoughtfully.

Sir Graham eyed Davis a trifle doubtfully, and asked: 'If you really are Myers, why did Sir Ernest send for you?'

'Surely you don't have to look very far for the answer to that question,' said Doctor Kohima somewhat sarcastically.

'No?' growled Forbes.

'Sir Ernest sent for Mr. Myers for precisely the same reason that you sent for Paul Temple. Simply to catch Rex. Correct me, Mr. Temple, if I'm mistaken.'

'You're quite right, Doctor. Mr. Myers has a reputation in America for investigating cases of a strictly confidential nature. He has his own peculiar methods – as most of us know – but he generally obtains results. So far as Sir Ernest was concerned, this case was strictly confidential.'

'Did you investigate this case alone, Mr. Myers?' demanded Crane slowly.

The American shook his head.

'No,' he replied quietly, 'I had a partner. It was really through her I came over here . . . after she had worked for some time to help Norma Rice, she'd had no luck, so she cabled me and I came over.'

'And the partner in question,' announced Temple, 'was a girl called Carol Reagan, better known to us as the girl in brown!'

Lathom jerked back in his chair.

'Temple, are you serious?' he ejaculated. 'You don't mean that the girl who followed me – and Mrs. Temple too – was nothing but a sort of amateur detective?'

Temple said: 'Hardly an amateur, Mr. Lathom. She was an extremely experienced and very courageous person.'

'But why did she follow me, Paul?' demanded Steve anxiously.

'I can tell you that, Mrs. Temple,' said Myers. 'We knew from the moment Temple took on the case that you would be in danger, and we wanted to make certain that you wouldn't meet with Norma Rice's fate.'

'Didn't you find my name written in the back of Norma Rice's diary?' asked Mrs. Trevelyan suddenly.

'That's true,' nodded Forbes. 'Also on a visiting-card belonging to Richard East.'

Mrs. Trevelyan glanced nervously from Forbes to Temple.

'Do you think I killed Norma Rice and Richard East, Mr. Temple?'

Temple shook his head.

'I know you didn't, Mrs. Trevelyan. For the simple reason that they were murdered by Rex – and you are not Rex!'

With a sigh of relief Mrs. Trevelyan relaxed in her chair. Doctor Kohima caught her hand and held it for a moment.

'Just a minute, Temple,' interposed Crane. 'If Mrs. Trevelyan isn't Rex, perhaps you'll tell us why – explain the reasons for all the strange things we've found out about her these past few weeks.'

Temple moved to a slightly more comfortable position.

'I was coming to that,' he said, quite unruffled by the inspector's challenge. 'Some time ago, Rex hit upon the idea of blackmailing Mrs. Trevelyan into supplying him with certain vital information about Doctor Kohima's patients. He knew he had obtained practically all the money he could extract from her, so he was prepared to take payment in kind. He knew that a psychiatrist would obtain information of an extremely confidential nature in the course of his professional duties. And that he would be bound to keep a record of his patients' – er – eccentricities. At first, Mrs. Trevelyan refused to obey these instructions, so Rex began to put on pressure, and in order to frighten her, he involved her in one or two situations which attracted the suspicions of the police.'

'So that they thought she was Rex,' said Lathom eagerly.

'Exactly, Mr. Lathom. You see, Rex didn't only black-mail people for money, at least not directly. He had a carefully organised plan of campaign which was highly ingenious in its way, making use of various minor victims in a bid for higher stakes. Frank Chester, for instance, was completely under his thumb, and had no alternative but to obey every order implicitly. Mrs. Trevelyan was in a similar position.'

Temple paused before adding quietly, 'So, for that matter, was Doctor Kohima.'

This was something of a bombshell in the little circle.

'Another drink for Mr. Lathom, Ricky,' said Temple, noticing his empty glass.

'Thanks, Temple,' said Lathom, then continued: 'You mean that Rex wasn't satisfied with getting the dope from Mrs. Trevelyan? He started to blackmail Doctor Kohima directly?'

'Does that sound too incredible, Mr. Lathom?' demanded Temple in a challenging tone.

'But are you trying to tell us that Mrs. Trevelyan was actually blackmailed into confessing she was Rex after that business at Haybourne?'

'That's just what I'm telling you, Mr. Lathom.'

'But surely Mrs. Trevelyan wouldn't incriminate herself as far as that, unless there was some other reason—' began Steve.

'Yes! Yes! There was another reason!' cried Mrs. Trevelyan.

'Yes, and a very potent reason. You see, Steve, Mrs. Trevelyan knew that Rex had started working on Doctor Kohima – and she happened to have fallen in love with the doctor.'

Mrs. Trevelyan dropped her head, then looked up quickly. 'It's true,' she breathed.

'By George!' exclaimed Forbes. 'That explains the silver pencil – the one that was planted beside the body of James Barton. Rex told Mrs. Trevelyan that if she didn't confess after the Haybourne affair that he would plant further clues.'

'Yes,' said Mrs. Trevelyan excitedly. 'I had a telephone message . . .'

'That is correct,' confirmed Kohima in a level tone. 'I was compelled to hand over that ticket for my car the night of that accident.'

'I had a pretty good idea of that at the time, Doctor,' smiled Temple. 'I didn't take any immediate action just then

271

because I needed more proof. And I preferred to await further developments. Which came all right, eh, Doctor?'

Kohima's expression changed. His customary pleasant voice now had a note of anger, and there was a distressed gleam in his eyes.

'When he made Barbara turn up at Haybourne on that damnable errand,' he rasped, 'I felt just about at the end of my tether.'

'Just as I guessed,' murmured Temple. 'You didn't mind paying him money up to a point – you didn't even stop at giving him information when he had you by the throat – but when he attempted to blackmail Mrs. Trevelyan into confessing that she was Rex, that was too much of a good thing, eh, Doctor?' He chuckled at the memory. 'You remember what I said? "You can lead a horse to the water, but you can't make him drink".'

Temple looked round his guests and said to Forbes: 'Talking of drink, Sir Graham, what about another whisky?'

Ricky came forward to take Forbes' glass.

'Well, Temple,' said Crane, somewhat reluctantly, 'you've certainly reduced the suspects to two – three, counting Ricky.'

Ricky looked up from the siphon and grinned, but made no comment.

'And not counting yourself, eh, Inspector?' said Temple.

'Good Lord!' exclaimed Crane. 'You don't suspect me, do you, Temple?'

'I won't say I didn't at one time,' admitted Temple. 'Particularly when I found you in the flat with the girl in brown. But I managed to check up your story quite accurately. And so, our suspects are reduced to one.'

He turned his back squarely to the mantelpiece, took a sip at his drink, and looked pointedly at Lathom.

272

'Well, Mr. Lathom?' he said quite pleasantly.

Carl Lathom simulated an air of aggrieved surprise. Then he burst out laughing.

'I suppose this is your idea of a joke, Temple,' he replied.

'Rather an unpleasant joke as far as you're concerned, I'm afraid, Mr. Lathom.'

'My dear fellow, the idea's too stupid for words,' protested Lathom. 'Why, good heavens, you saw that letter I got demanding two thousand pounds.'

'Certainly I saw it,' agreed Temple. 'But what precisely does it prove, Mr. Lathom?'

'Why, it proves I'm not Rex. How could I be? I don't write myself blackmailing letters.'

Lathom noticed that Crane and Forbes were watching him with considerable interest.

'It proves,' continued Temple deliberately, 'that Rex is quite fiendishly cunning, Mr. Lathom. That you planned to direct suspicion away from yourself and on to Mrs. Trevelyan. You take a lot of trouble with your little schemes, Lathom, and that's why they've met with more than average success. You went to the trouble to establish a nice background for yourself about some mysterious affair in Cairo, which was complete nonsense. You consulted Doctor Kohima as an apparently genuine patient – and all I can say is it's a thousand pities he didn't give you a shot of sodium pentothal and find out the real truth. It would have saved us a lot of trouble.'

'This is absurd!' exclaimed Lathom.

'At Doctor Kohima's,' continued Temple relentlessly, 'you fitted the girl in brown very nicely into your background, but you knew very well it was no hallucination. You couldn't make head or tail of why this particular girl should be following you, but your intuition told you that she must suspect something.'

'Carol was on to you, Lathom, right from the start,' put in Jeff Myers quietly.

'But she couldn't prove anything,' said Temple.

'Can you prove anything, Mr. Temple?' demanded Lathom defiantly.

Temple bent down and picked up the tongs, replaced a burning coal that had fallen from the fire, and turned to Lathom again.

'You'll be surprised,' he replied grimly. 'Let's go back to that night when we saw you in Luigi's. You overheard me tell Steve what Leo Brent meant when he said it was all done by mirrors. That's how you were able to bring off that nice little coup at Canterbury that nearly cost us our lives. However, let's go back to the night at Luigi's. When Ricky turned up and asked you to deliver a message to me you immediately realised the full importance of the message. You knew that Carol Reagan was here waiting to see me, and you knew that here was your chance at long last to corner her and put an end to her investigations.

'Before delivering Ricky's message you went outside and planted glass in front of my car, and it was only after doing this that you returned and gave me the message. As a result of the puncture you had a flying start on us when we left Luigi's, and of course the girl was already dead when we got back.'

'And I must say that was a quick bit of work,' commented Crane, recalling his visit to the flat on the night in question.

'Later that night,' Temple went on, 'I paid you a visit, Mr. Lathom, and it was then you made rather a stupid mistake. In fact, I was mildly surprised that a man of your obvious ingenuity should give himself away so easily.'

'If you mean that I referred to the fact that the girl had been shot, when I was only supposed to know she was murdered—' began Lathom, but Temple waved him aside.

274

'That wasn't your fatal mistake, Lathom. When I got in you asked me to have a drink, and ran through quite a list of wines and spirits. But you said, "I'm right out of port at the moment."'

'I can't see that proves anything.'

'Oh yes, it does. I made it my business to check up with Luigi that you had bought a bottle of port earlier that evening. If, as you said, you went straight back to the flat, you must have had a bottle of port, unless you deliberately smashed it and carefully placed the glass in front of my car. I checked that too, Mr. Lathom – I managed to find a piece of glass with part of the label on it, and Luigi recognised it at once.'

With a quick, cat-like movement, Lathom leapt to his feet, kicked his chair out of the way and backed a couple of yards. He stood facing Temple with his hand in his right coat pocket. 'Keep back – all of you – and if any one moves I shall shoot!' Crane made an involuntaiy movement, but Forbes restrained him.

'I'm afraid you're giving yourself away again, Lathom,' said Temple mildly.

'If you don't mind, I'll do the talking for a change,' said Lathom fiercely. 'And I think you'll find it quite interesting.'

He gave vent to a grim chuckle, and there was a queer look in his eyes.

'He's crazy!' whispered Mrs. Trevelyan, clutching Kohima's arm.

'Go on, Lathom,' said Temple softly. 'We're listening.'

'All right!' snapped Lathom. 'Well, Mr. Temple, do you know what killed Norma Rice and Sir Ernest Cranbury?'

'Of course,' nodded Temple. 'They were poisoned by an overdose of Amashyer or crailin.'

'Exactly. And, as you know, crailin is a delayed action poison that takes about twenty minutes before it is effective.'

275

'What are you getting at?' asked Crane angrily.

'Don't you know what I'm getting at, Inspector?'

'I'm damned if I do!'

'Then I'll tell you,' said Lathom. 'You may remember that Temple complained of the quality of the gin I gave him.'

'My God! You mean – you – doctored that drink?'

'Crailin!' nodded Lathom. 'Stay where you are, Mrs. Temple!' For Steve had made a movement towards her husband.

'You must have had a very low opinion of Rex if you thought he would listen patiently to all your theorising without having a trick up his sleeve!' said Lathom contemptuously. 'I've made certain of one thing, anyhow – the next time Rex operates he will not be annoyed by Mr. Paul Temple.'

'I wouldn't be too sure about that, Mr. Lathom,' said Temple quietly. He had remained quite motionless for the past few minutes, and his expression was inscrutable.

'I'm more than sure – I'm positive!' said Lathom savagely.

'Nothing is certain in this world, Mr. Lathom,' said Temple. 'If you'll take your mind back and recall exactly what happened when you gave me that drink, you'll see how fallible the human memory can be. I lifted my glass and wished you good health – which was a trifle ironical – and at that moment the front-door bell rang, and I left the room to let in Mr. Myers – without drinking.'

'But you came back and complained of the taste of the gin,' Lathom reminded him triumphantly.

'That,' explained Temple, 'was a little subterfuge, I'm afraid, Mr. Lathom, I was never very fond of the taste of water, so it wasn't difficult. You see, I had emptied your carefully prepared mixture down the kitchen sink before I opened the door to Myers.'

Lathom took an involuntary step backwards, tripped and staggered. At that moment a large object whizzed through the air from the other side of the room, and caught him neatly on the side of the head. Lathom collapsed and lay quite still. Forbes and Crane rushed over to him at once, and picked up the revolver.

'Jolly good shot, Ricky!' approved Temple.

'I am so sorry about the vase, Mrs. Temple,' apologised Ricky. 'It was the first thing to hand . . .'

'My dear Ricky, we're delighted! You forestalled what might have been rather an unpleasant moment,' said Temple. 'If Lathom hadn't tripped. Can't think what made him do that—'

'I can tell you,' said Steve with a smile. 'It was my ball of wool!'

Steve hardly set eyes on her husband until tea-time the next day, for he was up early and on his way to Scotland Yard soon after nine o'clock. He telephoned to her that he was lunching with Sir Graham and Lord Flexdale, and that he would be home to tea about four, when he would have cleared up most of the final details of the case. He arrived to find Steve sitting in the lounge before a large fire, placidly knitting. She looked up as he entered.

'Ring for tea, will you, darling?'

Temple rang the bell and spread his hands to the blaze. 'Well, we seem to have everything nicely tied up now,' he told her. 'I think Lord Flexdale was a bit disappointed he wouldn't be able to broadcast to the nation again.'

'You may have cleared up things at Scotland Yard,' said Steve, as Ricky brought in the tea and silently withdrew, 'but there are several points I still can't understand. About this little man, Davis, for instance. Ricky is still quite certain he was Cortwright.'

277

'Quite correct, darling. I asked him about that this morning. It seems he was working on a special case for the F.B.I. when Ricky saw him – and he was playing the part of a hick from the Middle West. Myers is rather proud of himself as an actor.'

'He certainly fooled us,' said Steve. 'But I can't think why he didn't take us into his confidence in the first place. That would have saved quite a lot of trouble.'

'I'm afraid that's a weakness of his,' said Temple, appropriating a scone. 'Insists on playing a lone hand. He thought he could clear up the Rex case on his own and take all the credit – then he began to see that it wasn't so easy. Myers has plenty of resource, but he got a bit out of his depth. He hasn't much use for the police, but he told me he was particularly anxious that I shouldn't jump to the conclusion that Rex was Mrs. Trevelyan, and abandon the case.'

'So he told you that he had seen Chester put cyanide in the flask, and produced that strange note.'

'Which was just a little ruse to keep me interested. Of course, he knew darn well that Chester had put cyanide in the flask – no one else at the hotel could have done it. I was quite amused really, because I'd already tumbled to the fact that the girl in brown was working in with Myers.'

'Then that night we went to Claywood Mill and Chester followed us,' began Steve.

'Chester was working under instructions from Lathom, of course, and he'd taken Leo Brent there that afternoon. As soon as Chester started tailing us that evening, Myers was hot on Chester's track.'

'And Sir Graham and Crane followed Chester!' smiled Steve.

'Exactly!'

The telephone rang and Temple answered it. There followed a cryptic conversation.

'Who was it?' asked Steve, as Temple replaced the receiver.

'Doctor Kohima.'

'Did he want anything special?'

'Yes, he wondered if you and I would care to act as witnesses.'

'Oh dear,' said Steve. 'Is he in more trouble?'

'I wouldn't be surprised,' grinned Temple. 'He proposes to marry Mrs. Trevelyan on Tuesday by special licence. I told him we'd be delighted to attend.'

Steve said, 'That means another new hat I'm afraid.'

'Remind me to get an advance on my book,' he smiled. 'By the way, Steve, isn't that a new piece of knitting?'

'Oh yes, I started it this morning.'

Temple helped himself to another scone.

'I feel rather pleased with myself over this Rex case,' he admitted. 'Did you see what the *London Graphic* said this morning?'

'Considering you marked it heavily in blue pencil,' said Steve.

'They described me as England's foremost detective,' went on Temple unheedingly, stirring his tea with a complacent smile and looking particularly pleased with himself. Then he glanced across at Steve and said rather curiously: 'Darling, I don't think that shade of blue is quite your colour. Why don't you knit a nice yellow jumper?'

'Because there's an old superstition about pink for a girl and blue for a boy,' said Steve. 'And this doesn't happen to be a jumper!'

'Blue for a boy?' repeated Temple, slightly dazed. 'You don't mean—'

Steve said, 'And you call yourself a detective, Mr. Temple!'

He looked at her incredulously, then at the knitting. For the first time he realised it was a baby's vest.

'By Timothy!' said England's foremost detective.